What Our Readers Are Saying. . .

"An absorbing, exciting novel with all the elements of suspense and romance to keep a reader entertained from cover to cover. I loved it and couldn't put it down until the end."
Carwin Williams, professor emeritus BYU, Executive V.P. of Family Literacy Centers, Inc., author of six books.

"Many people have gone through challenging times and survived. But there is a difference between survival and triumph. In *Angels Round About*, we feel intimately involved in the story of a noble young woman who transcends her difficulties with inspiring triumph."
Kaye Bingham, homemaker, Sunnyside, WA

"I got pulled in on the first page. The only thing I didn't like is that it didn't last longer."
Joanne Smith, teacher, Salt Lake City, UT

"This is such a wonderful book! I couldn't put it down. Now all the other teachers here are waiting in line to read my copy."
Phyllis Hooker, English teacher in Bangkok, Thailand

"This book was especially enjoyable to me because I grew up in the same area of Austria as the main character did, though a few years later. The author is very authentic in her tone and historical research. My Austrian friends and I had a great time reading it together."
Renate Johnson, tax accountant, Orem, UT

"It is no easy thing to manage true characters set within an accurate description of other times. In this book, personal struggles and joys are seen against a backdrop of European ideologies. The author handles well both the pains of reality and the triumphs of the spirit."
Carma de Jong Anderson, historical costume expert, artist, playwright. Provo, UT

"My favorite kind of reading—more like a biography than a novel! The story line pulls you along with well-defined and genuine characters. The contrast between the formal European and the easygoing Americans is very authentic for that time. Rather than being maudlin, or tugging at spurious emotions, this novel presents lives with a modicum of history, and in an uplifting, refined, unpretentious, and courageous way."
Elizabeth Wilson, grandmother, avid reader, Provo, UT

"A fascinating book! Enthralling!"
Dianna Bauer, computer design engineer, Franklin, MI

"I loved it. It made me cry."
Arianne Davis, anthropology student, BYU

W9-BZU-670

Angels Round About

Lorie Nicholes

A Novel
by
Lorie H. Nicholes

No portion of the book may be reproduced in any form
without written permission from the publisher,
Stellar Publishing and Distribution
P.O. Box 685
Heber City, UT 84032

10 9 8 7 6 5 4 3 2 1

Cover design by Lorie Davis and Ben Watson
Interior design by Rebecca Roane, Roane Design

Dedicated to

my Mom,

my friend on the other side.

✤ ✤ ✤ ✤ ✤

Acknowledgments

This is the fun part, where I get to thank the people who gave me so much.

Thanks to Orson Scott Card for giving me a day and a vision. To James Nicholes, Paul Lenhardt, and Renate Johnson for offering and checking historical accuracy. To every one of my readers and advisors who helped me to see straight. To Darla Isackson and Georgia Carpenter, editor and publisher, for faith and fun. To Walt Nicholes, Kathy Pitt, Arianne Davis, and Kay Bingham for essential moral support of many kinds. To Curt Fawson for letting me quit my day job and follow my dream. To Joanne Smith and Kathy Pitt for help with the cover design, to Arianne Davis for posing as Hildegard, and to my computer wizard, Ben Watson, whose skill made the cover a reality. And not least, to Jim, who never once said I couldn't do it.

Germany, 1938

*W*ith mounting fear, a dark-haired girl watched the Gestapo guards. She stood in line approaching a customs table at the German seaport of Cuxhaven. Between the tables prowled stony-faced soldiers, peering keenly at each traveler, waiting for an inspector to signal that one of them was trying to smuggle illegal goods out of the Fatherland.

Hilde took a deep breath, trying not to look guilty, suppressing panic, wondering what on earth she was doing here. Was she insane? Suddenly the whole plan seemed terrifying. She was only nineteen. She had thrown away a good job and left a young man who loved her. All because an apostle of the Lord had looked into her eyes and told her to go, and she had known with a burning of the Spirit that it was the will of God.

A man several places closer in line lifted his suitcases to the examination table. The inspector pressed the clothing away from the sides of the man's suitcase and patted the lining. Hilde exhaled softly, thankful she had earlier rejected *that* idea. Without mussing the contents, he felt between layers of belongings, asking the man to open this or that receptacle. Hilde's eyes flicked down to her shoulder bag for an instant. Would he look behind her father's photograph? It seemed such a foolishly obvious hiding place now. *Oh, please, Heavenly Father,* she prayed silently. *Make them blind.*

At the table, the inspector's hands stopped. They patted over a collection of socks a second time. He pulled one of the pairs apart and reached inside. Out came a fistful of bank notes. The man began to stammer. The inspector raised his hand, and a Gestapo guard stepped forward.

"Come with me!" he snapped at the horrified man, closing his suitcase and indicating a glassed-in office. Another guard took his place.

The inspector turned to the next passenger. "Put your suitcases on the table, please."

Why am I here? the girl asked herself again. She took a deep breath and answered, *Because this is where I am supposed to be.*

She thought of the beginning. Her reasons began many years ago. They began because she missed her papa so much she had opened the door to a missionary who looked like him. But she had let in more than a missionary. She had let in a new world, a new life, eternity.

❖ ❖ ❖

Vienna, 1923

*P*apa was wonderful! Four-year-old Hilde watched in gleeful anticipation as he and Mama's two brothers heaved and panted, lifting the piano step-by-step up the stairway to their new apartment in Vienna.

"Watch the corner! Watch the corner!" Papa grunted, straining to lift his end of the instrument up the final step. All three men groaned and heaved. At last the heavy piano sat safely in the upper hallway, and they all leaned against the walls to rest.

"I'll make sure the way is clear," the girl's mother, Rosa, said, turning toward their flat.

Hilde danced and sang in excitement. "We have a piano, a lovely new piano. Papa, when are you going to teach me to play it? Why can't I learn right now?"

Hans lifted her to sit on the lid of the upright piano while the other two men mopped their brows and caught their breath. "Because princesses don't learn to play pianos in hallways. The neighbors have to keep coming out and bowing, and they don't get anything done."

"Papa, you're so silly," Hilde giggled. "I don't mean right this minute. I mean as soon as we get it into the flat."

Rosa leaned out the door. "Hilde! Get down off that piano, and leave the men alone."

"But Papa put me up here."

"Well get down anyway."

"Yes, Mama." Hilde held out her arms to her tall, handsome father, who whirled her around before setting her on her feet. The girl ran to the end of the hall where a deep window seat was partly enclosed by heavy, floor-length curtains. "I'll wait here in my castle, and you can call me when you're ready to teach me."

Rosa sniffed. "Then you'll wait about two years, Hilde. You're much too young to start lessons yet. Grandmother Edler gave your Papa this piano for *his* pleasure, not yours. Hans, I have the floor cleared and swept. You can bring it in whenever you're ready. And I've made hot tea and cakes to revive you all."

When the piano was settled in place, Hans played rolling arpeggios and bits of classical pieces. He swayed from side to side with his eyes closed and a smile of pleasure on his lips. Hilde stood beside him, entranced by his flying fingers. "It's wretchedly out of tune, of course," he said over the music. "But what a delight to have it again. When I was a boy I played for two or three hours every day, and now I haven't touched a note since we left Mother's." Hans turned to his brother-in-law, Johann, as he played. "They wouldn't have taught you piano tuning, too, at your seminary, would they?"

"Sorry, Hans. All I've worked on is the organ. But I've watched pianos tuned often enough to take a shot at it, no guarantees."

"Anything would sound better than this."

"Can I play it, Papa?" asked Hilde.

"Of course. Come here." He lifted the little girl onto his lap and spread her fingers over the keys. "You must curve your fingers just so when you play. Do you see why Mama says you have to wait and grow a little? Your dainty little hands cannot yet reach the keys properly. But you can play a tune with one finger." He took her hand, extended her index finger, and guided her in the notes of *The Blue Danube Waltz*.

"Mama! I can play! Did you hear me?"

"Yes, dear. I heard. Now leave your papa alone and come to the table for your cake."

❖ ❖ ❖

Hilde's mother, Rosa, was a brilliant, driven woman. She had grown up in poverty on a farm near the city of St. Pölten. At the age of nine, little Rosa had been the only person available to help deliver her own mother's last baby. It was an event that was to direct the course of her life. Never again would she allow herself to feel so helpless or afraid! She was determined to become a physician in a world of men.

The Great War had given her the chance. With casualties of war mounting everywhere, doctors urgently required, and every able man called to fight, she and a few other women had been allowed to study medicine at the university in Vienna. There she had taken classes from the great Sigmund Freud, and observed and assisted in hospitals packed with the wounded. But she had not finished the course.

Against all her desires and expectations, she had fallen in love. The handsome, aristocratic young officer, Hans Edler, had left her breathless. She was not the first young woman during a war to find herself pregnant. The young man fervently admired the girl who defied the stuffy conventions of a society which he found chokingly obsolete. They married, and Hilde was born. Medical school was no longer possible.

The war had left the Austrian Empire dissolved and impoverished. Only respect and noble connections were now left to Hans's family. The young couple had nothing to live on except their salable skills. After a few years, Rosa was able to begin medical classes again, but on a radically limited basis. Even so, she clenched her fists and swore to continue if it took her a lifetime.

❖ ❖ ❖

Hilde's father, Hans, worked at various firms throughout Vienna, auditing their accounts for the government. Although her mother seemed forever busy with books and classes, whenever they were able, mother and child loved to spend an afternoon in a public park or garden before meeting Hans so they could go home together. One favorite spot was the Emperor's rose garden. While Rosa sat on a bench and darned socks or embroidered, Hilde played around her on the pavement or grass.

"Mama, why does the emperor have this great big fence around his palace?" asked the child, bouncing herself repeatedly against narrow bars which stood higher than a man.

"So he can have a little privacy from all the people like us who come to see his beautiful gardens. He doesn't want anyone to go peeking in his windows."

"But I *want* to peek in his windows. I want to go inside and see all the gold and jewels and crowns."

"Why don't we go look at those statues, instead," Rosa distracted her by pointing to an enormously high monument a short distance away with two mounted horsemen on top. Rosa walked across the courtyard while Hilde skipped beside her. The sun was warm on their skin, and, in fountains, water sprayed and splashed with cool, delicious sounds.

"That one up there on the right is Prince Eugene. He was a marvelous general who saved Austria from the Turks a long time ago. He was so gallant and noble, I have always loved him."

Hilde giggled. "You love a *statue?* I'm going to tell Papa that statue is your lover!" She put her hands over her mouth and laughed gleefully, her brown eyes twinkling at the joke.

Rosa smiled. "You silly girl. Let's go look at the roses."

"I already saw the roses. I want to go into the emperor's palace."

"Well, the emperor doesn't live there anymore. He moved out, and now it's the foreign ministry. And we aren't allowed to go inside, anyway." Rosa sat down again on the bench, her back toward the palace, and took out her needlework.

Hilde knew there had to be a way to get inside that fence. All she wanted was a look in the window. Surely the emperor must have forgotten a few things when he moved away. Everybody forgot things. She pictured a box of treasure lying neglected in one of those lower rooms, or maybe just a jewel or two that had dropped unnoticed to the floor. With both hands she grasped one of the iron bars as high up as she could reach. Her fingers fit around it easily. Pulling herself upward with all her might, she wrapped her legs around the bar and locked them together. To her surprise, she didn't slip, but hung there a few inches higher than she had stood. Again she reached up and pulled. It was working! She could climb! Slowly she struggled upward, delighting in her new skill. She was half way to the top when she hear a muffled exclamation behind her.

"Hilde! For heaven's sake!" Mama rushed to the fence, dislodged the disappointed child and set her on the ground. "You're nothing but a little hoyden! Look at your dress. Your apron's filthy!" While her mother brushed off her dress, a tall figure approached.

"Papa!" Hilde cried happily, tearing herself from her mother's grasp, and dashing across the sidewalk. Hans picked her up and tossed her shrieking into the air.

Rosa put her embroidery back into its bag and walked toward them. "Your daughter is determined to get us arrested for trespassing on the palace grounds."

Hans looked at Hilde fiercely, and said, "Tsk, tsk, tsk."

"Mama has a new lover," Hilde announced loudly.

Hans looked startled. His eyes flew to Rosa's.

Rosa said dryly. "It's the statue of Prince Eugene on top of the monument. I made the mistake of saying I loved it."

Hans chuckled and pinched Hilde's cheek. "What do you know about lovers, little one? Careful what you say." He put Hilde down, and she skipped in front of them as they left the palace grounds and walked down the sidewalk toward the street-car. "I was in my mother's neighborhood today, and dropped in on her," said Hans.

"Oh? How are things?"

"Her school is doing well. She has several new students. She brought up the subject of Hilde's education. Hilde is her only grandchild, you know. She feels very strongly about her 'proper upbringing.'" Hans wiggled his eyebrows up and down melodramatically.

The little girl, listening absently, thought about Grandmother Edler. She made beautiful dresses for rich ladies, and ran a school to teach other people how to sew. She always smelled good, and had pretty clothes and nice things in her apartment. But she wasn't as much fun as Mama's mother. Oma Reiner was the nicest person in the whole world.

"What does she propose? " asked Rosa. "Hilde won't start school until next year."

"She proposes that now is none too soon for us to begin applying for Hilde to go to Notre Dame de Sion."

"Notre Dame de Sion! Is she kidding! That's the most exclusive girl's school in Vienna! Nobody goes there but the obscenely wealthy and the excessively aristocratic. And the pupils and teachers only speak French! What can she be thinking?"

The tone of Hans's answer suggested the humorous disdain in which he held the rich, pretentious, and aristocratic. "She is thinking that her granddaughter carries the blood of ever so many generations of noble Vidosvalvys, and should be trained to carry it in an appropriately regal fashion."

"Well, to start with, we don't have the money."

"Mother offers to pay half."

Rosa walked in silent contemplation for half a block. Hilde paused just ahead of them to examine the trunk of a tree.

"We couldn't possibly . . . but it *would* be such an excellent education." Rosa sounded sorely tempted.

"I thought you'd like the aristocratic connections. You and Mother are one on that, at any rate."

"And with *that* school in her background," Rosa mused with growing enthusiasm, "she could become anything. Go to any university."

"Ah, yes. 'Making something of herself.' We know how important that is."

Rosa spoke challengingly. "Well, what's wrong with that? Why shouldn't she?"

"She should. But if you really want to consider this, you'll have to be willing to work as much or more than you do now until I get better established. Weigh it well, Rosa. It may come down to Hilde's education or your medical school."

Rosa's brow furrowed, her expression showing a mind torn by possibilities. Her steps quickened as they did when she was thinking through a problem. Hilde turned away and picked something off the trunk of a tree.

"Look at my fuzzy worms!" The child held out a hand containing three wriggling black objects.

"Caterpillars," corrected Hans.

"Hilde! Drop those dirty things! They have germs!" exclaimed Rosa.

❖ ❖ ❖

In the fall, Hilde was dressed in a gray uniform with a pleated skirt and white collar. She wore long black stockings and shiny black shoes with straps. Together she and Mama walked from the streetcar to the big school called Notre Dame de Sion. Mama was dressed in her very best clothes, and wore the real gold bracelet Papa had given her when they got married. It was Hilde's first day of school.

Girls from ages five through fourteen were educated at Notre Dame. A good many of them were boarding students from wealthy and titled families throughout Europe.

Hilde was uncharacteristically subdued as they approached the huge, magnificent building. She clung closely to Rosa's skirts. The front of the building was recessed from the street, allowing chauffeured limousines to approach and discharge their passengers. Amidst chattering girls Rosa and Hilde climbed the wide flight of steps to the large, glossy front doors, where a doorman opened one of the tall portals for them. Inside, the marble floors were polished to a mirror finish. Beautiful religious paintings were hung in gilt frames along the halls. Nuns in gray habits and white wimples drifted in various directions. One approached them.

"Good morning," she greeted with a French accent. "It appears that this young lady might be looking for the first grade. I'm Sister Magdalana. May I take you there?"

"Good morning, Sister. That's very kind of you. Hilde?" Mama gave her hand a squeeze.

Hilde dropped a little curtsy and said, "Good morning, Sister." She was too timid to look up, but she followed the instructions drilled into her.

"Well!" the nun said, smiling. "You are a very polite little girl, and Sister Haubinger is going to like you very much, indeed. She will be your teacher. Come along, please."

The first grade was a large, bright room with well waxed wooden floors and large rugs for the children to sit and play on. A tall, plumpish nun walked forward as they entered.

"Hello. I am Sister Augusta Haubinger, the first grade teacher this year."

Mama said hello and introduced them both.

Hilde glanced up at the round, smiling face, and remembered to curtsy. "Good morning, Sister."

Sister Haubinger knelt before Hilde and looked into the girl's shy brown eyes with her warm blue ones. "Good morning, child. Is your real name Hilde or Hildegard?"

"It's really Hildegard," said Rosa from above them. "But we have always called her Hilde."

Sister Haubinger continued to look into Hilde's eyes, giving no sign she had heard Rosa. Finally Hilde spoke. "My real name is Hildegard."

"Would you like me to call you Hildegard? It's such a beautiful name. It means 'guardian angel,' you know."

Hilde smiled and said softly. "Yes, please. I want to be Hildegard."

"Hildegard, if you will come with me, I'll show you where your seat is, and I'll give you your own slateboard and chalk and all the other things you'll be using in class. Would you like that?"

"Yes, Sister." Hilde released Mama's hand, and took the hand of Sister Haubinger. The woman stood up, and smiled at Mama.

"Frau Edler, if you will be good enough to wait just a minute or two, I would like to settle Hildegard and then have a few words with you."

Sister Haubinger took Hilde to a seat at a table, opened a drawer beneath, and showed her the items within which would be her very own. She pointed here and there around the room to explain where everything was.

"I'm going to be your teacher from now on," she said kindly. I will be with you this year and the next and the next for every class until you're a big girl and graduate. I'm sure I'm going to like you very much. And I hope you'll like me, too. Now, why don't you look at this picture book while I talk to your Mama a little."

Hilde already knew she would like it here.

❖ ❖ ❖

The first few months at Notre Dame were exciting for Hildegard. She got to work and play with other children, and do all kinds of things she never did at home. Each morning Rosa got up early to study for her two classes until an alarm clock reminded her to get Hilde up to dress for school. They took a streetcar across town, and walked the last four blocks from the streetcar stop to Notre Dame de Sion. Hilde chattered as she skipped beside her Mama.

"Will Uncle Peter come again soon? I want to see his horse. Why doesn't he ever bring his horse when he comes to see us? Mama, is Uncle Peter the tallest man in the world?"

Rosa dragged her attention from the day's concerns to the child at her side. Peter had been Rosa's closest childhood friend, and was now a gendarme, a mounted policeman in the countryside. He visited whenever he came to Vienna, and Hilde adored him. "There are probably taller men," she replied, "but last year he got an award for being the tallest mounted policeman in Europe. Which he thought was a silly thing to be awarded for, since he can't help being tall."

"I like awards," the little girl replied. "I want to have enough awards to hang all over the wall. Sister Haubinger says if I keep doing good I'll get an award for neat writing."

"*Well.* If you keep doing *well.* You must use proper grammar or you will sound lower class and Grandmother Edler will be very displeased."

"I'm glad I get to sleep at home. One of the girls who sleeps at school wet her bed, and they made her put the wet sheet over her head and walk down the hall to teach her a lesson. She was crying. I would have run away." The child prattled on about children and events at the school. She had been hearing dozens of things she had never heard of before, some from the teacher, but many from the other little girls.

One Saturday, Hilde woke before the sun. She didn't know if Mama and Papa were still asleep. She slid out of bed, and tiptoed to the door of their room, which was open a few inches. She pushed it wider, and looked in. Mama was lying in bed awake, but Papa was still breathing heavily. Mama smiled, and

Hilde quietly scampered to Rosa's side of the bed. Rosa lifted a finger to her lips as she raised the covers for Hilde to climb in beside her.

The child whispered, "Papa's still asleep."

"Yes, and we mustn't wake him," Rosa whispered back.

Hans mumbled and turned from his side to his back, pushing the covers from his bare chest.

"Papa's very hairy," Hilde observed, still whispering. "You aren't hairy." She looked at her father intently for several moments. "Mama, are papas different from mamas? A girl at school said they were."

Mama's eyes widened, and she stammered nervously, "Ahh . . . I don't know."

Lowering her voice still more to a conspiratorial whisper and leaning close, Hilde said, "Let's pull back the covers and look. Papa is asleep. He'll never know we did it."

Choking on a laugh, Rosa gathered Hilde into her arms, and slipped from the bed. "Let's go have breakfast, instead, little one."

❖ ❖ ❖

Hilde knew that Mama never ever cried, and that she didn't respect people who did. But during the next year, Mama often looked like she wanted to cry. Through closed doors Hilde heard many arguments between her parents which always stopped when she came into the room. They seemed to have something to do with Papa and other ladies, and Mama was very angry. At those times, the child knew it was best to stay out of sight. Sometimes Papa spent the night sleeping on the sofa.

Once there was a very bad argument that went on all night and frightened Hilde, who huddled in her bed behind her closed door. Papa was gone for a week after that, but when he came home, he was smiling and charming, bringing presents and flowers for Mama and a little toy for Hilde. Very soon they moved to a large new flat where Papa had his office right in their home.

He even bought Mama a beautiful set of bedroom furniture with a matching wardrobe and a dressing table with a large oval mirror that could tilt back and forth. It was her mama's pride. Things were better from then until summer.

Hilde loved summer vacation more than any other time because she got to spend it in St. Pölten with Oma and Opa Reiner. She looked forward to exploring in the woods with Oma, and knew Opa would take her aboard the big railroad engine he drove all over Europe.

The railway attendant held her small hand as she almost dragged him between the rows of seats. His other hand gripped her small traveling bag.

Passengers were collecting their belongings, getting ready to depart. The child could scarcely contain her excitement to be in St. Pölten for two whole months.

"Slow down, little Fräulein! I promised your grandfather I would take good care of you, but he won't be ready to walk you home until he has seen to his engine, and that could be a good while."

"Oma will be here!" Hilde grinned. "She always comes. She is the very nicest person in the whole wide world!"

The attendant smiled. "That she is, Fräulein. That she is."

And there was Hannah on the platform, as Hilde had promised, scanning the passengers that climbed down the steps of the several cars. Her eyes lighted when she spotted her granddaughter, and she ran to catch the child up in her arms.

"Thank you, Felix, for bringing my treasure safe and sound," she smiled at the attendant. "And here is a little something for your wife. Just take the bag off my arm, please."

The man smiled broadly. "Mmmmm! I smell hot apple strudel!* My wife will be lucky if it gets home untouched."

Hannah put Hilde down, and took the traveling bag from Felix. "Tell Jakob we'll be waiting at home with a good dinner for him, will you? And thank you again for watching Hilde."

Felix tipped his hat. "A pure pleasure that child is, Ma'am.

* *See appendix for recipie*

Thanks so much for the strudel." He turned and lumbered away to help other passengers.

Hilde grabbed Hannah's arm and hugged it to herself, her face a picture of blissful anticipation. "Oh, Oma, I'm so glad to be here. This is going to be the best summer I ever had! Is it too late for the strawberries? Can we go stay in Opa's hut in the woods?"

"There will be time for everything, darling girl. It's a little late for strawberries, but we may as well have fun looking, eh?"

"That's what I like about you, Oma. Mama only does things if she knows they'll turn out like she wants them to. You let me do silly things just for fun."

"Tell me, little one, how is your mama feeling? Does she seem happy or sad these days?" Hannah never made the mistake of underestimating either Hilde's intelligence nor her skills of observation.

Hilde's face sobered as she concentrated on an accurate answer. "She was sad for a long time last year. She was pretty mad, actually. She was mad at Papa, but she wouldn't tell me why. But he's been very, very nice to her, and now she's getting happy again."

"Do you like your new home?"

"Oh, yes," Hilde smiled up at her grandmother, squinting at the sun in her eyes. "I have a room all to myself. And Papa has a big office of his own, so he can work at home most of the time. That's very nice because I get to see him after school every day. He has a bed in his office, too. He says it's so he can take naps, but I know he used to sleep there every night. But now that Mama's happy again, he gets to sleep in her room." Hilde began to skip. "And our new flat is only five blocks from school. I can walk by myself both ways."

"And how is your Papa? Does he seem to like working at home?"

"I guess so," she shrugged. "He has lots of work to do. Sometimes Frau Bemmer comes to help him. She's his secretary and she's really old, and has hair that sticks out of her nose. But she's nice. And Papa has some bad teeth and has to go to a dentist lots of times. The dentist drills holes in them, and it hurts. If I ever get bad teeth I won't tell anybody. And Papa bought a typing machine, but I'm not allowed to touch it."

Hannah and Hilde chatted for the quarter mile until they reached Hannah's upper floor apartment by the mill stream. They stopped on the bridge to look, as they always did, at the big wheel turning slowly. Its narrow stream flowed through the paddles toward them, disappearing into a culvert under the road where they stood. An iron railing edged the bridge, and Hilde loved to lean over it, hypnotized by the moving water and the waving seaweed beneath.

That evening Hilde sat in her nightgown, curled in Hannah's soft arms. Together they read a book about some children who sailed into the stars in a wooden shoe. They took turns reading while Opa smoked his pipe, and snorted over stories in his newspaper.

The book finished, Hilde turned and wrapped both her arms around the old woman's neck. Hannah closed her eyes and smiled as she held the child close.

"Oma, if I am very good and help you a lot, could I stay here with you forever?" Hilde asked Hannah's neck.

"Why, sweet baby, I would love to have you stay here forever. But you would get very lonesome for your mama and papa. And I am afraid they could never be happy at all if you were not there."

"I could visit them," she replied logically, pulling away to look into Hannah's brown eyes.

"They need much more than a visit, dumpling. You may not think so, but your sweet face every day is the one thing in the world that brings them real happiness."

"I don't think so," said Hilde. "Mama is so busy with work and with school that sometimes she hardly talks to me. And Papa plays with me a little bit, but then he tells me to go do something, but there's nothing to do."

"Liebchen, how often do you talk to the sun? How often do you think about it shining?"

Hilde thought seriously. "Sometimes I say 'hello, sunshine' in the morning."

"Do you do it every day? Every week?"

Hilde shook her head.

"And yet," continued Hannah, "How often are you glad it's shining? How often does it feel good warming your shoulders, or telling birds to sing, or telling flowers to grow?"

"Always, I guess."

"Darling girl, you are like the sunshine in your mama and papa's lives. They may not talk to you or play with you as much as you would like. But you are like the warm sunshine in their hearts, and the birdsong and flowers in their lives."

Hilde thought about it awhile. She smiled tentatively. "Really?"

"Yes, precious. Really. And you are all those happy things to me, too." Hannah hugged her hard until she squeaked. "Now I think it's time to say your prayers and go to bed."

"Can we go to Opa's hut in the woods tomorrow?"

"Not till next week. But tomorrow I will make a picnic, and we will go to the woods and pick berries to put in Opa's pancakes."

"Good plan," muttered Opa over his pipe stem.

❖ ❖ ❖

Vienna, 1925

In November, Hans's secretary quit because her family was moving from Vienna. He advertised for a replacement, and interviewed half a dozen women in his apartment-office. Rosa was particularly taken with one very young applicant.

"She reminds me so much of my little sister, Theresia, who died of pneumonia. And she's so eager to please, Hans, even if she has very little experience. Did you notice how thin she is? She must be almost starving." Rosa's heart always went out to those less fortunate.

Margarethe Stengel was barely eighteen, and deeply grateful for the job. She was even willing to stay and cook supper on the days Rosa wasn't able to be home at a decent time. Fond of her admiring protégé, Rosa often invited her to stay and eat with the family.

As Christmas approached, Rosa was troubled that she had no gift for Hilde. Money was so tight there was barely enough for the essentials. For the previous month Rosa, who was a quick and excellent seamstress, had been working daily at the home of an enormously wealthy family, making special Christmas uniforms for the maids who would serve her employers' guests for a week of holiday parties.

When Rosa finished, Madam was pleased, but seemed nervous and distracted, complaining that she had far too much to do to prepare for the evening's entertainment. After a moment's hesitation, she asked if Rosa would be willing to stay a few extra hours and help decorate the tables for the banquet. Rosa laid out greenery around wonderful centerpieces featuring large, hollow chocolate bells. The confections were decorated in some magical way with sugar crystals arranged to look like swirls of hoar frost.

One of the lovely bells had a crack, and Madam demanded that the confectioner take it back; she would not pay for a cracked bell, even if the crack wouldn't show in the centerpiece.

That gave Rosa an idea. When Madam had departed, she asked the confectioner if she might buy the bell for a fraction of its original price. What a wonderful gift it would make for Hilde, even if it cost all the wage she made from the afternoon's work! He agreed.

Rosa rushed home with gladness in her heart. She could envision Hilde's delight when she saw the beautiful bell on Christmas eve. They always opened their gifts before Mass, and this year it was Rosa's present that would light the brown eyes with excitement and love. There was a little prick in her heart as she thought of Hans and Hilde together. It was always Hans who knew how to win the child's love. Hans knew how to play, to be foolish and charming, while Rosa always had to bring them back to reality. But this year . . . !

Rosa rushed straight into Hans's office to show him her find. Hans and Margarethe were standing close, and stepped quickly apart.

"Oh, Hans!" Rosa spoke in a low excited tone. "Wait till you see what I have. Where's Hilde?"

"We got her out of the flat for a few hours hours," grinned Hans. Margarethe was smiling too. A large box lay beside them on Hans's desk. "She's downstairs with Frau Head, making springerle cookies to surprise us for Christmas. I arranged it this morning. Now look! Come here, Rosa, and look what we found for Hilde." He turned to the box and lifted the lid. Tissue paper rustled as he lifted it aside. With a flourish he brought forth a beautiful doll dressed in a traditional Austrian costume. "Ta Da!" he sang as he held the doll for Rosa to see.

Her mouth agape, Rosa reached for the doll. "Hans! It's . . . it's beautiful! Where on earth did you get it? How can we afford it?"

"Afford it? Rosa, this is Christmas! I couldn't bear to have my princess with no present. And we were very lucky! While Margarethe was out job hunting yesterday afternoon, she saw a store that had dolls on sale. I had her pick one out. It didn't cost so very much, really, Rosa." His tone was cajoling. He circled her waist with his arm and drew her close for a kiss on the forehead."

Rosa felt a dull throb in her chest. "But Hans, if you wanted to buy her a doll so much, why didn't you tell me? I would like to have picked it out for her."

"Don't you like it, Rosa? Look, the costume is just like the ones they wear at the festival in St. Pölten. I was sure you'd like that one."

"It isn't that, Hans. . ." Rosa didn't know what she felt, just that suddenly her buoyant joy of the afternoon had dimmed.

"Well, never mind that," Hans changed the subject. "You rushed in here all excited a moment ago. What was that about?"

"Oh. Yes. I found a gift for Hilde, too. It's very pretty." She opened the box in which she had carried the bell, and gently lifted it out. "I got it for a marvelous price because it had the tiniest crack. You can hardly see it."

Hans and Margarethe oh'ed with appreciation. Hans took the bell. "Why, no, the crack is almost invisible. Oh, won't Hilde be delighted with this! This will be her best Christmas ever." Rosa smiled, but her heart hurt a little.

❖ ❖ ❖

Margarethe had been able to return to her home in the country for Christmas, and Rosa was glad. She liked the girl—they all did. But she wanted this Christmas to belong just to her family.

For Christmas Eve dinner, Rosa fried tender fillets of pork schnitzel.* Their bubbled golden crusts sent delicious aromas through the apartment. All four candles on the advent wreath were lighted above the table, and others glowed from the mantle over the fireplace. After the meal, Hans and Rosa sat on the

See appendix for recipie

floor beside Hilde as the child excitedly reached for her gifts.

"Two presents!" she exclaimed, delighted. "I'll save the big one for last! Oh, this is so wonderful!"

"Be very careful with that one," Rosa warned as Hilde turned the smaller package over in her hands. "It's breakable."

"What can it be?" Hilde trilled in anticipation, gently removing the wrapping paper. Her dark, bobbed hair swung down over her cheeks as she bent to lift the lid of the box.

"O-h-h-h-h-h-h!" she sighed rapturously. "Oh, this is the most beautiful thing I ever saw! Oh, Mama! It looks like a fairy bell!" She took the chocolate confection from its box and turned it from side to side so the sugar crystals sparkled in the candlelight.

Rosa smiled and ran her fingers down her daughter's cheek. "I'm glad you like it, Liebchen. Hold it very carefully. The chocolate is hollow inside, and it's fragile."

"Can I eat it?" she asked.

"Of course. That's what it's for. But perhaps you would like to keep it awhile first, to look at."

"Oh, yes! It's very beautiful," she said reverently. She laid it gently in its box, and placed it on the low table next to the sofa. She turned to pick up the other package.

"This is such a big box! I wonder what it is?" She untied the bow and lifted the lid. Her eyes grew wide as she gasped. Eager hands lifted forth the doll and held it before her. "Oh, Papa!" She didn't need to ask who had given her the doll. Clasping the doll to her bosom, she threw herself into her father's arms. "Oh, Papa, she's wonderful! She's just what I always dreamed of!"

Hans answered with his arms around his little daughter. "She is from both of us, Hilde." The child drew herself away and turned to hug her mother, too.

"Thank you, Mama. Thank you for the very best present I ever had in my whole life! I'm going to call her Sissi, because she is as beautiful as the Empress Sissi." Hilde rose to her feet, and holding the doll before her, danced round and round the room, singing a waltz melody.

Hans reached out to take Rosa's hand, but hers lay limp in his.

"I have something for *you*, too, Rosa," said Hans. He reached into his pocket and drew forth a small box. "Open it."

The box was covered in gold foil, and she lifted off the lid. Within, on a velvet cushion, were a pair of small gold earrings shaped like edelweiss.

Rosa looked up and smiled. "Oh, Hans. They're lovely. Really lovely. I hope they're only gold plate. They'd have cost a fortune if they were real gold."

"Don't spoil my fun, Rosa. They *are* real gold, and let's don't talk about whether we could afford them. Just wear them." He took them from the box and fastened them on her ears.

"Look, Hilde," said Mama. "See the pretty earrings Papa gave me." Hilde danced over and exclaimed at the baubles. Rosa stood up and held out her hand to take the child's. "Now, little one, it's time for us to get ready for midnight Mass. Did you take your nap today?"

"Oh, yes! Right before I . . . Oh! I made you a present at Frau Head's flat!" Hilde ran to her room and brought back a plate covered with a napkin. She lifted it to reveal several of the sculpted, anise flavored springerle cookies* traditional for an Austrian Christmas.

The three nibbled on the cookies as they crunched through the snow to the Cathedral. Rosa wondered at her growing sense of deppression throughout the service. The playful chatter of her husband and child only increased her negative mood.

Afterwards, Hilde was irritable from exhaustion. She complained about the cold, about wanting her doll, about having to walk.

"Hilde, can't you stop whining?" Rosa said crossly. "My head is throbbing, and I'm as tired as you are."

Hans finally picked Hilde up to carry her the rest of the way home and up the stairs.

---

* *See appendix for recipie*

"Get into your nightgown now, Hilde," said Rosa taking off her hat and coat.

"I want some more cookies," whined the seven-year-old. "I don't want to go to bed."

"No more cookies tonight. And pick up the boxes and ribbons you scattered around the living room. Go put your coat on its hook. And look! You've left your shoes and stockings here on the floor. What a mess! Put down your doll and pick up these things at once!"

Hilde scowled. "I *won't* put down Sissi. It's Christmas now, and I'm going to hold her all night!"

"I beg your pardon, young lady! You will *not* speak to me that way," said Rosa, her temper thinning.

"And I don't want to clean up the room! I'm not the maid. Miss Margarethe doesn't make me work. She's *nice* to me!"

Something in Rosa snapped. She reached out and grasped the arm of the doll. "How dare you disobey me! Give me that doll, and do what I tell you!"

"My doll! You're hurting her! Let go! Let go!" Hilde pulled and tugged at the doll. There was a ripping sound. Suddenly the doll's arm tore loose at the joint, leaving the doll's arm in Rosa's hand and flinging Hilde back against the table beside the sofa. The child's momentum knocked the table awry. The box with the bell in it toppled off, shattering the confection on the floor. Hilde stood open-mouthed and aghast, staring first at the broken bell, and then at the dismembered doll in her hand.

"Look what you've done, you wretched child!" raged Rosa.

"You broke my doll!" screamed Hilde. "You broke my bell! I hate you! I hate you!"

"How *dare* you!" cried Rosa, raising her hand and stepping toward Hilde. Hans caught her wrist and restrained her.

"Rosa, calm down!"

"I will *not* calm down! Let go of me! She has sassed and disobeyed me, insulted me, torn apart this doll we couldn't afford, and broken a bell that cost me half a day's wages! She deserves a sound spanking!"

"I will not let you hit her. Punish her some other way, if you must." His grip was painful.

Rosa glared at him, her eyes flaming. His did not waver. "Very well!" Rosa said through clenched teeth. She straightened and pulled her wrist from Hans's grasp. Her eyes burned with a fury born of a deep hurt she couldn't explain even to her-self. "You have been a very naughty girl, Hilde. Therefore, you will *not* take your doll to bed. Nor will you play with her again until we can have her repaired." Hilde began to wail. Rosa stepped forward and took the doll from her unresisting arms. "And you will not keep your bell, either. Since you broke it by being disobedient, it is no longer yours!" She bent and gathered up the largest of the broken fragments, then turned to Hans and growled beneath her breath, "And you can sleep in your office, since you value me so very little." Rosa strode from the room and slammed her bedroom door behind her.

✣ ✣ ✣

Hilde lay miserably in her cot, her sobs abated to hiccoughs. The door opened softly, and Papa came in. He sat on her bed and gathered her into his arms.

"Oh, Papa," she sniveled, "why does Mama hate me so much?"

"Shhhh, darling. Mama doesn't hate you. She was just very angry tonight. She works awfully hard, you know, and she gets tired."

"She was angry at me. She's *always* angry at me. I didn't mean to be a bad girl. And I want my dolly . . ." her sobs broke out anew.

"Hush, liebchen. You're not a bad girl. You were a bit naughty tonight because you were very tired. But I'll work on your doll tomorrow, and soon you can have her back. All right? Will you stop crying now, and go to sleep? Look what I brought you. I found it under the sofa." He held out his hand to show a large, curved segment of chocolate decorated with sugar crystals. Hilde's sobs stopped, and she sniffed. She took the confection from his hand, looked at it for a moment, then gazed up lovingly.

"Thank you, Papa. You're the most wonderful papa. I love you best in all the world, next to Oma." Papa chuckled. She put her arms around him and squeezed hard. Then she bit off a piece of the chocolate, and snuggled down into the covers. Papa tucked them up around her chin and kissed her on the forehead. "I love you too, princess. And make sure you keep that chocolate out of sight."

Vienna, 1927

*R*osa spoke to Hans as she and Margarethe brought food from the kitchen to the dining area at one end of the living room. "Can you get Hilde to the table, please, Hans?"

"I'm already at the table," giggled a disembodied voice.

Hans lifted the floor-length tablecloth to reveal Hilde underneath, just bedding down her doll on a needlepoint throw cushion from the sofa. She grinned up at him.

Rosa put a pot of stew on the table. "Hilde, please take your things out from under the table and go wash up."

"This is my cottage in the woods," explained the girl as she crawled out. "And Sissi is Rapunzel."

"Does that mean you're the witch?" asked Hans, "or the handsome prince?"

"No, I'm her fairy godmother, and I'm rescuing her from the witch."

"I think you have your stories mixed up," said Rosa. "Hurry up with your hands, and come and sit down."

After dinner Hilde played under the table again, while the grown-ups talked above her. Mama had made a nightgown for Sissi out of scraps she got from the big house where she went to sew every day. In a loving voice Hilde explained to her doll that it was time for bed. She carefully took off Sissi's golden cap, dirndl, and little shoes, and laid them neatly on a handkerchief, which served as a wardrobe. She noticed that Miss Margarethe, (sometimes Papa called her Miss Gretl) had taken off her shoes again, and was petting Papa's leg with her foot. Sometimes Papa's foot petted her back. She moved the handkerchief wardrobe over to the other side of her cottage so Miss Margarethe wouldn't accidentally kick it.

❖ ❖ ❖

By spring Rosa could no longer deny the evidence that her husband was having an affair with his young secretary. She had found impassioned and shockingly explicit letters from Margarethe to Hans. Sick to her soul, Rosa cursed herself for trusting her husband after the last two times, and felt black rage at the young woman whom she had helped save from destitution. Rosa's mother, Hannah, sorrowfully advised her daughter that enough was enough. She must seek a divorce, however painful and shameful it would be.

Rosa was devastated, paralyzed by fear of an unknown future without the man she had adored. Charming and handsome, Hans had been her only true love. By the standards of the level of society in which he had been raised, he was a man of honor. But that society had different moral expectations of its men. She could not continue to deceive herself that he would ever remain faithful.

Divorce was, unfortunately, an almost fatal blow to the reputation of any woman, regardless of the reason for the divorce. No more would such a woman be counted as an equal to other women, married or spinster. She would be avoided, shunned, and considered somehow dirty, almost criminal. Respect and admiration had always been the deepest cravings of Rosa's soul. Her heart failed her in contemplating the terrible consequences of divorce. It wasn't fair! But it was fact. And she could no longer bear betrayal.

In Catholic Austria, a divorce was only allowed when adultery was proven in a court of law. Margarethe's letters would serve. Those convicted were sentenced to six months in jail. Hans's mother, Madam Edler, humbled herself to beg Rosa to withdraw charges to avoid destroying her son's reputation and career with a prison record. He would never be hired again, she pointed out, and without a job he could pay neither alimony nor child support. Madam Edler promised to help keep Hilde in Notre Dame if Rosa would not prosecute.

Rosa agreed to withdraw charges from Hans, but not from Margarethe. So hostile was the air between Hans and Rosa after the trial, that he refused to speak to her when he collected Hilde for visits during the following months. In the spring he came more rarely, and then not at all. Hilde was worried and wounded, and missed her papa terribly. But no one explained anything to her. Rosa became bitter and quiet, except when she exploded. Hilde was almost afraid to be around her. The girl's heart trembled at the tearing apart of the people she most loved.

During a visit to St. Pölten in August, Mama and Oma were talking in the kitchen. In the parlor, just around the corner of the doorway, Hilde sat quietly behind Opa's big overstuffed chair. Beside her was a lamp table covered with a beautiful printed table scarf which fell halfway to the floor, a gift from Oma's brother Eduard, who traveled to faraway places. It was one of Hilde's favorite things, printed all over with fat roses, and bordered with silky, red fringe as long as her own hair. She loved to sit in the little cubbyhole between the furniture and the wall, and make braids of the fringe, or comb the long strands with her fingers. If she remained quiet, her mother and Oma would forget she was there, and talk about things they wouldn't say in front of her.

There was so much she couldn't understand. She was confused and afraid. Why wouldn't Papa come to visit anymore? She missed him dreadfully, and was heartbroken that he had stopped loving her. If only she could see him she would promise to be very good if he would come back home.

Mama was mad all the time. Hilde nervously stayed out of her way to avoid getting yelled at or spanked if she didn't obey immediately. After an outburst of anger, Mama would hug her hard and tell her she was sorry, that they had to love each other more than ever because they were alone now. Which wasn't true, because there they were, visiting Oma and Opa. And Uncle Johann and funny Uncle Richard came to Vienna a lot, and sometimes tall Uncle Peter. And they saw Mama's best friend, Aunt Steffie, and her boys, in the park all the time.

Mama went crazy when anybody talked about Miss Margarethe. Hilde didn't understand why at first, and when she asked about it, her mother got an awful look on her face. So Hilde was careful not to mention it again. But if she listened when Mama talked to Oma or Aunt Steffie, she could find out things. All morning Mama and Oma had been discussing money, and whether Mama was going to survive if all she had was something called an alimony, which was very small.

Hilde had braided all the fringe on the table scarf, and now she tried to braid the braids together, but they looked messy that way. Everything was messy. She slapped angrily at the fringe. She wanted to cut it all off. Her stomach hurt.

She heard Oma say, "And what about medical school now?" Suddenly everything got very quiet. After a minute, Mama walked across the floor and went out the door. There was no sound for awhile. Hilde crawled over to the door and peeked into the kitchen. Oma was there, with the apple knife in one hand, and her head bowed. The other hand was wiping her eyes.

Hilde jumped to her feet and ran to her. "Oma? What's

wrong? Why are you crying?"

Hannah put down the knife and looked at Hilde. "Oh, my poor baby. Come here to me." She gathered Hilde into her lap and held her tightly.

"Hilde, do you understand what's going on with your mama and papa?" she asked.

Hilde didn't know what to answer since she had learned that it was dangerous to know anything about the troubles with her parents. So when Oma held her away and looked into her face, she avoided the kindly eyes and looked down.

"Darling, look at me." Hilde looked up tentatively. "I'm afraid your life is going to be very sad for awhile."

Hilde's lips trembled, and her nose stung way up inside. She threw herself against Oma's ample bosom and burst into tears. Oma cuddled her close as though she were a baby and whispered soft words in a broken voice.

After a while, Hilde asked moistly, "Why is everybody mad at me? Nobody likes me anymore."

Hannah heaved a great sigh. "Liebchen, sweet baby. It isn't you. Your mama and papa have grown-up problems that are very, very bad. They can't live together anymore and be happy. So your papa has gone to live somewhere else.

"Is that what a divorce is?"

"You've been listening, little one. Yes. That's what a divorce is."

"Mama's friend, Aunt Steffie, got a divorce, but Uncle Fritzie still lives with her and Richard and Willie."

Oma breathed deeply again before she answered. "Yes, but Uncle Fritzie isn't the papa of Richard and Willie. He's a stepfather."

Hilde began to cry again. "I don't want a stepfather. I want my own papa. And I want him to live with us like he used to."

"I know you do, Hilde. And I wish it could be so. But it can't. It can't be that way ever again, do you see?"

Hilde didn't, but she nodded because it was expected.

"Darling girl," Oma said, rearranging her to sit up, and turning her so she could look right into her eyes, "there is a very important thing that you must do now. It is a very grown-up thing, but you are the only one who can do the job." Hilde bit her lower lip to keep it from trembling.

"Right now your mama is feeling sadder than she has ever felt in her life. And she's scared, too." This was news to Hilde. Mama had never been afraid of anything. Oma continued. "The one thing you can do for her better than anyone else in the world, is to be sure she knows that you love her. You do love her, don't you, Hilde."

"Yes."

"Do you love her very much?"

This was a puzzling question. Of course she loved her mother very much. She was her mama, wasn't she? "Yes, Oma."

"Well, she loves you, too. More than anybody in the whole world, darling. It may seem sometimes like she doesn't like you very much. She might act angry with you."

Hilde nodded, her mind full of such memories.

"But I want you to know something. I promise, now. You know I always tell you the truth, don't I?"

Hilde nodded soberly.

"I promise that the reason your mama is angry is because she is very, very sad, and she feels that nobody loves her. So she acts angry when she really wants to cry."

"Mama *never* cries," said Hilde.

"That's true. So I want you to remember that when she acts angry, it's because she needs to have love. This is a very hard, grown-up thing I'm telling you, Hilde. But I promise it is true. And you are the only person in the world who can help her feel loved. Will you try?"

Everything was awful, and Hilde's stomach was hurting again. But she would do anything Oma asked. With a quivering lip, she nodded.

"Darling, I love you so. And I will pray that God will make

you and your Mama strong enough to get through this. And do you know what? If you will ask God, He will put angels round about you to help you, and to help your mother. I promise this is true."

Angels? Oma never told lies, so it must be true. Hilde could do it if she had angels. She felt a little better.

On the way back to Vienna, Mama was very quiet, but more calm than before they went to St. Pölten to get rested. Together they climbed the stairs to the flat, and Mama fumbled with the key to the door. When they went inside Hilde could tell something was different. The door to the office stood open, and their footsteps echoed a little. Mama walked quickly to the office and looked in.

"He's been here! He's taken all his furniture and everything. How did he get in? I took away his key. How dare he come here without my permission! What else has he taken?"

Mama walked swiftly into the kitchen, looked around, then went around the corner into the bedroom. She made a funny sound, and then was quiet. When the quiet continued, Hilde went cautiously to her mother's room. The first thing she saw was that the bedroom was empty. There was a pile of Mama's clothes on the floor where the prized wardrobe used to be, and another pile of underwear and things on the other side of the room. They were in a heap, like someone just threw them there, which Mama would never, ever let anybody do. There were a few scraps of paper here and there, and some dust balls where the dresser and wardrobe had been.

The second thing Hilde saw was her mother. Her face was white, and her mouth was twisted up crooked. She stood sort of bent over, and she wasn't moving at all. Her breath was making strange little sounds. Distressed, Hilde ran to take her hand. "Mama?"

"He took it all. He took it all away." Mama's voice was thin and high like a little girl's. "He gave it to me. It was a love present to me. And now he took it all away." Her mother leaned against the wall and slid slowly to the floor. She began to whimper. Hilde had never seen Mama look that way. It frightened her. She ran to her mother's side and wrapped her arms around the woman's neck.

"Oh, Mama! Oh, Mama! Please don't feel bad! Papa can take away the furniture, but he can't take away our love!"

Rosa gasped, then uttered a choking sob. Her arms wound around the little body, and she hugged back. Oma had been right.

A few days later, Rosa stood back and surveyed the refurbishing of her bedroom. "Thanks, Johann. And Fritzie, you and Steffie are darlings to give me your old things. They will do just fine."

The two men were moving a chipped and stained chest of drawers back against the wall. Fritzie stepped forward with his handkerchief and wiped dust from the top. "Steffie says to remind you that the second drawer's broken," he warned. "Don't pull it out all the way or it'll fall on your foot."

"I can put a slat on the back of the drawer to stop that," said her brother, Johann.

Hilde stood at the bedroom door, swathed in an apron that came to her ankles. "Uncle Johann, Uncle Fritzie, come into the kitchen. Uncle Richard and I have made us a nice tea party with the strudel Oma sent."

Richard, the younger brother Rosa had delivered as a baby, was now a manly eighteen years, but, as ever, a hopeless clown. In the kitchen he was carrying a tray of things for their tea. Somewhere he had gotten an oversized paper chef's hat, and was wearing it pulled down completely over his eyes. "Help me, Hilde! I've lost my way!" He staggered around the kitchen, tipping the tray dangerously this way and that.

Hilde shrieked, and ran to grab his arm. "This way, Uncle Richard. I'll lead you to the table." He laid out the cups and food without removing the hat, deliberately stacking cups on top of the jam, laying the spoons and forks on the seats of chairs, and balancing the teapot dangerously on the table's edge. Hilde, giggling gleefully, corrected his false moves.

"Richard, take off that stupid hat," ordered Johann.

"What hat?" he replied. "I don't see any hat. In fact, I don't see anything at all." Hilde laughed until she nearly fell over.

Johann reached out and pulled off the hat. Richard blinked with astonishment, "Oh! There you all are! Won't you join me for tea?"

Later, as the men were leaving, Johann stopped by the door of the former office and looked in. "If you get a good renter from that advertisement, I'll nail the door to the office closed for your privacy and safety. It's a nice big room, and a good location. You should be able to ask a decent rent for it."

"Pray for me, Johann, " she asked softly, laying a hand on his arm. "I need so much now . . ." she choked to a halt. Her brother covered her hand with his own. He had always been a bulwark of faith to her, a man of deep spirituality. He nodded a promise.

Not three weeks later the room was taken by a Mr. Sodamar, a retired banker whose only joy and occupation in life were the endless practice of his violin.

When her two brothers visited shortly thereafter, Rosa had Johann tack a straw mattress against her side of the separating door, both to buffer the incessant concert, and to insure that *their* noises wouldn't bother Mr. Sodamar.

"Actually, he's quite good," Rosa commented. "It's just the non-stop nature of the concert. Now, if I hang a curtain over the mattress, it will give the illusion that we have a window behind it."

"I like Mr. Sodamar," Hilde piped. "I can dance all day while he plays for me." She twirled away in demonstration. "And he wears gray things on his shoes all the time," she commented through an arabesque.

"Spats," clarified Rosa. "He is a very proper banker, thank you, and wouldn't dream of being seen without gloves, bowler hat, and spats." She commented to her brothers, "He's a dear, and adores Hilde."

"Is he rich?" asked Richard waggling his eyebrows up and down.

"You can forget that one, Richard. He's a courtly old man, and we are charmed to have him, even if he serenades us to death."

"Well, at least he has his own entrance, and doesn't have to trail through your flat to get in and out." As Johann put his tools in a sack, he asked, "How's the financial situation, Rosl?" He used her childhood nickname.

Her face became grim. "Not good. Without Sodamar, we'd have been on the street at the end of the month." Her chin lifted in defiance. "But I'll make it. I always do."

"Yes, you always do." He leaned over and kissed her cheek before he left. "You can thank the Lord for that."

❖ ❖ ❖

It was December 6th, the evening of the feast of St. Nikolaus. Rosa's wealthy friend Steffie and her two boys had come to celebrate with Rosa and Hilde. Steffie announced in a bold and breezy tone that Fritzie was busy attending a meeting, but would join them later that evening. When he arrived later, she told the others, they would all share a lovely supper of good things she had brought.

The women sat on the sofa and chatted, covert smiles on their faces as they watching the children prattling and playing on the rug. At any moment they expected a sound at the door.

Soon it came: A firm knocking.

The children's eyes flew to the door. Rosa assumed a look of curiosity and called out, "Who's there? Who's that at my door?"

A muffled voice replied, "It is I, St. Nikolaus, with gifts for good little children."

Immediately the first voice was overridden by another male voice crying out in harsh tones, "Yes! Let us in! I want to get at the *bad* little children who live here! I can smell them through the door! If you don't open up right away, I will break down the door!"

Alarmed, the children scampered over to Steffie as Rosa went to open the door. The first of two men entered. He was dressed in long, ornate priest's robes of white, red, and gold. On his head was a tall mitered hat decorated with a heavily jeweled cross. Resting on his back was a lumpy sack, and he held a shepherd's crook in one hand. His long, white beard hung slightly askew, and Rosa stifled a smile.

Almost immediately another creature jumped from behind him into the center of the room, glaring and hopping around with exaggerated movements. This one was dressed from head to foot in a black, hairy suit. Over his face was a mask carved into angry eyes, hooked nose, and sharp teeth, with a very long red tongue hanging out. Horns protruded from his head. One hand held a heavy chain, and the other a small whip.

"Aha!" he cried. "There they are!" He lumbered toward the children, who ran screaming behind the sofa. However, their faces didn't look as terrified as their voices sounded.

"Stop, Krampus!" exclaimed St Nikolaus, blocking the hairy man with his staff. "You have no right to these children if they have been good. And I am sure they have been *very* good. Come to me, children. Let me talk to you." The children ventured timidly forth.

"No! No!" cried the figure of Krampus, the devil. "I want them for myself! I won't let them near you!" He capered and leaped about, shaking his chain, howling loudly, and darting at the children, who shrieked and ran from him. Saint Nikolaus seemed content to stand serenely and let Krampus steal the show.

The man in black glared at Rosa and Steffie, and growled, "Have these children been good? If they have not, I'm going to whip them!" He lunged forward, brandishing his whip, and the children screamed again and scampered behind the furniture. "You can't hide from me, you naughty children! Little girl, come out from there and take your punishment!"

Hilde crept out from behind the sofa, her face a mixture of fear and anticipation. Krampus bent and glared directly into her face. "You've been a bad girl this year, haven't you," he growled.

Hilde stammered with nervous excitement, "N-no, I've been a g-g-good girl."

"Well then, you've been a bad student, and done poorly in school!"

"No! I've worked hard. T-truly! I have the highest score in my class."

"Well, I know you've been mean to your mother, so I'm going to have to whip you!" He flicked his whip gently on Hilde's ankles several times.

Rosa stepped forward and laid a hand on the devil's arm. "Oh, no, Krampus. Hilde has been good to me. You must not whip her."

Krampus roared and turned to the boys, who had been watching Hilde's mock punishment with evident delight. "Then I'll beat these boys. One can see how naughty they are just by looking at them. Come here, you two, so I can beat you." He plumped heavily into a chair, and beckoned imperiously at them. They edged toward him, giggling. Putting his whip aside, he grasped them, one at a time, and laid them both, crosswise and bottoms-up, over his lap. "This makes me more efficient," he cried, "I can beat two at once!" And raising his whip he swatted them lightly over and over while they howled as if being tortured. "This is for disobeying your mother. This is for teasing each other. This is for playing instead of doing your studies."

Steffie cried out, "Stop, stop, Herr Krampus! Please don't beat them! They're good boys, and they've been very kind today. They gave their own spending money to some beggars!"

At this point St. Nikolaus chose to show some spirit. He

spoke sternly in an artificially deep voice, "Krampus, I forbid you to punish them. They are good children. Put them down immediately!"

"Hmmph! Very well. But I still say they are fooling you!" Krampus set the boys back on their feet, straightening their rumpled clothing.

"You are wrong, Krampus," insisted St. Nikolaus. "Anyone can see they are very good children, and deserve presents for Christmas. Come, children! And you, Krampus, you stay away from them!"

Krampus snarled and howled in frustration while St. Nikolaus opened the sack he carried and upended it. Candies and tiny trinkets and toys spilled out onto the rug.

The children dove at the treats, squealing with delight, clutching up as many as they could hold. A little horn bounced as it fell, and came to rest against Krampus's shoe. Hilde crawled over to pick it up, and looked long and hard at the devil's footwear. She snatched up the horn, and grinned up at Krampus.

"Ha, Ha, Krampus. I'm not afraid of you! You can't do anything to hurt me!" She jumped to her feet, wiggled her hips insolently, and stuck out her tongue at the hairy man.

Satan roared and brandished his whip at her. "You had better watch out, little girl! If you're naughty to me, I will whip you!"

"You can't spank me," she replied impishly. "You can't do anything to me!"

"I can't?" He seemed genuinely puzzled at this change of attitude. "And why not?"

Gleefully Hilde replied, "Because I know who you are!" She pointed down at the gray spats showing beneath his hairy costume.

The adults all laughed, and Hilde glanced at her mother, very glad to see her laughing again at last, seeming really happy.

✧ ✧ ✧

Vienna, 1929

The year turned, with spring and summer passing. Hilde became aware of the disappearance of small comforts they had formerly afforded. Mama was more often worried and irritable. In the fall Hilde was dressed in regular clothing and taken to a new school.

"Please, Mama, I don't want to go to the public school this year. I want to go back to Sister Haubinger." The nine-year-old had to walk fast, almost run, to keep up with her mother's long stride on the sidewalk.

"Well, that's unfortunate." Mama's face was grim. "There are a lot of things that you're going to have to do from now on that you don't want to do."

"But why, Mama? You got me new uniforms and everything. Why do I have to go to the public school?" Dismay had made Hilde bold. She never would have questioned Mama otherwise. Questioning Mama nowadays only got her into trouble.

Rosa stopped dead, and turned flaming eyes on Hilde. She answered in a low, angry voice. "Because your father is a selfish swine, and doesn't care what happens to you or me or anyone, as long as he can have what he wants. Now, quit dawdling, or we're going to miss the streetcar." And so saying, she grasped Hilde's hand and hurried her along.

Hilde trotted beside her mother for half a block. Rosa slowed to a stop and turned to her daughter with a sigh. "You might as well know, Hilde. Your father hasn't sent us any support payments since July. I went to see your grandmother Edler about it last Friday. She told me that your father and Fräulein Stengel have moved away to Hungary. They're going to get married there, and live there, and there is no Hungarian law that will force him to send us the support he owes us. He will probably never come back, since he would be in trouble with the law if he did. So, we are abandoned, Hilde. We are also totally broke, and Grandmother Edler cannot pay the whole tuition herself. And, that is why you are going to public school, instead of Notre Dame."

Hilde's mind couldn't grasp it at first. No more Papa? Papa would not come to see her anymore? No more half days in the park? That had to be the reason he hadn't come to visit after she came back from her summer with Oma. Hilde's eyes blurred with tears, and she stumbled on the sidewalk.

Rosa glanced down at her. "What is it?" She lifted Hilde's chin. "Are you crying? Oh, Hilde," she said, shaking her head, "it won't do any good. I'm sorry, dear, but that's just how things are." Rosa took her hand more gently, and continued to the street corner. "Look, now, there's our streetcar."

At the school, after Mama had filled out all the papers and gone, the teacher, Frau Drikker, led her before the class. To Hilde's frightened eyes, all the girls looked as if they knew each other and knew what to expect. They had already been there a week. But she knew nothing and nobody, and wanted to shrink away so they wouldn't all stare at her.

"Girls, we have a new student today, Hilde Edler." The woman's voice was brisk and cool. "This is her first year with us. She has been attending Notre Dame de Sion until now." She looked down at Hilde. "I trust, Hilde, that you will set us a good example in etiquette, which I know they stress at that fine school. Now, please take that empty seat at the front of row one. Girls, as I explained yesterday, today you will have an examination on paper so I can evaluate your skills and penmanship. We will be using your copybooks instead of slates. Please prepare your materials."

Hilde pulled her new notebook from her school bag. Paper was very hard to obtain in Austria, so students only used it for important things. She hunted in the bottom of her bag for a pencil. She was still looking when the teacher began.

"If you have nine blue balls, seven red balls, and twelve yellow balls . . . " She paused for a moment, and the class scribbled busily. Hilde was frantically trying to find her pencil. ". . . how many balls will you have in total?" The class scribbled again. Hilde found her pencil, but the lead was broken. She looked beseechingly up at Frau Drikker, who was attending another student and didn't notice her.

Hilde turned to the girl behind her and whispered, "My pencil lead broke. Is there a pencil sharpener somewhere?"

A cold voice spoke aloud, "Hilde, in this school, we do not speak aloud during examinations. You will please observe the rules."

"But my pencil . . . " began Hilde in consternation, holding up the item.

Frau Drikker interrupted, "Apparently you do not understand what I am saying. Therefore, you will stay in the room for ten minutes during recess." She then recited the next problem.

Hilde could do nothing but stare in misery and embarrassment at her empty paper as the teacher went on.

"Why aren't you writing the problems?" came the sharp voice from directly in front of her.

Afraid to look up, Hilde held out her pencil and whispered, "My pencil lead broke. I don't have another."

"Well, you might have said so. However, in this school you are expected to always have two extra pencils, sharpened and ready. 'Be prepared' is our motto. Girls," she spoke aloud to the class, "what is our motto in this school?"

"Be prepared," answered a chorus of voices.

"Humph! You can hardly do anything at all without a pencil, so the class will wait while you sharpen yours. The sharpener is next to the door."

Hilde arose, flushed and shaking, and walked before them all to the sharpener. She broke the lead by grinding too fast, and two or three girls snickered. Finally succeeding, she returned to her seat, pencil poised, wishing she were dead.

When the teacher began again, she felt at least a hint of confidence. She had always been good at arithmetic. Papa had helped her, explaining that at first he had been very bad at math, but practice and understanding had helped him to become better than all the other boys he knew.

"There are five automobiles heading south on the strasse. Eight other automobiles are heading north. They are joined by seven automobiles coming from side streets. How many automobiles are on the strasse at this moment?"

Hilde wrote in her careful script: five, over eight, over seven, with a plus sight at the left of the seven. She drew a straight line, and wrote the answer: twenty. She knew it was correct, and waited while the other girls scribbled busily away. After fifteen more problems she was feeling much better. She knew her answers were all correct, and Sister Haubinger had always praised her penmanship.

The teacher spoke, "Please pass your exercise books to the front and prepare to go out for recess. Today you will be doing calisthenics and relay races. Fräulein Gumph will lead you. Hilde, you will remain in your seat.

Hilde sat quietly with downcast eyes as the other girls filed out. Frau Drikker's busy pen checked and scribbled notes on the exercise books at her desk. A surreptitious glance out the window showed Hilde the class neatly formed in rows, following Fräulein Gumph in jumping exercises. She also saw her own notebook work its way to the top of the stack on the desk. Frau Drikker paused, looked closer, then looked angrily at Hilde.

"What is this you have done, Hilde? You have done only part of each problem. I can hardly believe that Notre Dame de Sion allowed either disobedience or sloth at their institution. Do you think you can get away with them here?"

Hilde was confused and almost too frightened to respond. Finally she managed to stammer, "I—I don't— But— what did I . . ."

"Speak up, girl. It is impolite to mumble."

"I'm sorry, Frau Drikker," Hilde attempted in as loud a tone as her trembling voice could manage, "I don't know what I did wrong."

"Come here," said the teacher. "Look! All you have put down is the problems. You haven't written *any* of the words of the story problems: 'red automobiles,' 'brown kittens,' nothing! All you have is the numbers."

Hilde's voice fell to a whisper again, "I'm sorry, I didn't know I was supposed. . . ."

"That's sloth! Plain sloth. You will stay inside for the rest of the recess period and properly complete your work. Here, take Britt's workbook. She has done all the problems exactly as they should be done. You may copy the words appropriate to each problem next to each of your own. But do not change your answers if they are incorrect! I hope you do better at arithmetic than you do at following instructions."

Hilde felt hot at the implied insult. She would *never* copy another girl's answers! She would never need to, even if she didn't mind cheating, because she knew she had them all correct. And how was she supposed to follow instructions she had never heard?

Without a word she took Britt's exercise book and her own, and returned to her desk. As she wrote the proper words next to each problem, her hand shook and spoiled the penmanship. The score she got when her paper was finally corrected was the lowest she had ever received, and she had to fight to hold back tears.

After school Hilde dawdled at putting her things in her school bag. Humiliated by the entire day, she was reluctant to be caught in the mass of girls who crowded out of the classroom the instant the final bell rang. But a group lingered on the steps of the school, and she had to pass through them.

"Why look at Miss Prim-and-Proper! She doesn't look like such a rich girl to me," spoke one girl sarcastically.

"But she must be," said another, "so we better imitate her

good etiquette, hadn't we? Parley voo, Miss Rich Girl." The speaker tilted her nose in the air and minced across the step.

"She doesn't even know how to do her story problems right," said a third. "How clever can she be?" The girls broke into laughter.

Hilde rushed through them, down the steps. Her lowered head and tear-blurred eyes made her unaware of a girl bending to tie her shoelace, and Hilde almost fell over her. "Oh, I'm sorry," she croaked. "I didn't see you."

The girl, who had lost her balance, scrambled to her feet. "You're Hilde, the new girl, aren't you. Hello, I'm Ava, and I'm new, too. I came only two days ago." She smiled.

"You did? You are?" said Hilde, hopeful at this first sign of friendliness.

"Yeah. Don't pay any attention to those cats on the stairs. They think they're the queens of the world, and they're nasty to everyone. Are you going to the streetcar stop? Come on, we can walk together." She linked her arm through Hilde's, and suddenly the world was not such a horrid place.

❖ ❖ ❖

Hilde never stopped hating the school all the time she was there. It was a stupid place! Most of the girls had terrible grammar and they spoke low German with accents Mama would have likened to street sweepers'. She would have thrown up her hands at their manners. Frau Drikker seemed to take sly satisfaction in pointing out that Hilde was no better than the rest of them. And some of the girls never stopped teasing her. But Ava was her friend. They smiled at each other across the classroom, and talked and played during the brief periods of free time after recess exercises.

The school was ugly, too, brown and plain and unadorned. Hilde painfully missed the mirror-like marble floors and gorgeously framed paintings at Notre Dame de Sion. They didn't have French lessons here, nor seem to care about art or music appreciation. And she truly missed the lovely, peaceful times each day when the entire school of Notre Dame went to Mass in the beautiful chapel. Most of all, she missed the kindly love of Sister Haubinger. But there was not one thing she could do about any of it.

Mama had not been able to find sufficient work for weeks— only a temporary cleaning job here or there. Sometimes she bought used clothing and re-cut the items to make dresses for herself and Hilde. There was never enough food to really fill their stomachs. Mother and daughter became increasingly thin. Hilde seemed all enormous eyes and bony arms and legs.

When Hilde opened the front door of their flat after school one day, she found her mother in the kitchen, looking through cupboards.

Hilde put her books on the table and slumped into a chair.

"What is it, Hilde? Rosa asked.

"Nothing," the child murmured.

"Were the children unkind to you at school?"

Hilde shook her head.

"Then what's wrong? You act as if your best friend died."

Hilde paused a few moments, then said quietly, "I'm just hungry."

"Well, that makes two of us," sighed Rosa. She put an arm around her daughter, and pressed her close for a moment. "I'm sorry, Liebchen. I'm hungry, too. I'm going to St. Pölten tomorrow to get some vegetables from Oma. Tonight we have a little rice . . ."

Rice with nothing. Again. As Rosa took out the pot, she stopped and stared at it thoughtfully for several minutes.

"Hilde, *you* might help get us a little food tonight."

Hilde looked questioning. "Me?"

Her mother's lips were grim, but she straightened her shoulders and looked at her daughter. "Sometimes we have to do hard things. Embarrassing things. Things we would never do if this were a better world."

Hilde knew it well, and waited for the rest.

"You know Mr. Lindburg's meat market? The one on the Hapsburgstrasse?"

" Yes. You never go there. You said they have poor quality. You like Mr. Pruze's better."

"I do, but Mr. Pruze won't give us credit anymore until we pay him. And we can't pay him until I get some work. But Mr. Lindburg hardly knows me, and doesn't know you at all." Her lips tightened again. "We're going to go there together. I am going to stand outside, across the street. I want you to go inside and ask Mr. Lindburg if he has any soup bones he will give you for nothing. He might. Anyway, he would have more sympathy for a child than for a grown woman. And you're small enough to look about six. It's our only hope. Are you brave enough to do this?" She held out her hand to Hilde, and the girl took it. Together they walked from the building.

Hilde went into the store with her stomach churning and her face red. There were three other customers, and Hilde shrank into a corner and waited. When they were gone, the butcher asked what he could do for her. She whispered. "Do you have any soup bones you were going to throw away?"

"I'm sorry little fräulein, I can't hear you. Come a little closer and tell me again."

Hilde burned with shame but spoke a little louder. "A soup bone? Do you have a soup bone? I-I can't pay anything for it." Her voice choked, and her eyes glossed with embarrassed tears. The man didn't answer, but stood looking at her over the counter for a few moments. Hilde hung her head so he wouldn't see her face.

"Little fräulein, have you had any dinner today?"

She shook her head, still looking at the floor.

He muttered, "Poor little thing." Then more strongly, "Yes, I think I have a soup bone here I was going to save for my dog. But she's so fat she doesn't need it. I might as well give it to you."

Hilde heard paper tearing and crinkling as he wrapped something up.

"Thank you very much, sir," she said as she took the package.

Rosa was waiting in the shadow of a doorway when Hilde came out with the brown wrapped package. Rosa jerked her head in the direction of the nearest corner, and walked ahead around the corner.

When Hilde joined her, she held out her hand for the package. "What did you get?"

"I don't know. He said I was 'a poor little thing', and gave me this."

Rosa opened the wrapping and smiled. "Look, Hilde! He gave us a soup bone with plenty of meat on it. He is a man with a good heart." Hilde smiled too, looking up for approval. Rosa gave her a big hug. "You did well! I'm sorry you had to do it, but now we will have some nice beef soup with rice. Come on." She rewrapped the package, and took Hilde's hand. They both walked home with lighter steps.

It wasn't the last time Hilde went begging, by any means. But Rosa made sure they ranged a wide area. She said there was no sense in wearing out the sympathy of the same shopkeepers.

❖ ❖ ❖

One of Hilde's favorite people in the world was Uncle Peter. He wasn't really an uncle, of course, but she loved him as dearly as any of her real uncles, and she knew he loved her, too. He only came to Vienna every few months, but he always visited, and brought hot cinnamon buns! Enough to last them two or three days!

After Papa had left them, she had heard Uncle Peter talking to Mama in the living room when they thought she was playing in the other room. He asked Mama to marry him, and said he would love them both and take care of them. But Mama said she didn't love him that way, and begged him to always remain her friend. So Uncle Peter had kept on coming, always bringing them nice things to eat, or something pretty, like a little bracelet for her, or some flowers for Mama. After what she had over-heard, Hilde had watched Uncle Peter more carefully. She saw that Peter often looked at her mother in a way she had never noticed before. But now she understood.

During one visit, Rosa sat on the sofa with her legs tucked under her, sipping a mug of steaming tea. "We have to move, Peter. We can't afford to stay here."

Peter sat on the chair across from her with another mug, his long legs stretched before him. Beside his chair lay Hilde, books spread out, doing her homework on a slate, and then copying it correctly into her notebook. "Where will you go?" he asked. "Every place in town is outrageously expensive, and the rents go up every week."

"That's why I don't plan to stay in town." Her eyes unfo-cused as she thought about the plans she had mentioned to Hilde a few times. "Even if I have a little work now, I don't want to take a chance on the future."

"What do you mean? What are you thinking?"

"Peter, I miss the country. Painfully! Who'd have thought I would miss so much the life I constantly complained about as a child?" She smiled. "I miss the dirt and the seedlings, and food! Having food I grew myself! Oh, the fresh vegetables, and . . . " she shrugged. "I miss just grubbing around. I miss fresh eggs. I miss being wakened by roosters. I miss *physical* labor, the kind that makes you so tired at day's end that sleep is a refreshment like delicious wine."

"Well, I'll be!" Peter grinned. "When did you get this mag-got into your brain? You haven't 'grubbed around' since you were Hilde's age. Not since you came to Vienna."

"A lot you know! What do you think I did during all my school breaks? Sat home and let the peasants wait on me? Do you imagine for a minute Papa would let me lie around the house?"

Peter chuckled. "Not likely! Huh! Imagine that! The wom-an wants to go back to her humble beginnings."

"Well, not that, exactly. The whole thing is because I simply cannot afford to live here in Vienna anymore. Food costs the earth, and that's providing I can find anything for sale. Our rent goes up likewise, in spite of Mr. Sodamar, who adores us, and has offered to pay us more if we would stay."

"You already told him? Before you told me?" Peter assumed a mock expression of hurt.

"Peter, I've been mulling this over for months. Months when you haven't been here, or I would most assuredly have mulled it over with you."

Hilde glanced up to see Peter taking her mother's hand, and looking at her in that special way. "Rosa . . ." he began.

"Please don't, Peter," she interrupted him gently. "You know how I feel. You are the best man I know. You deserve a good woman who treats you like the prince you are. Which I never have, if you'll recall. Answer me honestly, now. You travel all over the countryside, in and out of dozens of villages and towns. Haven't you met one single, kind, attractive, good woman? I'll bet there are hoards of them languishing for an interested glance from you!"

Peter regarded her noncommittally for a few moments, then changed the subject completely. "If you've been thinking of moving for several months, you have some fairly concrete plans by now. What have you found?"

Rosa gave up and chuckled. "My, you are good at evading that issue. But, since you ask, there are a few places over on the other side of the Danube, out where they have the market gardens. I've seen a few little cottages, dilapidated though, a thousand years old. Possibilities, but . . ."

"But?"

Her face became animated. "Last week I found an advertisement for a piece of ground. It's right near the Danube, on a little tributary that feeds into it. Five acres. Not so far away from the city. I went to see it. It would be perfect. There is a little woods that covers half of it—so pretty! And plenty of ground already cleared to build a house and plant a good big garden."

His eyebrows soared, "*Build* a house? It doesn't have a house?"

"Oh, Peter, I can build a little house. It doesn't have to be glamorous or big. Just a couple of rooms will do. I found a place not too far away where I can get used lumber and windows and things salvaged from torn-down buildings. And for practically nothing! All I need is enough for Hilde and me. How hard can that be? Especially with Papa, Johann, and Richard to help me?"

Peter shook his head. "Rosa, does anything daunt you? Do you ever look at anything and say to yourself, 'I'd better not try that; it's too risky. It's too hard'?"

Rosa sobered. "There are plenty of things I've tried and failed at, as I have proven during the last decade of my life." She straightened defiantly. "But I'm not rushing into this blindly. I know it will be challenging, but this is something I can do. Something that will heal my soul. It's worth the risk and the work."

"How will you buy the land?"

"I don't have to buy it. It's on lease. A ninety-nine year lease from the county. Nobody can buy or build anything substantial on it because it's on the bank of the Danube and the water table is too high. It's ridiculously inexpensive, all things considered. Mama and Papa will help me with the initial payment. And with the price of produce being so high, I know I can grow enough every summer to help pay the lease. Besides, I'll still have my sewing and cleaning and other jobs in town."

"It doesn't sound to me like you consider it an option. It sounds more like a decision. Would you like to take me out to pass approval on it before I go back to Carinthia?"

Rosa grinned. "Oh, Peter! Would you?"

"Can I come, too?" Hilde asked, expectantly.

"Of course," they said in unison.

❖ ❖ ❖

The ground was leased and the plans drawn up. The foundation would be laid in early spring. Rosa expected to start a garden as soon as the ground was workable. She would tackle most of the building in spring and summer, and move in by fall. Meanwhile, she and Hilde would remain in the apartment in the city. Hilde would continue to attend a public school.

Rosa took every job she could find to save up for building materials. The house would be two stories high someday, but she could only build the ground level at first. That would consist of a large kitchen, and a living room which would double as a bedroom for the time being. They could move in as soon as the lower rooms were covered, and build the upper level when they were able.

Later on, when the upstairs could be afforded, it would be two roomy bedrooms. Rosa would join the two levels with a wide staircase attached to the outside of the house. Perhaps not the greatest in luxury, but easy and inexpensive, and the stairway could later be enclosed. An outhouse would stand apart from the house, further from the river, and they could use a tin tub in the kitchen for bathing. A hand pump at the kitchen sink would bring water in from the river. Rosa's progenitors had survived on far less for centuries, and so had Rosa. She was not above going back to such basics if it would ease their financial straits, get her back to the land, and help heal her heart from the ache associated with the apartment Hans had once shared with her.

❖ ❖ ❖

Hilde was studying at the table in their Vienna apartment when a knock sounded on their door. Mama was in the bedroom packing belongings they wouldn't need until the next year, after the house was finished and they had moved. She called to Hilde to answer the door.

Hilde opened the door and stepped back, confused and disbelieving. The young man at the door wore a tweed suit, a white shirt and tie, and carried books in his hand. But his face! He looked almost exactly like Papa! Could it be? But he looked much younger than Papa had been the last time she had seen him. And his hair was different. She had missed Papa so! Tears pricked at her eyes.

The man smiled at her nervously and said something she couldn't understand at all. Hilde was unable to answer. His voice was a little higher than Papa's. He spoke again, this time with a look of distress. Hilde thought she understood a few words, but he said them wrong. Something about "mother" and "come."

The girl continued to gape at him for a moment, then, leaving the door wide, ran to the bedroom. Mama was sorting clothes and folding them into crates. Hilde was breathless, her eyes wide. "Mama, there's a man at the door. He looks just like Papa, but I don't think he is Papa. And he doesn't know how to talk!"

Puzzled and slightly alarmed, Mama went into the living room. There in the open doorway was the young man. She gasped, her hands flying to her mouth.

"Who . . . who are you?" Rosa breathed.

The young man uttered gibberish, then turning his panic-stricken face away, called in another language to someone they couldn't see, farther down the balcony. "English?" murmured Rosa. Another voice answered, and footsteps quickly approached.

A second young man appeared in the doorway. He was shorter, with dark hair, also dressed in a suit and carrying books. "Good morning, Madam." He nodded to Rosa. His German was heavily accented.

Hilde pointed at the taller young man, and burst out, "Is that my papa?"

The second youth was completely taken aback, but answered, "No little fräulein. That's a friend of mine, Elder Chambers. I'm Elder Hasslem. We're missionaries." He looked to Rosa, perplexed.

"Oh, please forgive little Hilde," said Rosa in a slightly breathless voice. "We're both completely surprised. You see, your friend looks so very much like my husband. Or, at least, the way he looked when he was younger. She hasn't seen her papa for quite some time, and I think she is confused."

The young man who spoke German smiled, and repeated her explanation in English to the other young man. The man who looked like Papa blushed and laughed, and then spoke slowly and haltingly to Rosa and Hilde. His accent was nearly unintelligible. "Hello. I am glad to meet you. My name is Elder Chambers. I am from the United States of America."

Rosa was instantly fascinated. "From America! Oh, please, you *must* come in! I've never met anyone from America before. My name is Frau Edler, and this is my daughter Hilde. Please, won't you sit down?"

The two young men sat on the sofa. They looked so earnest! Neither could have been much older than her Uncle Richard, who was still in his teens. Hilde continued to look at the one called Elder Chambers. She sat on the floor by the sofa and gazed up, searching his face. He glanced down at her, and smiled nervously.

"You say you're missionaries from America? " asked Rosa. "But what are you doing in Austria? We're a Christian country."

The shorter one answered. "We're missionaries from The Church of Jesus Christ of Latter-day Saints. Perhaps you've heard of the Mormons?" he asked. Rosa shook her head. "We have a wonderful new message for Christians and non-Christians alike. Do you believe in God?"

"Of course." Rosa replied. Hilde was barely listening. She let her hand creep over to lie against the coat of the young man who looked so much like her father.

Elder Hasslem continued, "Do you think that if God really loves his children, he would talk to them, tell them what he wants them to do?"

"I'd like to think so. But the state of the world makes it rather obvious that he doesn't."

Elder Hasslem smiled as if she had just answered brilliantly. "It certainly looks that way. But that's only because most people aren't listening. Our message is that he really *is* talking to people these days, just as he used to do thousands of years ago. And the way he speaks now is through prophets, just the way he always has!"

❖ ❖ ❖

How odd! How interestingly strange! Rosa's mind went over the peculiar message of the Elders as she hurriedly packed items into boxes and barrels. Her curiosity had always been too easily piqued, and she had talked to the young men for nearly three hours. Now she'd have to rush through the packing she had planned to take the whole afternoon, in order to get to her cleaning job by 6:00.

Prophets, for goodness sake! She envisioned a bearded, robed man presiding over a flock of followers in the deserts of America, and shook her head. The concept of a modern-day prophet might have an element of logic, if it weren't so absurd. If God really did care . . . if He really didn't change . . . The young men had read scriptures from the Bible, and from some other book she had never heard of. It occurred to Rosa that although she had gone to Mass all her life, she had never read the Bible. Her brother, Johann, had, of course, when he was studying to become a priest. Sometimes he discussed various religious topics with her. But, of course, how would she ever have had time to read anything but her medical books? She hmmphed aloud.

And how could such a farfetched idea be anything but silly? At best, it was wishful thinking. Wouldn't such a claim be widely known? Wouldn't the newspapers have said something if God were speaking to some prophet?

And this story of a boy in New York. Rosa smiled cynically. She had asked the elders why God would appear to a mere teenager and tell *him* how to establish the "true" church. They had replied something about innocent faith, open-heartedness, and an uncontaminated mind. They had mentioned the young Samuel, and Joseph of the colored coat.

"Ridiculous!" exclaimed Rosa, as she changed into her work clothes. At that point in their discussion, she had turned the subject from religion to America, and had questioned them with fascination about fantastic red deserts, cowboys (which apparently didn't exist the way the talking pictures showed them), and American customs which seemed outlandish to Rosa. The conversation had been so absorbing she had asked them to come to see her again. She would only be here for another few months, until the roof was on her little house. And unfortunately, she *would* have time to talk. She had far *too many* hours when there were no calls for her services in Vienna, and when it was still too cold to do much work on her house. At least these boys might provide an interesting diversion.

Rosa chuckled. The mystery of Elder Chambers inability to speak had soon been solved. He had just come to Austria two weeks earlier, speaking virtually no German. He was supposed to learn as he went along, listening to his partner and going from door to door, spreading his "gospel." Rosa no longer wondered at the gibberish he had spoken at the door, nor at his panic when she and Hilde couldn't understand a word. But how amazing that a complete stranger from the other side of the world should look exactly like Hans!

Rosa buttoned her blouse and slipped into her work shoes. "Hilde, are you ready? Frau Head downstairs will give you supper. And don't forget your books. You have a test tomorrow."

They walked down the stairs together, and Rosa bent to kiss Hilde's cheek.

"Mama," the child asked, "you said Elder Chambers could come and visit us again. When do you think he'll come?"

"I don't know. Don't worry about it." As she walked to the streetcar, Rosa felt a moment of concern over Hilde's fascination with the young man who looked so much like her father.

Two weeks later Rosa found herself irritated and amused at the same time. How had the missionaries ever talked her into this? Here she was in a congregation of Mormons, flanked on both sides by the young elders, listening to a group of overly friendly people belting out a song with an enthusiasm which would have been considered vulgar in the Catholic congregation she occasionally attended.

Truth to tell, neither she nor most of her family had felt satisfied by religion since her brother Johann had been expelled from his seminary at St. Gabriel on false charges. A girl had accused the novice priest of carnal knowledge with her, and claimed she was carrying his child. In spite of Johann's pleading denials, they had believed *her*, and required Johann to marry her. The prejudiced and unjust priests at his hearing had convinced *Rosa*, at least, that whether or not there was a God, *those* particular leaders certainly weren't inspired to discern truth from falsehood.

After the terrible verdict, only her mother had still faithfully attended Mass, though in another congregation. She never said so, but Rosa knew she carried heavy resentment toward the priests for their judgment. Her father went only rarely. The younger children didn't care either way.

Johann had struggled mightily with anger at the unfairness of the priests. He had argued and wept with Rosa on several occasions over his wrestlings with the question of religion, truth, and forgiveness. But bitterness was utterly foreign to Johann's nature, and his heart had always belonged to God. After two years of rebellion and lengthy soul searching, he had returned to sporadic church attendance with their mother.

Rosa had struggled with her own feelings. She had needed God so desperately during her agonies over Hans's infidelities. She had prayed in intense and constant earnestness, and sometimes felt strokes of comfort. But what good had any of it done? Hans went right on seeing other women. Maybe there was a God, but Rosa had a hard time believing he cared about individuals. Her involvement in organized religion had dwindled to infrequent holiday attendance.

This Mormon service was foreign to everything she was

accustomed to. Everybody chattered noisily with each other before and after the meeting as though they were long lost friends.
Every single person, she would have sworn, asked her name and
wanted to know all about her. She was invited to dinner on the
spot by at least four families (all of whom she gracefully de-
clined). Astonishingly, they had no priest! And, of all things,
the members themselves gave sermons, quoting from scripture,
and acting as if they had every right to voice opinions on gospel
subjects. She had never heard of such a thing!

There were religious instruction classes for every age, which
all the members attended, and in which praying, arguing, and
laughing seemed equally acceptable. Hilde was delighted when
she came from her class, showing Rosa a little picture of Jesus
her teacher had given to her. Rosa shook her head at the whole
bizarre thing, and was glad she and Hilde would be moving
before these Mormons could become more intrusive.

✤ ✤ ✤

It had rained for days, delaying Rosa's little crew from putting the roof on the first level of the house. Every delay was
worrisome now that fall was approaching. But now Rosa's father had a weekend off, and had come at dawn with her brothers,
Johann and Richard. They were in the act of hoisting the first
heavy beam to the top of the walls when Rosa heard her name
called from the dirt path leading to the house.

"Sister Edler! We finally found you."

"Oh, no," Rosa muttered quietly to her men. "It's the Mormon missionaries. I purposely didn't tell them where I was
building. But they've tracked me down." She had told her family a little about these strange people, and assured them she was
nothing more than curious.

"Want me to run them off?" asked Rosa's short, gruff father.

"Don't be rude, Papa," she barely had time to answer before
the young men were upon them.

"We've come to help," they beamed, as cheerful as the rosy

morning sunshine. "We knew after all this rain you'd need some extra hands to get back on schedule." Rosa noticed they wore work clothes, and one carried a heavy sack. What different creatures they looked without suits and ties.

"Mein Himmel! That one *does* look like Hans," Papa murmured to Rosa. Then he spoke aloud in his usual abrupt and cynical tone, "Do American missionaries know how to build anything?"

The young men weren't aware of the snub. Elder Hasslem answered, "Of course we do! Elder Chambers grew up on a farm where he had to do everything from plow the field to build barns. And I spent the two summers before my mission working with construction crews on public buildings. We're ready to go!"

"Well, this is no public building," Papa retorted. "If you think you can help, you'll have to follow my orders and not get creative. I don't suppose you have any tools."

"They are here!" Elder Chamber's German had improved dramatically. He opened the sack and took out two hammers and a saw. "Some of the members loaned these to us. We have also a square, and a level, and a . . . a . . . what?"

He looked beseechingly at Elder Hasslem, who replied, "Plumbline."

Johann decided to rescue them from Papa. "That's good! Come on over here and I'll show you what we're doing."

Within an hour it was obvious the two extra men were heaven sent. With all five of them cutting, hoisting, and hammering, and Rosa marking lumber and running back and forth with tools and cans of nails, the roof was up by just past noon. The men were ready to start on the shingles.

"Lunch break!" cried Rosa, hauling a sizable basket from the shade of some bushes. She wore pants borrowed from Johann, a scandalous innovation which had raised the eyebrows of the scattered neighbors during the past few weeks.

The missionaries shifted bashfully from foot to foot. "Uh,

we knew you didn't expect us, so we brought our own food. But we have plenty, and we'll share it."

Papa's eyebrows raised slightly. Rosa recognized his approval that these young men weren't moochers.

Papa had brought a huge pot of Hannah's potato salad, and half a dozen large chunks of strudel. Rosa took several quart bottles of herb tea from a shallow spot at the edge of the river, a short distance from the house. The Reiner men were impressed when the missionaries reached into their sack and withdrew a slightly smashed loaf of bread, and two or three thick end pieces of sausage, massive enough to slice and put on the bread for sandwiches. Elder Hasslem grinned as he held them out to Rosa, pleased they could add something as valuable as meat to the meal. "Compliments of Brother Brighten, the butcher. He gave us the sausage, and his wife baked the bread."

The missionaries offered a prayer on their food, and they ate heartily. Afterwards, the men napped in the shade for awhile. Rosa cleared away the meal, and put the remaining bottles of herb tea back in the cool shallows of the river. She, too, sat and dozed a few minutes against a tree, until Papa woke with a yawn and commanded them all back to the job.

In the late afternoon, Rosa walked smiling through her two rooms. The position of the hammering above indicated that the shingling was half done. Next week the wall boards would go up, and they would install the windows and door. At that point the furniture and boxes could be brought from the city. It would only take a few more weekends. The inside could be finished after they had moved in. Rosa felt more happy and excited than she had for years. Sunlight, slanting through the west window frames, shone on more than bare boards. It shone again on her life.

❖ ❖ ❖

Vienna and Alland, 1930

The following autumn, after they had moved into the little house, Hilde caught a severe cold. Occasional coughing in October increased in November. By December the child was racked with coughs, and often had a fever later in the day. Rosa took her to a doctor for an examination. They sat together in the doctor's office after Rosa had put Hilde's dress back on. She heard them talking about her, but was too fuzzy minded to really understand.

"I cannot be absolutely sure at this time, Frau Edler, but I believe your daughter here may have tuberculosis. I'm very sorry," the man said.

"Tuberculosis!" exclaimed Rosa, dismayed. "But where. . . ? How. . . ?" That filthy public school, of course! My poor child! Are you sure?"

"We can't be absolutely certain until we have performed tests of her saliva under the microscope. But if she has the bacteria, well . . . She will need a great deal of experienced care before she will feel better. And I am required to tell you that even if we only *suspect* tuburculosis, the law prohibits her from going back to school until either we have proved it is not tuberculosis, or until she becomes free of symptoms. In any event, she is a very sick little girl. She needs constant care at this point, and should not expose other children, regardless of what the infection is."

Rosa put her arm around her daughter. "But what am I to do? I have to go to work. Of courseI want to stay at home with her, but we would have nothing to live on."

"Ah, that is a worry. I see," said the doctor, smoothing down his bushy mustache. "Well . . . There *is* a sanitorium in Alland that takes children. It's called the Kinderheilanstalt." He sorted through a drawer, and came forth with a card which he handed to Rosa. "The costs are largely defrayed by the state."

Through the haze of several indistinct days, Hilde felt her mother's hands gently bathing her, massaging her chest and back with camphor, heard her voice singing softly in the dark of night. She heard her mother talking to people, sounding anxious.

Then, finally, they sat on a train that was puffing and chugging through the snowdrifts. Hilde felt cold and hot, and her chest hurt all the time. It was terrible when she coughed. Slow tears streaked her flushed cheeks.

"Please, Mama. I don't want to go away," she croaked. "Why can't I stay home with you?"

"Leibchin, Liebchin, I'm so sorry! I don't want you to go away, either." She drew the girl onto her lap and held her close. "I wish I could stay at home all the time and take care of you, but then we wouldn't even have enough money to pay the rent and buy food. I'm grateful to God that the sanitorium will pay most of the costs. But I will have to find more work than I already have just to pay our little share of the expenses. Darling, don't cry. I'll miss you, too! Oh, I'll miss you so much! If only there were some other way! But there isn't, sweetheart. I can't work to support us, and stay at home with you, as well."

"But what about Oma?"

"How could you stay with Oma, dear? She's getting older, and her rheumatism is very bad this winter. She loves you and would try her best, but caring for you would be a great hardship for her. And, besides, wouldn't it be dreadful if you passed your illness on to her?"

Hilde buried her face in the pillow Mama had brought with them. She was miserable and frightened. She wouldn't know anybody at the sanitorium. She tried not to cry because it would start her coughing. She took short sobbing breaths, and wished with all her heart that she were with Oma. Or with Papa. Her tears sprang afresh as she thought of her darling Papa, who didn't want her anymore.

She must have been asleep when they arrived at the sanitorium. She remembered only faintly the nurses dressed in gray and white. She sensed being lifted and moved uncomfortably, and woke briefly to pain when a coughing spell seized her. The bed they put her in was white and cold. The room was gray and cold. She couldn't stop shivering. Someone's warm hands caressed her awake. It was Mama.

"Hilde, I have to leave now." She was gathered into her mother's arms. "You're going to be all right. You're going to get better here. I'll visit you as often as I can." Mama placed a soft kiss on her forehead. "Be a good and obedient girl, and you'll get well faster. I'll write you letters when I can't come." Mama's gently laid her down, and tucked the blankets under her chin. "I love you, darling. Go back to sleep now. Sleep and get better."

The days and nights flowed together for the first week. The nurses brought her hot soups and bitter medicines, and helped her eat until she felt strong enough to feed herself. She did feel a little better after awhile. The nurse said her fever had gone down.

Days and days passed. She was supposed to rest, and she didn't really feel like doing anything else. But it was so boring. If the day was clear, she was taken to a room with walls all made of windows to bask in the sunshine. Some of the windows were opened part way, and a little cold, fresh air came in. She was covered with a warm blanket, and that felt very good.

There were other children on the sun porch, too, but their chairs were kept far apart. The nurse said it was so they couldn't spread infection. They were all ordered to rest themselves. If they talked they would become excited, and that would not be good for their recovery.

Hilde gazed longingly at the others and wished that they would at least look back at her. They all looked so thin and sickly. She wondered if she looked that way too. She felt so lonely. Sometimes in the evenings, when she lay in her bed in her cold gray room, she pulled the covers over her head and cried.

Mama could only get free to come twice, but she brought several books, and sent letters saying that she loved and misssed Hilde. The books were nice. Oma wrote letters every week, full of funny stories, and that was best of all. But the days were long and the nights were longer. And the weeks went on and on. Hilde huddled in a ball and stared out the window. Inside, she felt as cold and gray as her hospital room. Quietly she whispered prayers. "Please, God, please make me get well so I can go home. Please send Mama or Oma to visit me. Please make my papa come back. Please, God, isn't there anybody to love me?"

One day in the sun room there was a girl she hadn't seen before. She was a little older. As Hilde looked toward her, she looked back and smiled.

"Hello," said the girl. "My name is Ilse. What's yours?"

"I'm Hilde."

"Where are you from? How long have you been here?"

"I live in Vienna. I've been here three months." Hilde could feel her lip quiver as she said the last words. She was embarrassed that her eyes filled with tears.

Ilse watched Hilde for a few moments, and chewed on her full lower lip. "I've been here six months. I used to be upstairs, but they moved me down this week. I'm supposed to get more sun, and they don't have a sun room upstairs."

Hilde was shocked. "Six months! You've been here half a year? How can you stand it?"

"It's not so bad when you get used to it." She smiled. "It's sort of nice in a way. I have seven brothers and sisters at home, and my aunt lives with us, and she has five children. I'm the oldest, so I have to take care of all the little ones. This is the most quiet and restful I've gotten to be in my whole life."

Hilde's mouth dropped open as she did some quick addition. "You have thirteen children in your house!" She tried to envision thirteen children in their old flat in Vienna. Or even in their new house in the country. You wouldn't even be able to move! She couldn't imagine what it would be like living with even *one* other child, although she had wished a thousand times she had a brother or sister. But *thirteen*!

Ilse laughed at her expression, which led to a fit of coughing. A nurse rushed in to check her, and saw Hilde's anxious face.

"Have you two been talking? You know you are supposed to lie here quietly and rest. See what happens if you don't follow the rules?"

The chairs in the sun room had backs that could recline, so the children could rest better, and wheels so they could be rolled to and from their rooms. Lying still in their chairs was the first rule of the sun room. Not getting excited by talking to other children was the second. When Ilse's coughing had subsided, the nurse raised her chair back, and wheeled her from the room. A disapproving glance at Hilde seemed to say, "See what you have done."

After that Hilde looked forward eagerly to her hours in the sun room, each time hoping Ilse would be there. She even prayed fervently that God would make tomorrow sunny, so she could see her new friend. But it sleeted for a week before she got to go there again. Ilse was pushed in a little later and positioned not very far away. Afraid to anger the nurses, Hilde only smiled at her, but put her whole heart into the smile. Ilse grinned back, and murmured, "I'll talk to you if I want to. What are they going to do to me if I disobey? Send me home?"

Hilde covered her mouth and giggled at this outrageous defiance. She had never conceived of disobeying authority and felt naughty at the thrill it gave her.

"When will you get to go home?" asked Hilde softly.

"I ask them that all the time. They say I can't go till I can spend a whole week without coughing." Her shoulders drooped. "That could be months and months. I really miss my family. Mama and Papa and Auntie come to visit me every week. But it isn't the same. I miss the noise and the playing and even the fighting." She grinned. "And there's a lot of that, you bet. Mostly I miss the little ones, the babies."

Hilde thought of Ilse surrounded by laughing, crowding, playing children who all loved her. She imagined what it would be like to have someone visit every week. Her eyes filled with tears that rolled down her cheeks. She turned her head away.

A moment later she felt a soft touch on her shoulder, and looked up to see Ilse standing beside her chair.

"Hilde, you're crying. Did I say something to make you cry?"

"I'm not crying," she said, quickly dashing the tears from her cheeks with her hands.

Ilse sat down beside her. "Yes you are. What's the matter?"

The tears began to roll again. Hilde's hands reached out to touch her new friend. "It's just . . . it's just that I'm so lonely. And I envy you having all those grown-ups and children who love you." Once started, the words seemed to flow out with no more control than her tears. "And they come and visit you. Nobody ever visits me. I'm so lonely! And my papa went away and will never come back. And I can't visit Oma 'cause I'm too much trouble. I wish I were dead!" Her shoulders shook with sobs which quickly turned to coughs. A couple of other children in the sun room turned their faces to look curiously at the two girls.

Ilse put her arms around the younger girl, and pulled her close. "Oh, poor Hilde. I'm so sorry you feel bad. I'll be your friend. Honest I will. I'll even come and visit you."

Hilde laughed wetly. "How can you come and visit me? You're already here." Ilse laughed too, but continued to hold her for a few more minutes. Hilde's tears subsided, and she hugged Ilse back. "Will you really be my friend, Ilse?"

They heard the click of nurses' heels echoing toward them in the empty hallway. Ilse gave Hilde a quick peck on the cheek, and rose. "You'll see," she said with a mysterious smile, and tottered a little unsteadily back to her chair.

As Hilde was rolled to her room, she felt totally exhausted. Her chest hurt. That must be why they wouldn't let the children talk. But she didn't care. She would do it again if she got the chance. Ilse was wonderful!

The next two days were wet and cloudy again, and Hilde had to stay in her room. She missed Ilse. She missed everybody. She lay in the nighttime silence of the sanitorium. Except for the dimmed lights coming in from the hall, her room was dark. Hilde curled underneath her blankets too miserable to even weep.

Suddenly she felt a hand pat over her covers. Startled, she pulled back the blankets and sat up. The illumination from the hall silhouetted a figure beside her bed, too small to be a nurse. "Ilse?"

"Shhhh. Yes, it's me. Move over. I've come to sleep with you."

"What? You can't sleep with me. It's against the rules," whispered Hilde.

"Says who? I never heard anybody say the patients couldn't sleep together. Did anybody tell you that?"

"No, but they put us all in separate rooms . . ."

"Well, then, move over. I said I'd come to visit." She giggled as she scrambled up into the bed.

Ilse snuggled next to Hilde. Lying on her side, she put one arm firmly around the younger girl, and pulled her close until they were nested together.

A great wave of love and warmth flowed over Hilde. Wordlessly she squeezed the arm that surrounded her. *Thank you for Ilse, God*, she whispered in her mind as she drifted off to sleep.

In the morning, the sounds of cleaning women moving about in the halls awoke both girls. "How are you going to get back?" whispered Hilde.

"Easy," replied her friend. "We've only been two rooms apart all this time. I'll just wait till the coast is clear, and scoot right back to my bed. They'll never know."

"Oh, Ilse," cried Hilde softly, hugging the girl tightly. She couldn't say more.

Ilse smiled and hugged her back. "That's the first night I've been warm enough since I got here. I'll be back."

The girls slept curled together from that night on, each comforted and warmed by the other.

One May afternoon, Hilde was surprised by unexpected visitors.

"Hello, little fräulein," said Elder Hasslem, walking into her room with a thin, gangly young man she didn't know.

Hilde, who had been slumped against a pillow in bed reading one of Mama's books for the twentieth time, sat up, eyes alight. "Elder Hasslem! What are you doing here?" she leaned to the side and looked around him toward the door, as if expecting someone else.

"I'm sorry I couldn't bring Elder Chambers. He's still back in Vienna, but I promised to say hello for him. I've been transferred to this area, and this is my new companion, Elder Luke, from Idaho, in the United States." He gestured to the gangly one, who smiled and nodded. "When your mother heard I was coming to this part of the country, she told me to be sure to visit you. I was glad to know I would be able to see you. And look, I brought you something from the whole branch in Vienna." He opened his satchel, and brought out a large, folded paper with writing all over it. He unfolded it until it covered half the bed. "It's on newsprint paper, see? Everyone in the branch has written you a get-well message. And the little kids have drawn some pictures for you."

Hilde was delighted, and read every message. "Get well soon! We miss you at church. We hope you'll be back with us soon. Your mother comes to church often, we hope that very soon she will be able to bring you, too. You are our friend; we pray for you. God bless you." And on and on. There were children's drawings of smiling faces, people holding hands, bears, flowers, birds, and quite a few scribbles she couldn't decipher. Hilde looked up with shining eyes. "Why did they send this to me?" she asked.

"Because they care about you and love you. And they want you to get well."

Hilde felt a lump in her throat, and read every message again. It made her tired, sitting up and holding the big paper, and she slumped back on the pillow.

"We have something else for you, too, if you want it," said Elder Hasslem.

Hilde coughed several times before answering, "What?"

"We can give you a blessing, to help you get well."

Hilde thought of the priests at Mass, dressed in beautiful robes, making motions with their hands while chanting words in Latin. She wondered if these Elders would do the same thing.

"How do you do that?"

"It's in the Bible. Elder Luke, will you read it, please."

The other young man thumbed through the pages, and cleared his throat twice before he read. "Is any sick among you? let him call for the elders of the church; and let them pray over him, anointing him with oil in the name of the Lord: And the prayer of faith shall save the sick. James 5:14."

Hilde looked up at them. "If you do that, will it make me well?"

"It will if you have faith that Jesus can do it."

Hilde considered this for a few moments with a faraway look. "All right," she said. "I want you to bless me so I'll get well."

The gangly elder poured a drop of oil into her hair. They both put their warm, heavy hands on her head. Elder Hasslem asked the Lord to make Hilde well soon. He asked that she would know how many people loved and prayed for her. He told her to remember that God loved her very much, and was watching her all the time, and would send angels to comfort her. Then they said Amen, and took their hands away.

"I'll get well now," smiled Hilde.

Elder Hasslem cupped her chin in his hand and looked into her eyes. "Yes, I believe you will."

That night as Hilde and Ilse lay cuddled together, Hilde said a prayer in her mind. *Dear God, thanks for sending the Elders to bless me so I'll get well. And please, won't you make Ilse well, too. She's been here ever so much longer than I have, and she misses her family very much. Thank you. Amen.*

Six weeks later, after Hilde had been in the sanitorium eight months, both girls were released with clean bills of health. They would never meet again, but Hilde would remember Ilse with love for the rest of her life.

For months after she had returned from the sanitorium, Hilde begged and pleaded to be baptized a Mormon. Half-heartedly, Rosa argued that the ten-year-old was too young to make such a decision for herself. But finally, confessing that she couldn't actually see that it would do any harm, she consented. She commented that most of the members were a good influence, seemed particularly honest and sincere, and all went to great lengths to take care of each other, including herself and Hilde. So, in November, the Elders and several members came out to her house on the Danube, and, in spite of the cold, Hilde was baptized in the river.

During the Christmas season, two letters came with a Vienna postmark, both addressed in the same hand. One was directed to Rosa, the other to Hildegard. The child was ecstatic. Only Oma had ever sent a letter addressed to herself alone, and this was not from Oma. As Rosa opened hers, Hilde cut open the end of her own, careful not to tear the envelope. Each of them withdrew a Christmas card.

"It's from Elder Hasslem! Just for me! A Christmas card just for me!"

Rosa was reading hers. "Mine is from Elder Hasslem, too. He wishes us all kinds of good fortune, and says that his mission is over, and he is on his way home. He invites us to visit him in the United States if we ever go there. How kind of him." Rosa smiled.

Hilde's message was somewhat longer. Hilde grinned hugely as she read it. "Look, Mama, Elder Hasslem told me that when I grow up I should come to America to go to college. He said he would be my sponsor, and I could live with his family. Oh, Mama! Could I? Could I go to America and go to college?"

"I think we'll have to wait and see, Hilde. Nobody knows what the future will bring."

❖ ❖ ❖

A few weeks later, Rosa came home looking unusually excited and happy. She picked up her daughter and whirled her around. "Hilde, the most marvelous thing has happened! I didn't tell you sooner, because I wasn't sure. But now it's for certain, and you're going to die of joy when you hear!" Rosa set her daughter down and told the story.

"A week ago I was walking down the street, not looking where I was going, and I almost knocked down someone who was standing on the curb. Who do you think it was? Mother Agathe from Notre Dame de Sion!"

Hilde's jaw dropped in amazement. "The Mother Superior?"

"Yes! And she asked me why she hadn't seen you in two years, and where were you and how were you, and said all kinds of nice things about remembering you. She asked why you had left Notre Dame. I was too embarrassed to say that we didn't have enough money, but somehow she got it out of me and made me promise to come to see her the next week. So I went today. I ended up telling her about the divorce, and about how you hated public school and got so sick there you had to go to the sanitorium.

"Anyway, she told me you had too good a mind to waste, and has offered you a scholarship to come back to Notre Dame! Right away! What do you think about that!"

Hilde had listened breathlessly, and could hardly think, let alone speak. "Go back . . ." she whispered breathlessly. "Oh, Mama!" She burst into tears and threw herself into her mother's arms.

Of course the old uniforms didn't fit. Rosa combed the pawn shops until she found clothing made of closely matching fabric.

She spent all her scant earnings on the items, unpicked them carefully, and made Hilde two new uniforms. Mother Agathe had advised Rosa where to buy used school books, and they were able to prepare Hilde to reenter the French Convent school within a little over a week.

The evening before Hilde was to return, she stood before the long mirror her mother had fastened to the back of the living room door. Rosa had bought it cheap, because it had a crack, but it served its purpose as well as new. Rosa was pinning up the hem.

"There's just one thing, Hilde."

"What?" the child asked, distracted by the image before her and the anticipation that whirled through her mind.

"The Reverend Mother is not going to let you go to Notre Dame if you are not a Catholic. You will have to give up the Mormon church. You are to go to confession tomorrow at Notre Dame, and tell the priest you made a mistake. You are young, so you may tell him you didn't know what you were doing, and that you now sincerely embrace the Catholic church forever."

"But Mama, that would be lying. I think the Mormons are God's true church."

"Oh, Hilde," Rosa was exasperated, "How can a child know whether any church is 'true' or not? Anyway, that is simply beside the point! Whatever you think, child, I am instructing you to obey me and make your confession. Do you understand?"

"But, Mama . . ."

Rosa interrupted. "Look, Hilde, I'm as fond of the Mormons as you are. They are fine and lovely people. But think of it logically. In Vienna there are two million Catholics and only about a hundred Mormons. How could it be logical that two million Catholics are wrong and a hundred Mormons are right? The Mormons are friendly, and kind, and persuasive. But millions of people can't be wrong on an important issue like this."

Hilde pressed her lips together in a tight line and looked at her shoes, saying nothing.

Rosa recognized the signs of stubbornness. She sighed. "Let me put it to you this way: either you can accept Catholicism and go to Notre Dame, or you can stay a Mormon and go to the public school. There *are* no other choices. Which will you take?"

Hilde chewed her lip for several moments to stop its trembling. "I'll confess to the priest," she whispered.

❖ ❖ ❖

Vienna, 1931

In 1931 the Austrian Kreditanstalt crashed, followed by other stock markets throughout Europe. Millions of people lost almost everything—another devastating tragedy added to the dismal economy which had never recovered after the Great War. The treaty of Versailles had required that the German and Austrian people had to repay the war debts of the allied nations, a crushing burden. During the years after the crash, such deep poverty blanketed Europe that over ten million people died of malnutrition and starvation. Members of the nobility and admired celebrities waited in bread lines with everyone else.

In the elections of 1932, Adolph Hitler brought his Nazi party into Austria to sway the country's elections. He promised that if he were elected Chancellor of Germany the following year, he would bring prosperity and unity among all German-speaking peoples. There was chaos in the streets of Vienna, almost a small scale civil war between the followers of Hitler and the followers of the popular Christian-Socialist leader, Dolphus. Dolphus was elected. By 1933, he brought a law to pass banning Nazism from Austria. Hitler swore revenge. In 1934 the small, mustachioed master of persuasion was elected German Chancellor, and, very soon after, Dolphus was assassinated. No one ever proved a connection to Hitler.

Rosa was thankful for the next two years that she had moved into her little house when she did, and could raise some of her own food in the summer. Austria had a huge population, but comparatively little farm land, so her produce brought in good money. But when she sold most of it, as she often had to, there was never enough left to satisfy her own and Hilde's hunger. The girl had become proficient at looking forlorn and begging scraps from a butcher here and a grocer there. Credit at the shops was increasingly hard to get, and mother and daughter had both learned to hide quietly behind furniture when bill collectors came knocking on the door and peering into windows.

Rosa desperately needed a job! She was pacing down a city street, holding a newspaper full of want ads, when she heard her name called.

"Frau Edler? Rosa, is that you?"

She turned to see a nicely dressed woman tripping toward her. It took a moment for Rosa to place the familiar face. It was Frau Osten, the wife of the general under whom Hans had served as aide during and after the Great War. For three years Hans had attended the general while he worked to restore order to war-torn Europe. Constantly thrown together for the next two years, Rosa had slipped easily into the unofficial role of assistant to Frau Osten, helping her plan and execute receptions and dinners and carry out the hundred other chores that fall the lot of a diplomat's wife.

Frau Osten was wreathed in smiles. "Frau Edler! I can't believe it! You haven't aged a day in the last six years." She embraced the younger woman in a cloud of perfume.

Rosa had been genuinely fond of the general's wife and she returned the embrace sincerely.

"What are you doing here?" they asked simultaneously, and then laughed. "You first," said Rosa.

"I'm working right here, at St. Michael's, with the Karitar-socialis." With a beautifully gloved hand, the woman gestured toward the cathedral across the street. "I'm head volunteer. You must have heard of our service to help feed the more deserving poor."

Rosa remembered reading about it in a discarded newspaper. Several dozen wealthy women, women who had not lost their fortunes in the Crash, had established a kitchen to cook and disburse food to the priests and monks, artists, musicians, professors who were out of work, and aristocrats without independent wealth—all of whom were starving as inexorably as millions of the common people.

"Why, yes, I have heard of it. It's a wonderful thing you're doing," she replied.

"You know, I'd be simply delighted if you'd come in for a minute and let me show you around. I'm rather in charge of the whole affair, and awfully proud of it."

"I'd love to see it," said Rosa. Frau General Osten put her arm through Rosa's and walked with her across the street and through a side door. They entered an enormous kitchen with a vaulted ceiling soaring three stories above. Two dozen women, wearing aprons to cover their nice dresses, were stirring great pots, or cutting up meat and vegetables. Several men were hauling buckets of water and cases of vegetables.

"My goodness!" exclaimed Rosa in awe of the size of the busy place.

"Amazing, isn't it?" agreed Frau General Osten. "This huge kitchen used to serve the monastery here, but they've loaned it to our organization to use during these hard times." She walked with Rosa around the room, pointing out various work stations. "Actually, this kitchen is the heart and center for twenty-six distribution points. We do all the cooking here, then each of these women delivers the amount of food which has been ordered by the different stations, and stays there to oversee its distribution. If we didn't watch everything in person, most of the food would end up on the black market."

"This must be the most enormous undertaking!" exclaimed Rosa. "How on earth do you manage it all?"

"Actually, it's getting to be more than I *can* handle. Every few weeks we add another distribution point. This afternoon I'm afraid I'm going to be forced to go to the employ . . ." She stopped, turned to Rosa, and looked at her keenly. "Frau Edler," she paused a few moments, as if deciding on her words. "When you were with me in Hungary, you were an enormous help on many occasions. Would you . . . ? Are you . . . ? Forgive me if I'm being forward, but are you employed at this time?"

Rosa's eyebrows shot up.

"What I mean," the general's wife hurried on, "We really need a full-time manager for all this. I was going to the employment bureau to start looking for someone, but as I think of it, I believe you would be an ideal person for the job. That is, if you aren't already involved elsewhere."

Rosa was taken by surprise. "I . . . that is . . . ah . . . I have a number of small jobs from time to time. Nothing permanent," she smiled in embarrassment. "In fact, nothing very dependable at all."

"Would you consider this? Consider giving it a try? It would mean managing the whole kitchen, keeping records and accounts, overseeing the cooks and volunteers. Oh, there are a million things that have to be thought of. It isn't a very easy job. And it wouldn't pay very much. But you could take food home with you every day. It's all donated, and there are always leftovers. And I know from our experience together that there's nothing you can't do if you set your mind to it."

It didn't take Rosa thirty seconds to decide. "Frau General Osten, I would be absolutely delighted to accept your offer." She paused, flushed, and looked down. "But there's something I think you ought to know. You may not want me."

The older woman's brows drew together in question.

"You see, I'm . . . My husband . . . We had rather a lot of

problems in our marriage. My husband and I were divorced. I don't even know where he is."

Frau Osten looked at Rosa a few moments. "I'm so sorry. I suppose these things happen. But what difference could that make to me?"

"Would you hire a divorcee?" Rosa asked. "A lot of places won't."

"Unless it has addled your brains, I can't see why it should affect your abilities."

Rosa could hardly believe Frau Osten's casual acceptance. "Then I accept! When do I start?"

"If you're available right now, I could show you around and explain things. Then tomorrow, we can start planning a way to get everything organized. Oh!" she clasped Rosa's arm. "This is going to be marvelous! You'll see! Come upstairs with me." She began unpinning her hat as they climbed a spiral stairway to a balcony several meters above the floor, which protruded into the high room.

"I chose this high room as my office because, even though it's small, one has a good view of everything that's going on below. You can even see delivery trucks through that window, and then be able to hop right down to supervise the unloading."

Rosa gulped. She had obviously plunged in over her head. But she straightened her shoulders. *I've cooked all my life, and I've supervised children all my life. I've learned a hundred new facts and processes in a single week at the clinic. Learning how to do this can't be that hard. I will make it work or die trying.*

For a week Frau Osten worked closely with Rosa, expressing pleasure when Rosa saw an easier or quicker way to handle this thing or that.

"I knew you were a perfect choice!" she exclaimed, beaming at her own cleverness.

Within a month Rosa had mastered everyone's name and job. She had regularized hours and mapped out more efficient procedures for ordering, preparing, and delivering the food. The wealthy ladies stopped in her office as they arrived, leaving their jewelry and furs with her for safekeeping, all of them quite friendly and cooperative. Rosa, for her part, was surprised and humbled to acknowledge the generosity of women this rich and privileged, who donated hours every day doing chores they would have relegated to their cooks and maids at home. After spending the morning cooking, they recovered their finery, and each with pots and baskets of food, rode in their chauffeured limousines to appointed distribution spots. And they seemed to consider it fun!

To them, it must be a little like playing dress up, she thought.

Her work was challenging and satisfying, and Rosa felt genuinely valuable. She was pleased to bring home a good supper for Hilde and herself every day. True, the pay was pitiful, more a token of thanks than a wage. But if they were very careful, it sufficed for their most basic needs: shoes, used clothing, coats for the winter, pencils and notebooks for Hilde.

❖ ❖ ❖

Vienna, 1932

Hilde was thirteen when she came home from school one afternoon to find Rosa standing by the river, shading her eyes from the bright spring sunshine and glancing here and there around the lot. She seemed to be trying to work out some problem. The girl left her school satchel on the outdoor stairway which led up to the new second floor of the house and waded through the long grass to her mother.

"First of all," said Rosa, as if she and Hilde had been discussing some plan together for an hour, "we'll have to scythe down this forest of grass. I wonder if we should try to build a little, sort-of jetty here?" She waved her hand toward the bank of the Danube.

"We just finished building the upstairs, Mama! Don't you want to rest a few minutes before starting another project? What are you thinking of now?"

"I'm thinking of you, dear. Look at yourself, blossoming into quite a pretty young girl."

"Somehow I can't bring that together with grass and jetties," Hilde said.

"Don't be fresh, dear. What I'm thinking is that you'll be out of school in a couple of years, and we need to be cultivating a few nice families. Especially those with eligible sons."

Hilde puffed impatiently. "Mother, I'm *only* thirteen. I really don't want to think about that yet."

Rosa's mind had wandered. Hilde could see her looking into some glorious future and continued her questions. "And the grass? The jetty? What do those have to do with meeting people?"

"Parties, Hilde! Picnics! We need to fix up the yard along

the riverbank so we can invite over guests who are acquainted with better things. We may not have a mansion here, but very few people have anything like our lovely setting. Our guests will love coming to visit."

"Guests like who?"

"Like all the excellent and cultured people I've met through my kitchen management. I've told you about a lot of them. There's Count Sternberg who has become my good friend," she ticked them off on her fingers, "a wonderful violinist from the opera who has two teenage sons. The Greek ambassador has a young assistant who is very handsome . . ."

"The Greek embassy comes to the Karitarsocialis to get food?"

"Certainly not! They graciously send some of their staff to help in the kitchens once a week. They feel the service helps promote their relations with Austria. Anyway, there are numbers of well-to-do women who volunteer there who have families, and who have expressed respect for me. Yes, and a few officers who help us coordinate with other government agencies. I'm sure some of them must have sons." Her thoughts drifted away. "A boat would be a wonderful thing. Anyone would love a little paddle out onto the water. It's so pretty here with the willows bending over and making little grottos."

Hilde left her mother planning her grandiose schemes. Sighing deeply, she waded back to the house. Her father had told someone (so long ago), that her mother was hungry to prove she was more than a peasant in every way, and would never be satisfied until everyone believed she was a born aristocrat. Once in a while Hilde worried that it might be true. She furrowed her brows.

Mother is two people. One is so practical and hard working. She isn't afraid of anyone's opinions, and goes ahead and does things that would scare anybody else. She'll work till she drops, then go back and work some more. She thought of her mother dressed in men's trousers, hauling and hammering great pieces of lumber with sublime disregard for the neighbors' opinions.

The other person is as snobbish as any of the girls at school who come in their chauffeured autos. She wants so much to be viewed as a fine lady. She feels so important when she has rich or famous people around her. Or even ones who used to be rich or famous. Maybe if I don't say a word, she'll loose steam, and forget about this whole plan.

Hilde had reached the stairs, picked up her satchel, and climbed up to the little balcony from which two doors opened onto their separate bedrooms. It was a hot day. In her room, Hilde took off her wool uniform and looked down at her body. She supposed she *was* "blossoming." Her breasts were growing, and were terribly tender. Mama had told her long ago about a woman's time of month, so that wasn't a surprise. But it always hurt her tummy awfully. Mama had warned her that first time that now she must be sure and not let any man touch her body in personal places, or she could get pregnant. *So why was Mama so anxious to have young men hanging around now? Stupid!*

She slipped on a loose cotton dress, and laid out her books on the little table in front of one window.

And buy a boat? Hilde was dismayed. *Every time we buy something new, we get into trouble. Can't she subtract? Can't she figure out that her wages minus a boat would leave us in the hole? Again? Where does she always think the money's going to come from? How is it she can manage the finances of that enormous kitchen but can't keep track of the little bit we have?* Hilde felt she'd die of shame every time they had to hide from the bill collectors. It made her feel dirty and crooked.

"Well, all these plans certainly aren't for *me*, whatever she wants to think," Hilde muttered. "She just wants a chance to brag about building this house with her own hands and to cozy up to all those *important* people."

She sat down at the table, but her mind wouldn't focus on the book. *I'm glad the house is done. It's a good enough house. But I've been to birthday parties for some of those girls, and their homes make this place look like a shack. I don't really care. But I wish Mama would be realistic.*

She opened a notebook, and checked her pencil for sharpness. "Picnics and parties." She grumbled, shaking her head.

They eventually did have parties of a modest sort. The guests were usually middle-aged, rather than young, but always charming and pleasant. Hilde more frequently played serving maid than debutante, which was fine with her. When she admitted she enjoyed the get-togethers, Rosa said, "You see. Trust your mother."

The bill collectors became more frequent, too.

Hilde and her Uncle Johann walked in the woods on a warm Saturday afternoon. She loved this man, such a center of calm and kindness. Only a year or so ago she had learned the real nature of the tragedy in his life. Even as a tiny child she had seen that he and his wife Katarina were nothing like each other, and had to struggle to get along. But she never knew why.

At the time of her own parents' divorce, when she first realized that people who were married could actually hate each other enough to break up a family, she had asked Oma if Uncle Johann and Aunt Katarina were going to get divorced, too. Oma had replied cryptically that they would not, because Johann had learned to forgive the unforgivable. It wasn't until a year ago that she had found out the whole story.

Johann had yearned from his boyhood to become a priest, and had worked diligently to gain that end. He was only a year from ordination when a pretty sixteen-year-old neighbor had lied to everyone, claiming Johann had raped her, and she was pregnant. She was so convincing at the trial held before the leaders of Johann's seminary that he had been dismissed from the school and forced to marry the girl. Had a court of law found him guilty, he would have faced execution. The life he had planned was ruined.

When she had asked Uncle Johann the truth of the story, he did not seem shocked nor offended, as most grown-ups would have. He didn't tell her she was too young to ask about such things, but explained the story with patience and honesty.

Johann had burned at the injustice of the forced marriage. Raged at the seminarians who had accused him falsely. However, the reason he had chosen to become a priest in the first place was because he loved God with all his heart. When the scriptures told him he must forgive his enemies, he had really tried. Tried and failed, again and again.

When the child that Katarina bore died at age two, Johann finally learned the truth behind his wife's lie: Katarina had been so badly abused in her home, that she would have done anything, told any lie, to get away from it. And the kindest person she had ever met was Johann. For that reason alone she had chosen to blame him for the illegitimate child she carried. She confessed that she had stupidly hoped she could make him love her after the wedding. Certainly she had not been thinking clearly to believe such a thing. But the truly desperate seldom do.

Johann had told all of this to his young niece. He explained that when he finally understood the extent of Katarina's tortured childhood, he began to feel the first stirrings of forgiveness, or at least sympathy. Time and mighty prayer and the grace of God had gradually done the rest. And finally Johann and Katarina really had created a child of their own, the lovely little Johanna. She was the very image of her father, an intelligent, appealing, sparkling little sprite who held together parents who had nothing in the world in common except one child.

At last Hilde understood what Oma had said so long ago. So large was Johann's soul that he really had learned to forgive the unforgivable. He was a man who had determined to serve God, even in such a distant and peculiar way as his life had forced upon him.

And on this beautiful summer day, as Johann and Hilde walked together in the dappled woods, it was serving God and honoring her spiritual feelings which deeply disturbed Hilde's peace. She had asked Johann to take this walk with her. She knew she could ask her uncle anything, and he wouldn't shame her or put her off.

"Uncle Johann, are you still sorry you never got to be a priest?" When he remained quiet, Hilde waited. He always thought things through so he could give a true answer.

"I wanted with all my heart to become a priest," he finally replied. "But it's not quite right to say I'm sorry that I didn't. Life has not been easy the way it turned out. Your Aunt Katarina and I have struggled for years to get along together. And it nearly killed both of us when the baby died. I loved the little thing, even if he wasn't my own. But later when our little Johanna was born, it all began to seem worthwhile. I can't even imagine life without my little girl; I love that child more than my own soul. And then, the work I do is interesting and has value. Of course, it would have been interesting and valuable if I had become a priest. Maybe harder, if I'd been a missionary priest in some primitive outpost. I suppose, to answer your question, that if I wanted to break my heart about my loss, I could. But I'm learning to take life as the Lord serves it." He glanced down at her. "There must be a reason you're asking me this."

Now it was Hilde's turn to formulate her feelings into thoughts he would understand. She wasn't sure she understood them herself, except that she felt troubled. "Do you hate the Catholic church for what they did to you? Not believing you? Making you get married when it wasn't your fault?"

"I did hate them. Sometimes I still feel resentful. I never hated God, though. He knew I was innocent. And he's too much a part of me. I can feel his loving. I can see his loving all around me. It was very hard to forgive the church, but I've tried."

"Do you think the Catholic church is wrong?" she asked.

"Wrong? Wrong about what? They were wrong about me, but that was a bunch of people, not a whole church. What is it you're thinking?"

Hilde twisted a stem of grass she held, her brows furrowed. She looked at her uncle, wondering if she should ask him not to tell anyone about what she was going to say, but decided that would be an insult. Johann *never* told.

"You know when I became a Mormon?"

He nodded.

"When I wanted to go back to Notre Dame, I had to go to confession and say I'd been wrong to join another church."

He nodded again.

"And Mama told me I mustn't ever go to the Mormon church again."

Another nod.

Hilde pulled the grass in two. "I disobeyed her. She doesn't know it, but I've kept on going. I go to Mass at school every day, so I don't see why I absolutely have to go on Sunday, too. Mama never goes. She just sends me by myself. So whenever I have the money, I take a streetcar into Vienna and go to the Mormon Sunday School."

Johann remained silent.

"We talk about doctrine there. I never even knew what doctrine was before, because Mass doesn't teach you anything—just a lot of Latin words. But that's all the Mormons talk about; doctrine, basic beliefs. Even the littlest Mormon children learn what they believe from the time they're in kindergarten. It's interesting, too. It's stuff that really matters. Then on Monday I go back to school, and sometimes I ask the nuns or the priest questions about Catholic doctrine. And you know what?" she asked.

He raised his eyebrows in inquiry.

She flung the grass away. "They don't know! They don't know, or they say it's a mystery, or they get mad and say I should accept things on faith. Sometimes Father Francis quotes me something from St. Jerome or St. Augustine, but I can't understand it at all."

Johann spoke. "That's why priests go to school for many

years before being ordained. Some of the doctrines are very difficult and complex."

"But, Uncle Johann, the doctrines of the Mormon church are so easy to understand. And they read right out of the scriptures to back up their beliefs. Mama says the Mormon doctrines can't be true because there are about 500 million Catholics in the world, and only a couple of million Mormons."

"So you're asking me, good old well-educated Uncle Johann if the doctrines of the Catholic church are true or not?"

"I figure that if anybody has thought it all through, it must be you."

Johann smiled sadly. "Well, little one, I've thought it through, all right. Especially when those priests judged me falsely. And do you know what I decided?"

She looked at him keenly.

"I decided that I don't know, either. There are some things I just can't swallow, and other things that glow with truth. I can't make one sweeping judgment that covers everything. But there are some fundamental things I *have* learned, and those are what I base my faith on. The first thing I've learned is that God loves us, whether we're religious or not. He loves us all the time. He knows who we are, and answers our prayers if what we have asked is wise. And I've learned he expects us to do the best we can to be kind and honorable to other people. Those are the doctrines I hang onto, no matter who teaches them, or who disagrees."

She felt a sort of bigness well up inside. "I believe that, too, Uncle Johann. I have such a good, warm feeling in my heart when I think about God loving me. I feel safe and loved when I say my prayers." But then she remembered what she had really come to say. Her body grew uncomfortable, and her voice choked up when she added, "But I'm a cheat and a liar, and I can't stand it anymore."

"Why? Because you've been attending two churches and can't make up your mind?"

"No, because I've let Notre Dame believe I'm a full-fledged Catholic. I go to confession every week and never say a thing, but I feel awful. If I admitted I went to the Mormon church, they wouldn't let me stay in school there." Her expression grew grim. "But I would rather die than go back to that horrid public school! And both churches teach that you should stand up for your beliefs, even if you get tortured or killed. I mean, that's what all the martyrs are about in the first place!"

She stood before him in distress, and he put comforting hands on her shoulders. "My darling little girl, that is a hard decision."

They walked in silence awhile, until Hilde said, "Uncle Johann, what shall I do? I really *do* want to do what's right. But I'm not *sure* what's right. Except that lying is wrong."

"I can't make up your mind for you," he said, "but I can tell you one thing." He considered his words for a few moments before he spoke. "I've decided that living in conflict with your principles is the most miserable kind of life you can live. And it sounds as if the only principles you're sure of right now is that God loves you, and that you need to be truthful, honest. That's not a bad start."

He breathed deeply, and ran a hand roughly through his hair before he continued. "Hilde, do you know how strange we are, you and I? We both seem peculiar to most other people because loving God goes clear through us. It isn't a Sunday hat we take off when we get home from church. If you're like me, you'll go on caring about what's true, and seeking it out all your life. That's good. It breeds tolerance. I go to Mass because I love the music, and the words have always seemed to me like sublime poetry . But I think I could go anywhere else and feel my love for God just as strongly. That's what gets me through."

He put an arm around her shoulder and drew her close. "Hilde, God doesn't answer all of our questions at once. So, in justice, he doesn't expect us to know all the answers from the beginning. I truly believe God will only hold you accountable for what you *do* know. Examine your heart. Be true to what you *do* know." They walked in silence for a few minutes. "And, Hilde, never stop seeking to know more."

Hilde considered his words for many weeks. Reluctantly she stopped attending the Mormon church.

❖ ❖ ❖

It was a hot afternoon when the long kayak overturned and Hilde first met Ferdi Graff. The yell and a splash on the river brought her running from the garden to find a young man several meters from shore, splashing and floundering against the upended bottom of the paddle boat.

"Are you all right?" she cried. "Do you want me to throw you an inner tube?"

"Curse it all!" He stopped splashing a moment to turn toward her, one hand on the kayak. "Do you have a rope?"

"No. . . yes! I have a clothesline. Will that do? Can you swim?"

"Swim, yes! Drag a two-man kayak with me, no! I'm afraid if I let go it will float away. I'd be grateful for your clothesline."

Hilde dashed across the yard to the coiled line her mother had not yet mounted on its posts. Instantly she was back. "Do you want me to tie the end to something?"

"No need for that. Just hold on to one end and throw the rest out to me. I can pull my boat along with me if I have something to pull against." He was awkwardly trying to keep hold of both boat and paddle and to stay afloat at the same time.

Stepping on one end, Hilde threw the rest of the coil. It flew about three meters and fell into the water. "Oops! Let me try again." It took her four attempts before the line got near enough for him to grab, and then only because he had been swimming nearer her a few centimeters with every stroke.

When he had a good hold, Hilde took the slack line and pulled it toward herself. Slowly the young man and his boat were drawn to the river's edge. When his feet touched bottom he tossed the paddle up the bank to Hilde and tried to pull the kayak aground. But the bank was sloping and slick with mud, and he had a hard time staying on his feet. It became obvious that he would have to turn over the boat and empty out the water before he could pull it ashore. He tried with futility several times while Hilde alternately called suggestions and laughed at his struggles. Finally she took off her shoes, slid down the bank, and together they emptied and righted the craft.

By the time they secured the boat to a protruding root and struggled up the bank, both were laughing, smeared with mud, and thoroughly soaked. They flopped down on the grass, grinning and panting. Ferdi's hair, very long in the front, was plastered against his face and head, and his ears stuck out between the strands. There were smears of mud on his cheeks and stubbly chin, as well as on both arms. His legs were caked to the knees. Hilde was sure her appearance was similarly unappealing. Each time they looked at each other, they broke out laughing again.

"Thank you for rescuing me," he smiled at last, wiping his hand on a pant leg, and holding it out to her. "I'm Ferdi."

She took the hand and grinned back. "Hilde. Hildegard Edler."

He pushed his stringy, wet hair off his forehead, and tilted his head toward the little house. "Do you live here?"

"Yes, my mother and I. She works in the city—oh, here she comes now! Mama! Over here!" Hilde waved her arm, and Rosa spotted her.

Ferdi leapt to his feet and gave a courteous bow to the woman walking toward them. Rosa's eyes were wide, her shock and disapproval obvious as she scanned the two before her.

"Mama, this is Ferdi. He overturned his kayak, and I threw him the clothesline and pulled him to shore. I'm afraid we both got rather wet."

Rosa's voice was brisk and disapproving. "It looks as if both of you have been wallowing in mud. Hilde, go in and clean up immediately." She turned to Ferdi. "I'm very glad you aren't hurt, young man. If you'll be so good as to take my clothesline back over there by that pole, I'm sure you are also eager to go home and clean up."

Ferdi thanked her, replaced the clothesline, and slithered back down the bank to his slender boat.

From time to time during the summer Ferdi paddled his kayak over to visit Hilde or help with the gardening. Rosa remained aloof until she learned he was the son of a judge, just beginning at the University of Berlin, and home for the summer. His family lived in a large, impressive house downstream a kilometer. After that she welcomed him.

Hilde enjoyed Ferdi. She'd never had a friend who made her feel at once lighthearted and grown-up. True, he was quite old. Eighteen. He was manly and handsome in a strong Teutonic way, but was so playful and casual she looked forward eagerly to his visits. They could talk about anything. Ferdi wanted to go into the army, although his father was insisting on law, with an eye to politics.

"I just don't want to die of boredom in some dingy courtroom," he said, lying on his back chewing a stem of grass. "But I'll bring Papa around. I always do. The favored son, you know." He grinned. "What about you?"

"I don't know, exactly. I hope to go to the university, too, eventually. The nuns have sort of hinted that I might win a scholarship. But there isn't anything that fascinates me right now."

"The university! I'm impressed. Especially if you don't *have* to go. Women have it made. Find a good husband and take it easy."

"Maybe. But I haven't been overwhelmed by the number of good husbands lying around waiting to be picked up. Watching my mother struggle has pretty much convinced me I'd better have *some* kind of career, just to be safe. Teaching, maybe. My teacher, Sister Haubinger, is wonderful. I wouldn't mind being like her. But not a nun, of course."

"I love being at the university," he said, turning onto his stomach, and propping himself on his elbows. "Not actually the studying part, but the life! All the fellows! We have drinking parties, and go singing through the streets in the middle of the night. And there are always rallies and things going on. Things you could get excited about if you wanted."

"You aren't going to be like those idiots who get their faces cut in a duel, are you?' she teased. "Men are so stupid!"

"I might. It's a badge of courage. Everyone respects you."

"Other *idiots* respect you."

"Women are such spineless pacifists."

Hilde had been absently tugging up handfuls of grass, and had amassed quite a pile in front of her. "I'll show you pacifists," she said, scooping up the heap and dumping it on his head. Both leapt to their feet and dashed across the yard, Ferdi yelling threats, and Hilde laughing. Although she was small, she easily outdistanced him.

Circling the pig sty, and momentarily out of sight, she grabbed the handle of a large ladle sticking out of their full rain barrel. Stooped with it behind the barrel, she had only a moment to wait. As Ferdi raced around the corner, she stood and threw the water in his face. Ferdi gasped and coughed. Hilde doubled up laughing. Grasping her around the waist, Ferdi picked her up and set her into the waist high water of the rain barrel, where her laughs turned to shouts of shock as her skirt floated up around her.

"Serves you right, brat. Come on, I'll get you out." He plucked her up, knocking over the barrel.

"Mama will kill you for that," Hilde laughed. "That was the wash water."

"No she won't. I'll charm her. Now, what do you say we find some towels."

They squished toward the house together, Ferdi's arm around Hilde's shoulder.

❖ ❖ ❖

Vienna, 1934

*U*ncle Peter sat between Rosa and Oma Reiner at Hilde's graduation from Notre Dame de Sion. Opa Reiner had not been able to come. But Johann was there. And Aunt Luisa, Mama's pretty youngest sister, was on Oma's other side.

Nearly two years ago, Peter and Rosa had quarreled, and he hadn't visited them for nine months. The argument had arisen when Peter told Rosa she had abandoned her ideal of wanting to serve humanity as a doctor, and had become a social climber, instead. Mama had ordered him out of her house. But they kept running into each other in St. Pölten, and finally called a truce for the sake of Hilde. Now they were friendly together, but their special closeness seemed a thing of the past.

They all watched proudly as Hilde accepted her diploma, and applauded enthusiastically when the students rose and stood together at the end. As a beaming Hilde approached her family, she was caught and hugged by various classmates, then by each of her family when she arrived at their seats. Peter seemed as proud of her as if he had been her own father, and presented her with a small, intricately engraved gold locket as a gift.

She exclaimed at its beauty, and added, "I hope your picture is inside." She opened the small heart. "It isn't! Uncle Peter, how could you give me a locket without your picture?"

"It never occurred to me you'd want to wear a picture of an old man around your neck when I happen to know at least two young ones who are mooning over you at this very moment."

"Oh, phoo! You aren't old! And if you mean Ferdi and Philip, they aren't my sweethearts. You are!" She threw her arms around his waist and hugged him hard. "Thank you, darling Uncle Peter. But I demand that you give me a little photo of yourself to put inside—within this very month. Promise?"

He promised, and Luisa stepped forward with a little package of her own.

"Aunt Luisa, this is beautiful!" Hilde cried, unwrapping a delicate lace handkerchief. "I'll wear it to your wedding!"

"That won't be for months and months," her aunt replied. "I hope you'll have a few parties before then, what with all these rich and famous people you're hobnobbing with." Luisa smiled knowingly at Rosa.

At that moment Mother Superior, Sister Haubinger, and one of the directors of the school approached the group. The family met them with smiles and little bows and curtsies.

Mother Agathe took Hilde's hand in one of hers, and Rosa's hand in the other. "We cannot congratulate you enough on your fine daughter," she said to Rosa. "Hildegard, you have made us very proud." She released the girl's hand to reach into an invisible pocket and bring forth a white envelope, which she handed to Rosa. Smiling, she went on. "Frau Edler, we are very happy to present to you this letter which we have only today received from the board of directors of the Gymnasium of St. Mary's. Hildegard has been accepted as one of the students deserving of a scholarship for advanced study at that fine school."

Hilde put her hands to her lips, and her eyes glowed. Beside the Mother Superior, Sister Haubinger was grinning with complete delight. Mother Agathe went on. "All the details are in the envelope. Her continuation in school will depend from semester to semester on the excellence of her work. But we feel confident from what we know of Hildegard that she will continue to make us proud of her." The Reverend Mother shook Hilde's hand, and Sister Haubinger enveloped her in a great hug.

After a few other comments and congratulations, the women went away. Hilde turned with joy to her mother. "Oh, Mama! Isn't it wonderful! Just what we've always wanted!"

Rosa's smile was a little tight. Hilde realized with a jolt that it must have pained her mother to have had to struggle for years for a schooling she passionately craved, while Hilde was being offered an open road.

"We'll discuss it when we get home, dear," was her reply.

Later, as the guests were milling around, Rosa and Hannah went for more refreshments. Luisa, Peter, and Hilde stood chatting.

"Oh, Luisa! It's so romantic! You're going to be a bride, and go to England, and live on a gorgeous estate!"

"Well, it's plenty romantic, anyway. I adore my Tom. But it isn't exactly a big estate. It's just a house and office on the edge of the Royal Golf Course. Tom gets it because he's the pro, you know, as well as the manager. He'll live there and be available whenever any of the members want special lessons."

Peter chuckled. "I can hardly believe there are people who actually make their living from playing a game."

"Oh, the Brits are mad about sports. They consider golf serious business. You'd just be surprised how rabid some of them get about one silly little shot!" She smiled. "But I'll kill you if you tell Tom I said so. He's the worst of the lot. I suppose he has to be, as a professional. I'd never even have met him if he hadn't been in Austria on tour. And there I was, serving at the country club. He was so cute, holding his little plaid cap and looking so serious. So I winked at him. You know the rest!" She took a sip of punch.

"Maybe you aren't the only one who'll be getting married," said Hilde smiling sideways up at Peter.

"Don't look at me!" he exclaimed. "We aren't ready yet."

"Well, when are you going to be ready?" the girl insisted. "You've been seeing that woman for simply ages. If I were in love I would want to be married right away."

"That's because you're too young to know all the complications that have to be taken care of. There's no hurry."

"Tell me about her," said Luisa.

"Well, Elise is a lovely woman. . ."

Hilde interrupted, "With long blond hair."

". . .with whom I feel peaceful and contented," he continued, ignoring Hilde's remark.

Hilde and Luisa looked at each other knowingly. He had loved Rosa years ago, and *she* had certainly given him no peace or contentment.

Peter went on. "She's an excellent cook! She writes me interesting letters about whatever is happening at home or her village. Her family likes me. We'll get around to marriage some time. Why rush it?"

Hilde sighed mockingly. "Oh, Uncle Peter! What a deathless romance!"

A laugh and a bright inflection brought their attention to Rosa, who was walking toward them speaking animatedly to Hilde's male philosophy teacher. Rosa was obviously arguing with him, and loving it. Her eyes sparkled. Her lips moved quickly. The expressions on her face shifted rapidly from humor to hauteur, to deep interest. Still slim and shapely in a new flowered dress, her body swayed gracefully across the grass while her shoulders and hands made expansive gestures. Hilde glanced at Peter in time to catch an odd expression on his face before he turned abruptly away.

❖ ❖ ❖

Late that afternoon Rosa and Hilde returned to their house while the others went their separate ways. Her mother's constraint on the way home made Hilde nervous.

As Rosa removed her hat and put it on the wardrobe shelf, Hilde began to wash up a few dishes that had been soaking in the sink. She felt her mother standing in the doorway behind her, watching her.

"Hilde, I want you to know I'm proud of you for being offered a scholarship." Her voice had an odd tone, the way it sounded when she was about to say something unpleasant. Rosa walked to the side of the sink so Hilde would have to look at her. "I'm afraid I've had to make a difficult decision. We've both been hoping for this scholarship, and I've done a lot of thinking about it. My conclusion isn't what either of us would want, but in the long run it will be the best for us both. I'm very sorry, but you aren't going to be able to accept the scholarship."

Hilde turned astonished eyes toward her mother. "What?"

She held up her hand to forestall Hilde. "Wait. Let me explain. For the last ten years of your life I have willingly given up my own dreams so you could go to a good school. I have worked several jobs at a time for years so that we could simply survive. But we have barely managed more than subsistance."

Hilde felt as if the ground had dropped out from beneath her. She could scarcely breathe. Her mother rushed on.

"Hilde, neither of us want to go on living the way we have. I have decided that in order for us to secure a better future, we are going to have to make a dramatic change in our plans. At last you have reached an age where you can contribute to the long range improvement of our lives."

Hilde interrupted, "But you've always wanted me to . . ."

Rosa's lips were thin and her voice bitter as she raised it over Hilde's. "I know perfectly well what I've wanted for you. I'm sorry, but we can't always have what we want right now, as you certainly know. If your father had supported us as he should have . . . If I had been able to get better jobs . . . If I had been able to finish medical school instead of scrambling for every pfennig. . ., I would have been very glad and proud to have you go on to whatever heights you can reach." Rosa plucked up one of the cups Hilde had set to drain, and wiped it briskly with a dish towel.

"So I have figured out a plan, and it's a good one. It will work!" She emphasized her point by clicking the cup firmly onto the shelf, and picked up another. "I am going back to medical school full time. In order for me to do so, *you* must get a decent job, so we can survive." She put another cup beside the first. "I should be able to finish in about two years. *Then* we'll have plenty of money so you can do whatever you want. So you see, it isn't as if I'm saying you can't *ever* go on. You just can't go on *now*."

Hilde's hardly heard the last few sentences. Her throat was tight. It was hard to breathe. She had to get away from her mother before she screamed or threw something.

Whirling, she raced from the room and out the door. She ran and ran down the path beside the river. She could hardly see through her tears and stumbled through a growth of tall reeds to a secret place she knew she could hide. Dropping down to a mossy hillock in their center, she gave way to grief. How could Mama do this to her! All these years she'd worked so hard! Mama had bragged about her to those high- class friends and sketched bright plans about her future. It couldn't be true! It couldn't! Oh, if only Ferdi were here now! He'd understand! Three more weeks until he'd be home! How could she go on? Maybe Uncle Peter could make Mama see. No, Mama wouldn't even listen to *him* anymore.

Curling into a ball, Hilde wept her heart out, her mind racing down every avenue that might lead her mother to change her mind. But it was useless! Mama never cared how she felt. Mama did what Mama wanted to do, and pity Hilde if she ever talked back or got in the way! Maybe she could run away to Oma. She'd write to her, anyway. Nothing left in life. Nothing but a gray, featureless future.

She stayed in the willows until dusk. If Mama called her, she didn't hear and didn't care. When she got home she saw her mother through the front window, sitting anxiously in a chair and tapping her fingers. *Let her worry*, thought Hilde. She quietly climbed the outer stairs to her room and locked the door.

Three weeks later she still felt desolate when Ferdi got home from college. By that time darling Sister Haubinger, who felt as bad as Hilde did herself, had helped her student find a good job right away. The girl was hired as assistant to the cook in a restaurant owned by the nun's sister and brother-in-law, with promises of promotions if she did well. Her new bosses, the Spannegels, were awfully nice to her, but she had to work hard ten hours a day peeling onions until her eyes streamed, and chopping vegetables with sore, chapped hands.

But life during her evening hours was better. Mama only had a few hours each week to spend at home, now that she was back in medical school. And when she was there, she displayed a pleasantness and enthusiasm Hilde never remembered seeing before.

Best of all was her day off whenever Ferdi came over. They swam and paddled his two-man kayak, or sometimes read novels to each other under the trees. When he chose to go out with his older friends, she missed him.

Mama had continued to throw little parties now and then for impoverished friends of artistic or noble bent whenever she could get credit with the grocer. So, of course, there were still bill collectors and nasty letters from creditors. Hilde shook her head, but realized with some pride that her small, steady wage kept them afloat.

❖ ❖ ❖

At the end of summer, Hilde lay dozing in a hammock, the late afternoon sunshine slanting through the leaves and warming her. She felt a presence, and opened her eyes. A woman stood a few paces away, smiling at Hilde tenderly. She was dressed all in white, and seemed to be glowing. The low angle of the sun gave an ethereal golden radiance to the leafy shrubbery around her. The woman tilted her head to the side, her smile increasing.

The drowsy girl lifted her head. "Are you an angel?" she murmured curiously. The woman laughed gaily, proving her corporeality, and spoke. Her voice was bright and cheerful.

"I'm sorry I woke you. You look so beautiful lying there. Like a French painting."

Hilde swung her feet to the ground, pleasantly embarrassed.

"You caught me napping, I'm afraid."

The woman stepped forward, holding out her hand. "You don't know me. I'd better introduce myself. I'm Sister Negrinni, from the LDS church."

"Oh!" Hilde was surprised. She hadn't seen any of the members for years. "Uh, won't . . . won't you please sit down?" She indicated a lawn chair made of stout willow branches, and then jumped up. "But let me wipe it off, first . . . your white dress . . ."

Sister Negrinni thanked her, waited while she dusted the seat, and sat down. "I wanted to meet you, Hilde. I've only been a member myself for a couple of years, but I've been told some very nice things about you."

"You wanted to meet *me*?" Hilde was puzzled.

The older woman smiled. "Yes. You see, you're fifteen now, and we have a wonderful program for our teenagers. It's called 'Beehive Girls.' You know, for 'busy as a bee?' I've been asked to be the new leader. And when they told me about you, I wanted to come in person and invite you."

Hilde cast her eyes down and felt herself redden. "I'm . . . afraid I haven't come for a long time. You see . . . Well, I got a scholarship to a really nice Catholic school. And . . . I had to quit going to the Mormon church." She looked up hopefully. "But I've graduated now."

"Oh, that's no matter at all," said Sister Negrinni, breezily. "This isn't a Sunday sort of thing, anyway. It's just a lot of fun with girls your age. We do handicrafts and learn all kinds of skills. There are first aid and service projects. And we go camping . . ."

"Oh, I *love* camping!" exclaimed Hilde, thinking of the Reiner family and their excursions in the woods by St. Pölten.

"Well we would *love* to have you," Sister Negrinni smiled. She gave Hilde the times and dates. Meetings were usually on Wednesday evenings because most of the girls had work or school during the days.

"I'll be there next Wednesday," promised Hilde, remembering that on Wednesday evening her mother always studied late at the university library.

The Beehive meeting was delightful. Hilde loved the other girls, the atmosphere, and just having fun. But she didn't mention it to Mama. Why bother her with trivia when she was so busy with her studies?

One evening the program called for the girls to learn lace crocheting. Hilde was pleased to be asked to show the others some of the skills she had learned at Notre Dame.

She explained to the girls, "We weren't ever allowed to have idle hands at my school. Every week, sometimes twice, we would be given special lectures by the priest on getting along in life. You know, how to deal with men, or employers, and things like that. He was really great. Or we had music appreciation classes. Anyway, while we listened, we had to make crocheted lace."

Hilde displayed some of the things she had made: doilies, antimacassars, and dresser scarves. She grinned. "Most of the girls were from very rich families. The only kind of work that would be considered ladylike for them was making something decorative. Not too useful for staying alive or getting a job. But kind of fun if you have spare time. Which I don't! Ever!" The girls laughed, and Hilde felt happy and appreciated.

After class, Sister Negrinni asked Hilde to stay a few minutes.

"Hilde, have you ever read the Book of Mormon?"

"No. I don't have one."

"I want you to have one," the older woman said, handing her a small volume. "And I would be very pleased if you would read it and tell me what you think."

Hilde accepted the book with surprise and delight. "I'll read it, Sister Negrinni. And I'll give you a book report next time I come."

"Don't read it all at once. Take your time. There's a lot there to think about. Do you have a Bible? There are a lot of cross-references, and you should pay attention to them."

"Yes, of course we have one. And I'll do that." Hilde opened the cover. Inside was a message:

> To Hildegard, a lovely young woman:
>   Remember, only when you are unafraid of truth can
>   you find it.
> Love, Magdalana Negrinni.

Impulsively, Hilde put her arms around the woman. "Thank you for caring about me, Sister Negrinni."

❖ ❖ ❖

Mama rarely had parties anymore. Too busy. But it was Aunt Steffie's birthday, and Mama had invited a few of their "better" friends to celebrate for an afternoon luncheon party. Steffie had been Mama's best friend for years, since the '20s when she had been even poorer than they were and emaciated from constant hunger. Mama had brought her vegetables from Opa's garden to help her little family survive. Now, of course, Steffie's family was terribly rich. One might read in the newspaper about people winning the national lottery, but it had seemed such a remote fairy tale until Steffie actually had! Being rich made no difference in Steffie's friendship for them. The only difference was in her figure, which had quickly grown rotund from frequent stuffing with rich foods. She was a darling, as were her husband and sons, and Hilde loved her like a second mother.

The pretty dirndl Mama had made for Hilde's sixteenth birthday last year had been pawned to pay a few little debts. But Mama had got it out of hawk a week ago for Steffie's party today. Both of them had been horrified that the dress didn't fit anymore, and Mama had complained at Hilde's added height and developing figure. As if she had done it on purpose! Honestly!

But, of course, Mama was very clever with sewing, and had inserted plackets of harmonizing material down the bodice front and back, and around the waistline. With a border around the skirt and a ruffle on the sleeves, she had made it into quite a different dress; one that fit nicely. For now. Hilde had two or three such dresses in her wardrobe. But so did nearly everybody else in these strained times. The trick was to make the insets look fashionable rather than necessary. Hilde had to give Mama that. She knew how to "make a silk purse out of a sow's ear."

Luckily, the October day was unusually mild. They would be able to eat outside, which was more lovely than ever with the sun shining on the colored trees. The food was exceptionally good and Mama had made a beautiful cake. Everyone they had invited came, many of them dressed in their Austrian national costumes; and a few of the guests brought wine for the adults. Everything was set out in a buffet so neither she nor Mama would have to serve.

Philip Prokalpi was there. The handsome young assistant to the Greek ambassador obviously liked her and came often to visit, even though the parties of former years had ceased. They wandered together to the hollow under the willow tree, but she made sure they stood in a spot where the others could see them. Philip was beginning to give her amorous looks, and Hilde wanted to be cautious until she knew how she felt about him. He was a worldly twenty-two.

"How are things at the embassy?" she asked. "Are they recognizing your brilliance yet?"

Philip was gorgeous and must have known it. Melting brown eyes, curly dark hair like one of those ancient statues the Greek embassy displayed so proudly. His profile was statue perfect, too, and even under a suit his body showed muscular as a bull. Too bad he wasn't taller, but she was tiny, so it didn't really matter. His lips were sinfully curvy, and he spoke with an accent that made everything seem exotic. She smiled up through her lashes because she knew it made him catch his breath.

He shook his finger gently at her. "Don't you do that, little girl, unless you're willing to take the consequences."

She raised her eyebrows innocently. "I don't know what you're talking about. Here, let's sit down, and you tell me what's happening in Greece since King George dissolved Parliament." That would distract him. He was awfully conscientious about his politics and patriotism. He became immediately serious.

"The Communists are gaining strength and popularity, even with parliament dissolved. It makes me very uneasy," he said pulling up a long weed. "And we don't know what to think yet of General Metaxas as a dictator. The king still hasn't named a date for new elections, and our constitution has no more meaning now than so much paper." He shook his head and looked at her intensely. "At least Metaxas is a strong leader. Greece has been confused and weak from the day she declared herself a republic back in 1923. But I worry. I dislike dictators on principle."

Philip went on in a similar vein until Rosa rang a bell and announced the birthday cake. It was a lovely almond bundt cake, drizzled with white frosting. In the center of the cake was a large, beautifully carved birthday candle called the Labenskerze—the candle of life. Someone played traditional birthday songs on a mellow wooden recorder while they all sang to Steffie. Philip grasped Hilde's hand and squeezed it.

Steffie stayed on in the late afternoon when everyone else had left. Her husband had gone into town earlier to pick up some theater tickets, but promised he would come back and retrieve her before evening.

"He knew I'd want to sit around and gossip, " Steffie admitted. The plump woman cheerfully dried dishes while Rosa washed and Hilde put away.

Glancing out the window, Hilde saw a man in a black suit coming down the main road, a large book under his arm. "Mama," she said, stepping back and nodding at the window.

Rosa glanced out, froze, and began to breathe quickly. "Hilde, lock the doors and windows." She turned to her friend with a wry smile. "Steffie, you're about to do something you haven't done for over ten years."

"What's happening? Rosa, stop pushing me! Who is that man?"

"That is Herr Rupert, an old and not-at-all dear friend of the family. He is a very unkind man who likes to torment us, and we are going to hide so he won't know we're at home. Thank heavens we don't have any lights on yet. Let's see," she turned around, considering. "I'll have to take the sofa. Hilde, you're behind the chair in the corner, and make sure your skirt isn't showing. Steffie, you get the wardrobe. It's the most comfortable." Rosa opened the door, pushed the coats aside and gestured for Steffie to climb inside.

Steffie was scandalized. "What on earth are you doing! Rosa, I'm not climbing into that wardrobe! I'll muss my hair, and I just had it done this morning!"

Rosa took Steffie's shoulders, anguish and pleading on her face. "Steffie, this is horrid for me to do to you on your birthday. I'm sorry! I'm *so* sorry! But if that man finds us here, he'll serve a summons, and we'll be in desperate trouble. Please, darling! Just remember your years before the lottery."

"Rosa! Why didn't you tell me things were so bad? Yes, yes, *yes*. Don't push. I'll get in. But only for you! I would never do this for anybody else!" Rosa helped arrange the plump woman as comfortably as possible, and closed the door. "Don't move," she hissed. The door pops right open if you bump it from inside."

"How do you know?" asked a muffled voice.

"Shhhhhh," Rosa admonished as she jammed herself full length between the sofa and the wall.

A moment later there were footsteps outside, and a firm knocking on the door. A pause. The knocking became a banging. "Frau Edler! Frau Edler! I know you're home today! Open this door!" More banging. "Frau Edler!"

The steps left the walk and rustled through the bushes at the side of the house. Hilde made herself smaller and held very still. He would be at the window now. She could hear the faint brushing sound against the glass as he placed his hands around his eyes to peer in. She held her breath.

"I can see you hiding. You might as well come out!" cried the man's voice. He was lying. Rosa had checked any number of times to see how much of the room one could see from that window. Soon he left and circled the house to the kitchen. She heard him rapping on the glass and calling their names. Then his feet went up the outside steps to the landing above, and he pounded on both their bedroom doors. He might open them and look inside, but the law took a dim view of his actually going in and searching. And without a warrant, he couldn't impound anything he found up there.

Down the stairs and around the house he went once more, looking in windows, but not bothering to call out. Finally, with a few muttered curses, he left. They could hear his footsteps crunching down the gravel of the path.

Rosa spoke softly, "Stay where you are, Steffie. Just a couple more minutes. Hilde, check on him."

Hilde crept out from behind the big chair and ran quickly into the kitchen. She crouched and looked through a little crack between the curtain and the wall, but was careful not to disturb the fabric. The crack was maintained just for this purpose. Sure enough, Herr Rupert was mostly hidden behind a large tree, watching the house. After a few minutes he gave up and went away.

"All clear," said Hilde in relief.

Rosa wriggled out from behind the sofa, and opened the wardrobe door for Steffie, who huddled wide-eyed within.

"Goodness!" she said. "I had forgotten how frightening that can be." Her voice became cross as her friend helped her out. "Rosa, how long has this sort of thing been going on?"

"Your hair looks fine, Steffie. Not a curl out of place."

"Don't try to evade my question, young lady. What is going on?"

"'Young lady.' I like that. I must be all of three years younger than you."

"You've got yourself in debt, haven't you?"

"Well, Steffie, what's new? How on earth can anyone live these days without going into debt? In fact, I was going to talk to you about that very thing. No, not my debts—yours."

"I don't have any debts. I'm a millionaire."

"You're a ninny. And so is your husband. Steffie, I want you to sit down right here, because I have something important to tell you."

Hilde perched on the arm of the chair and watched the two women on the sofa.

"Steffie," said Rosa, taking her friend's hands. " I may be a fool about the way I spend money, but at least I know exactly where I am. I suppose you and Fritzie still don't have a book-keeper. No, I thought not. But I've been watching you, and keeping a rough estimate. You've probably spent half your money already jaunting around and having fun."

"Why shouldn't we? We suffered long enough!"

"Yes, darling. But you're going to start suffering again if you aren't careful. Airplane trips to Paris! Dinners that would cost me a year's wages!"

Steffie looked down guiltily and pulled her hands away.

"Oh, Steffie! I'm not nagging you. You deserve to have fun. But you need to think a little of the future, too. Look! For what you spend on one little vacation, you could buy a farm and make enough money in a few years to pay for the farm, and keep on paying you afterward for the rest of your life." Rosa jumped up and walked over to a shelf, from which she took a newspaper. She sat down again, and spread the sheets open to "Properties for Sale."

"Look here, Steffie. I saw this at the library, and went right out and bought a copy. Look here, and here. Here's a dairy farm, house, cattle, land, everything, and the owner's widow is selling because she can't keep it up. It's a steal, and would keep you in money for as long as you both live."

"Rosa, don't be an idiot! I don't know anything about cows,

or farming, and that certainly isn't the way I want to spend my time!"

"Not *you*, Steffie. You could hire a manager to live there, and he would take care of everything. You could just count the money as it comes in."

Eyebrows drawn together, Steffie looked at the ad with a mixture of repulsion and fascination.

"And Steffie," Rosa continued softly, sensing her advantage, "food is one thing that never goes out of style, never stops being needed. The land never goes away. Even if all your cows died and the grass died of drought, you'd still have the land! What do you have left after an airplane trip?"

Steffie spoke slowly, her eyes still on the paper. "Rosa, you think too hard."

"Steffie, *you* think too soft. Will you give it some thought? Show the paper to Fritzie?"

As if on cue, a motorcar crunched up the road. Steffie sighed in relief as rescue drove into sight. She folded the paper and put it into her large bag. "I don't *care* to think about it, but I probably should." She put on her coat, and gave Rosa a hug. "Thank you so much, dear, for a *truly* memorable birthday party."

She embraced Hilde, too. "You look lovely today, Hilde. You're positively blossoming. I'd watch that young Greek, though. He looks like a famished animal, and you're the meal he has his eye on. He's much too old for you. I think you should wait for my Willie."

Hilde chuckled. "Good-bye, Aunt Steffie. Happy Birthday. Tell Richard and Willie hello for me next time you write."

For some unaccountable reason, Herr Rupert ceased to bother them after that. Hilde wondered if her mother had noticed, since she never mentioned it. But the girl formed her own ideas about why their credit was suddenly good again at various stores.

❖ ❖ ❖

Vienna, 1936

"What do you mean you can't come over and listen to my records Friday night?" Ferdi was honestly perplexed. "They're new."

Hilde explained patiently as she finished arranging the Christmas greenery around the mirror on the wall. "I'd love to, Ferdi, but I'm going to the opera that night."

"Your mother didn't mention it when we were talking today."

"I'm not going with my mother."

"Well, then, whom?" Ferdi sounded impatient.

"With Philip Prokalpi, if you insist on knowing."

"Prokalpi? That pretty boy? Whatever for?"

"Well, for goodness sakes! Why not? He asked me, and I love opera. And he's no more a boy than you are."

"He asked you on a date? You're going on a date with a Greek errand boy?" Ferdi's voice sounded irritated.

"Ferdi, Philip is an assistant to the Greek ambassador, and he's quite charming—although a little intense." She paused and assumed an innocent expression. "And he finds me ravishing, which is very nice."

"He told you he finds you ravishing? You're only seventeen!" Ferdi's brows drew together.

"Why not?" Hilde was amused to see Ferdi grow a bit jealous. "Is there an age requirement for ravishing?" She allowed a hint of a smile. "And what's more, he finds my eyes like stars and my lips like tender plums."

"Tender plums! What nonsense!" Ferdi began to pace around Hilde's front room. "He told you that? How can you stand the oily fellow!" Another turn around the room. "And just how does

he know they're so tender!" The question was more an accusation. "You certainly never let that roué kiss you, did you?"

"Ferdi! Of course not! I suppose he *imagines* they're like tender plums. And just why is this 'errand boy' suddenly a 'roué?'"
Hilde perched on the arm of the big chair, struggling not to
laugh. "Are you my big brother to protect me from improper
advances?"

Ferdi stopped in front of her, glaring down at her for a long
moment, then raked his fingers through his dark blond hair.
She tried the trick of looking demurely up through her lashes,
the way she did with Philip. She wasn't expecting for a moment
that he would grip her arm like that and pull her to her feet. She
was astonished as he put his free hand behind her head and
brought his lips down on hers. The sensations that enveloped
her when he did it turned her world upside down. Lightning
raced down through her stomach, then melted her insides to a
puddle. Her arm stole hesitantly around his neck, and she leaned
close against him.

He kept his arms around her after he released her lips and
pressed her cheek to his chest. She exhaled a long sigh. There
was nothing to say. His heart thudded rapidly beneath her ear.

Ferdi's voice was a little strange when he spoke. "More tender than plums. Much softer. And much sweeter." They held
each other for several minutes, neither of them wanting at all to
move.

A door upstairs opened. Rosa was coming down. Ferdi lifted Hilde's chin, and placed a swift kiss on her lips. "Looks like
you ravish *me*, too."

He released her as Rosa's feet clacked down the stairs.

When Rosa walked into the front room, Hilde was sitting
in the big chair, and Ferdi was examining the little nativity figures on a side table.

That night Hilde couldn't sleep for hours. Every time she
thought of Ferdi's kiss, delicious sensations raced through her
insides. She had liked Ferdi a lot, even had sort of a crush on

him last summer. But he had always treated her like such a child. Hilde smiled luxuriously and hugged her pillow all night.

Ferdi came over every day during the holiday, and Rosa began to give them knowing looks. When he returned to Berlin, he wrote her every week until Easter vacation. Hilde had never felt so exuberant about life.

❖ ❖ ❖

On a train trip together from St. Pölten to Vienna, Rosa rode beside her younger brother, Richard. Home at last from several years in the French Foreign Legion, Richard had enlisted in the Austrian army. She explained to him that she had nearly reached her lifetime goal. Her last three classes would be finished in a few months, and she would go before a medical board of review prior to graduation.

"About time!" was his reply. "Seems like you've been taking classes for fifteen or twenty years. I trust everything is right, proper, and approved for graduation after all your fits and starts. What do your advisors say?"

A little chill went up Rosa's spine. "They haven't said anything. What should they say? I was admitted in 1921, and I've been methodically working my way through the required classes every year I possibly could since then."

Do you mean you haven't checked your status in all these years! Darling sister, you may think *I'm* the irresponsible one, but hadn't you better ask someone where you stand in regards to being graduated?"

"Hmmph! That's the army talking, all right," she deflected. "Ask permission before you blow your nose. My professors see me and teach me every day. I'm practically a fixture in the school after all this time. If there was anything I needed to know in order to graduate, I'm sure they would tell me."

"I hope you're right," he replied.

❖ ❖ ❖

It took Hilde an hour and a half in each direction to go between home and her work at the cafeteria. She walked half an hour to the bus stop, then rode twenty minutes into town. The streetcar in Vienna took another forty minutes, but at least she didn't have to change cars. She didn't mind the trip; it was a good time to read.

In front of her she held the scriptures Sister Negrinni had given her. Deeply absorbed, she occasionally stopped to underline a passage, or gaze into space and ponder. Sometimes a seat mate would peer at her reading material, raise an eyebrow, and look away. She didn't mind. A feeling of warmth and rightness grew and deepened within her as she read her way through the book. She felt whole, secure, and full of joy.

Sometimes, when she had been reading, then looked up, it was if she momentarily saw the other passengers with eyes that were not her own. The eyes of God, she knew. Each man and woman looked so ordinary on the outside. Maybe *they* even thought themselves ordinary. Every one of them, like her, had pains and worries, wishes and hopes, and weaknesses great and small. Yet in the eyes of God they were each so dear and precious, cherished for their uniqueness. Each held within a greatness of their own! Every one of them worth dying for. Yet, each so caught up in the concerns of the moment they couldn't see the wonder of themselves or of each other.

I wish . . . I wish I could reach out and touch that woman over there with the sad face. That old man with his sleeve pinned up who is missing an arm. I wish I could make them feel what I feel inside. But I'm such a coward. They'd think I was crazy.

Nevertheless, she smiled sweetly at the old man, and he smiled back.

The more she attended the little LDS congregation, the more she thought, *I want to be this way. Like them. I like the way they keep trying to be good and do good, even after they make mistakes. I want to care the way they care for each other.*

She had tried tentatively to tell her feelings to Ferdi. She loved him so. She wanted them to feel alike on this. But he never seemed to hear her. It worried her. She thought of poor Uncle Johann. Nobody had to tell her how miserable a marriage could be when one partner loved God passionately and the other never gave him a thought. And it wasn't as if her aunt and uncle didn't *try* to work things out. Yes, it had started with a lie. But she could see how hard they both wanted a happy home for little Johanna's sake. Together, they were like a bird and a fish. They simply had nothing in common except for their little girl.

I desperately do not want to be like them, she thought. *The spiritual part of me has to be accepted. I can talk to Uncle Johann or Oma about how I feel, and they understand. But what if Ferdi looked at me like Uncle Richard or Aunt Luisa do? As if I'm speaking Chinese? Or like Mama, who just changes the subject? I couldn't bear it!*

She settled in her mind that she would talk to Ferdi again. Somehow she would make him see how important this was. How joyful! How vital!

But when he made a special trip home in May for his father's birthday, he had enthusiasms of his own to discuss. "My father will be glad I'm finally taking an interest in politics! Of course, it isn't necessarily what *he* supports right now, but that's because he doesn't understand it yet. One people! One German-speaking people that will create a civilization so remarkable and advanced it will last a thousand years! Berlin is wild about the idea. People who have been starving and discouraged since the war are holding up their heads again. Feeling pride again!" He put his arm around Hilde's shoulder as they paced down the path by the Danube. "I tell you, Hilde, it's a revolution! One where intelligence and fitness and inventiveness will triumph over weakness, slovenliness, and degeneracy. One people united with the best and purest ideals since the world began!"

Hilde had been nodding and murmuring assent. But she couldn't let that last statement pass. "Ferdi, I'll be glad if we can all unite in a better kind of life than we've had. But I don't think ideals of nobility and purity started with Herr Hitler, even if so many people are crazy about him. If you'll recall, goodness and purity and sharing and loving were preached a couple of thousand years ago in Palestine. By someone who didn't need to shout to convince people."

Ferdi looked at her blankly a moment, and then laughed. "Are you talking about Christianity? Ah, yes, and what a proud tradition that has of doing good! The Holy Wars. The Spanish Inquisition. Every so-called religious sect burning the members of the others at the stake for heresy. A fine plan, Christianity. But Hilde, it has *never worked!* Here we have something practical, with a strong leader people can see and hear and touch today! No, religion is too weak. It doesn't have the power to change whole governments, systems, the world . . ."

"Well it would if people lived it!" interrupted Hilde. "All those horrors you mentioned . . . they went wrong exactly because somebody tried to *force* their ideas on other people. Being better than you are can only start *inside* of you. Christianity can only change the world one person at a time. It might be slow, but it's *real* and *true*."

Ferdi smiled crookedly with one eyebrow cocked. "And look how far the world has come by now, with this 'real and true', and 'one person at a time' Christianity. Now don't get all upset. I know you're fond of religion, and that's all well and good. But if we are going to conquer the weaknesses of the world, we are obviously going to have to do it in a more efficient . . . " he paused, seeing the thunder on her face, "let's say, 'in an *additional* way,' all right? Can you accept that? Maybe we've reached a point in this modern age where people can be inspired to find better and quicker ways to change mankind. Call it a *supplement* to religion, if you like. Is that a remote possibility?"

"To be honest, I don't know. I don't understand it that much, but it doesn't feel entirely good to me."

"Hilde, any change is frightening—even changes for the

better. But will you think about it? Will you read the literature I brought you?"

"If I get time," she replied unenthusiastically. This was obviously not a golden moment for discussing her love of God and the gladness in her soul. Later, when he held her and kissed her, and whispered words of tenderness and love, very little else seemed to matter.

✤ ✤ ✤

Hilde drew the kitchen curtain aside to see more clearly. Her mother was striding—no, *stalking* down the lane toward the house, her aspect peculiar even from a distance. A chill gripped the girl. The satchel of papers Mama had taken that morning for her medical board review was not with her. Hilde waited tensely for her mother's arrival. But Rosa didn't come into the downstairs. She stomped immediately up the outside steps, threw open the door to her room with a crash, and clomped across the floor. Hilde heard dragging sounds, and the banging of the wardrobe doors. She waited nervously for several minutes, then crept out of the kitchen and up the stairs.

Rosa was pulling things out of drawers and flinging clothes from the wardrobe into a suitcase on her bed. The expression on her face was stone.

"Mama?" said Hilde timidly from the doorway. No response. "Mama, what's happened?" A long pause while Rosa bent to retrieve shoes from under the bed. "Where are you going? Mama, please talk to me. What's wrong?"

After a few moments Rosa responded in curt tones. "I'm going to St. Pölten. I don't know how long I'll be gone."

"But wh . . ."

Rosa interrupted, her voice hard as her expression, "I don't want to discuss it. Leave me alone."

"Mama, what about Steffie and the celebration party tomorrow?"

"Call her from work in the morning. Tell her it's off. Please leave." Her head jerked toward the door.

Hilde stole back down the stairs, her insides churning. Something terrible. It could only be . . . She sat frozen in the living room, listening to the noises above. Steps down the stairs. The outer door jerked open. Rosa took her coat from the wardrobe. She wore pants and a sweater and sturdy shoes. "You needn't worry about me," was all she said as she shrugged on her coat and headed out the door.

Needn't worry? thought Hilde, frightened and distressed.

❖ ❖ ❖

The cacophony of the wheels vibrating beneath Rosa didn't hold a candle to the cacophony of her thoughts and feelings. *How could they do this to me! How dared they! More than fifteen years!* She saw again the eight doctors lined up on chairs behind two tables. Most of them knew her, had taught her. Had praised her grasp and insight, even while tearing her apart for this or that misdiagnosis, or wrong answer. They had turned on her! All of them! It wasn't fair! Not just! Her responses had been mostly correct, they had admitted that themselves. Then why this stupid obsession with rules, rules, rules?

Rosa turned her body toward the window, resentfully grateful to be almost alone in the railroad car. Her faint reflection in the glass was ugly, and she looked away. Fists clenched and unclenched in her lap. Eyes burned. Breath was difficult past the persistent lump in her throat. Far, far away . . . Go into the woods alone. Up on a mountain. Climb a mountain alone until she was exhausted. Too exhausted to think or feel. *Unfair! Hideously unfair!* Her rage boiled. She could barely suppress a scream of outrage.

Duback's nasal voice echoed in her brain, " . . . have to repeat the earlier classes . . . Outmoded procedures . . . Modern advancements . . . Reputation of the university to consider . . . Light of the medical world . . . Must understand . . . Surely only two more years, perhaps three . . . No appeal . . . No appeal . . .

No appeal . . ."

She left her suitcase with Hannah, who knew what day this was and wisely asked no questions. Rosa took only a pack of essentials and a thick blanket for a few days of rough living; a thing she had done plenty of times in her youth. She hadn't even considered food until Hannah wordlessly stuck a sack of sandwiches and apples into her pack.

Rosa was gone four days. The weather was fortunately mild. When she returned she was physically exhausted, hungry, dirty, bitter, but mostly resigned. Mostly.

Hannah fed her when she came in. There was a calming spirit of quiet, unquestioning acceptance about the older woman. While she ate, Rosa heard the bathtub being filled. Hannah put towels on the chair beside Rosa and said, "I'm going shopping for a couple of hours." The older woman pulled on her jacket, tied a scarf over her hair, lifted her basket and left.

In the bathroom Rosa undressed, dropping her clothes on the floor. The water was hot, and stung her foot as she immersed it. She lowered herself an inch at a time, gasping as the heat assailed her skin. Slowly. Slowly. It was almost too hot for breathing. Definitely too hot for thinking or feeling. Without her volition, every emotion and conjecture numbed to silence under the enervating heat.

Rosa lay a long time, senselessly inert, until the bath began to cool. Languidly, mindlessly, she washed her hair and lathered her skin. Submersing, she waved her head from side to side, the movement of the water rinsing her hair like the tide flowing through underwater grass. Finally, slowly, she sat up, drained part of the water, then turned on the left tap again until it was as hot as before. A numb lethargy had stolen into her bones.

After a long time she heard the front door open and her mother clanking around in the kitchen. With a deep sigh Rosa knew she would have to come back to reality. Pulling the plug, she rose to dry. "Mama," she called a few minutes later, "would you bring me my suitcase, please?"

She put on clean underwear and clothing, and gathered her damp hair into a tail as she had done as a child. Putting her dirty clothes in the laundry basket, she hung the towels to dry.

Mama was sitting in the front room, but a goulash was simmering fragrantly on the kitchen stove. Everything was so normal. Rosa stood in the doorway and looked at the familiar scene. In her favorite overstuffed chair, Hannah sat knitting. Without a word Rosa walked to her and sank to the floor, tucking bare feet beneath her. She laid her head in her mother's lap. Hannah silently stroked the damp hair.

"Oh, Mama . . ." Hannah continued to stroke her. After a few minutes, Rosa spoke again. "It's all so wrong. So wrong. The waste is horrifying. The disappointment hurts terribly. But I can't bear . . . can't possibly bear . . . the humiliation." She rested for awhile, relaxed under her mother's gentle hand. Her voice was tired. "You know I'm talking about my board exams."

Hannah murmured assent.

"They could have told me sooner." She shrugged. "Maybe they tried. I wouldn't have listened. I *couldn't* listen. I gave everything I had for so many years. I couldn't even *think* of having to do it over." She raised her head, her eyes pleading. "But Mama, I kept abreast! I answered all their questions so well. They said I did! It was all a stupid matter of policy! *Policy! Rules!*" When she began to feel the mounting rage that had consumed her in the mountains, she consciously held herself still, breathed deeply, closed her eyes. "It doesn't matter. Nothing I think does any good. Nothing matters. Oh, Mama!" Her head dropped again.

They were still sitting as it became dark outside. Hannah reached to turn on a lamp on the table next to her. Finally she spoke.

"Have you decided what to do, Rosl?"

"That's the worst of it, Mama. I've been struggling toward this one goal for so long, it's like my life has been cut off. I have never given a single thought to what I would do if it turned out this way. What else am I good for?"

Hannah chuckled. "My daughter asks what she is good for. Oh, well now, let's see: 'Woman needs career, has studied medicine, designed dresses, made clothing, built a house, knows how to farm and breed animals, has run a kitchen for thousands, keeps books and cooks well, knows how to entertain in style, isn't afraid of anything, hard work included, knows how to live on nothing, and will fight dragons to protect what she believes in.' Hmmmm. What kind of job could such a woman find?"

Rosa laughed shortly in response, then sighed gustily. "Maybe. For all the good it does to try to find a decent job in Vienna." She became serious. "But Mama. I cannot stay in Vienna! I cannot! Not just finding work. The humiliation! I've told everyone forever that I would be a doctor. Boasted for so long! Oh, there will be such gleeful snickers behind my back! 'The arrogant Rosa was dreaming all along, just as we expected! Couldn't do it! Who did she think she was!'" Rosa shook her head violently. "People never approved, Mama. You know they didn't. And now that I've failed, they won't care why. They'll simply have a circus laughing at me! Ohhhhhh!" She groaned and turned her face to bury it in Hannah's lap. "I can't go back!" She mumbled thickly. "I can't, I can't, I *cannot go back!*"

She lifted her face again, distorted with fresh agony. "Oh, and the bills! The bills I've run up! So sure! Telling everyone I would start my practice soon, and pay everyone off! Oh, Mama, I'll be sent to jail! I can't pay *anyone!*" She leapt to her feet and paced around the room, clawing her hair loose with anxious hands. "What in this living hell am I going to do?"

❖ ❖ ❖

Hilde was queasy with apprehension and uncertainty about her mother, until she received a short note from Hannah.

"So, I finally learn she's rambling around alone in the hills," the girl grumbled as she scrubbed her way down the stairs. "Well, good for her! It can only be one thing, of course. Her board exam must have fallen through somehow." Hilde dumped the dirty water onto the bushes at the foot of the stairs. "Why won't Mama tell me anything! Does she think I'm still a child? What kind of 'child' could support two people for the last three years! Why can't she *talk* to me?"

Finally returning to the house on the Danube, Rosa was morose and silent, and never broached the subject of her absence. Her bitterness and despair darkened the house. Hilde went every day to the restaurant, while Rosa worked with grim and furious energy in her garden, seeing and speaking to no one. The girl felt constantly on her guard, wary of arousing Rosa's quick wrath, wishing her mother would look for a job, but not daring to mention it. Rosa wouldn't talk to anyone. *This can't go on,* thought Hilde. *We simply cannot go on this way.* "Oh, Lord," she prayed fervently. "Save my mother. Save us both!"

One afternoon Hilde found her mother radically changed. Her eyes were bright, almost feverish, and her cheeks were two patches of red. On her knees before the front room wardrobe, she rooted through the old shoes and galoshes stored at the bottom. Hilde eyed her uneasily.

"Hilde! Dear! I'm glad you're finally home!"

Hilde hadn't been "dear" for two months.

Mama continued, "Look on the table. Wonderful news from Luisa! She's going to have a baby!"

Hilde picked up the letter and read.

Dearest Rosl,

I have the most amazing news for you and Hilde! I'm pregnant! What do you think of that! The baby's due about Christmastime. I didn't plan on it happening for another year if I could help it, but here we are, Tom and I. He's thrilled to pieces, because he's nearly thirty-four, and all his married friends have been poking fun of him for years. I wasn't at all glad at first. Dreadfully ill, in fact, throwing up all day. But Tom has been so darling, spoiling me, and bragging to everyone, and bringing me whatever treats I feel I can eat. It's rather fun having everyone make a fuss over me. But that's the only *fun part. I cannot imagine how Mama did this seven times, counting the miscarriages! I swear it will be the last for me!*

Anyhow, I don't know how you managed to do any-thing *while you were pregnant! Especially look at dead bodies and sick people! Ugh! I gag just thinking about it. In fact, I gag at everything and anything. I am absolutely wretched! Which only makes me miss home the more. I wish to heaven Mama could come and take care of me. And she would, too, but Papa would have a complete fit and threaten to strangle her or something.*

I've been continuing my study of English as much as I can, so I can make friends and have some kind of social life. And I've been doing pretty well, too. Even Tom says so. But when you feel miserable, you don't care about any-thing—certainly not about verb tenses. And that's a double reason why I'm lonely and miserable. Oh, Rosa, just to hear somebody speak good German! To be able to answer them like an intelligent person instead of an idiot! How I wish I could talk Mama into coming, just for a few weeks! Or even you.

Our house here is just fine. It's nice and big, and looks right out over the golf course, which is like the most enor-mous, beautifully kept meadow with trees and streams and things. Tom works with all kinds of aristocrats and rich people. He gets a good salary, and tips, too. He said I could hire a girl to help me if I want, and I would in a minute if I could bear to sit up and interview anyone. I think he misses having good meals, but he can always eat at the clubhouse. I can't eat anything, myself, and the smell of cooking simply kills me!

Oh, I'm absolutely exhausted! I take a dozen naps a day. I have to go rest now. I've written to Mama with the news, of course, and I'll mail both of these with the afternoon post. They deliver mail twice a day, here. Isn't that something?

Please, darling, write to me soon. Write to me every day! I miss everybody so much I cry all the time. But then I seem to cry about everything. I can hardly wait till this is over, though I can't imagine how I'll care for a child. I've hardly ever touched one.
  All my love,
  Luisa

"A baby!" cried Hilde. "Oh, how wonderful! But she's *so* sick! Poor Aunt Luisa! I wish there were something we could do for her. I could write to her a couple of times a week, I suppose, although I don't have anything interesting to say."

Rosa had collected several shoes and was examining their soles keenly. "I plan to do something *very* helpful, and very *immediate*," she exclaimed with more life in her voice than Hilde had heard since spring. "I am going to England to take care of her."

Hilde's mouth dropped open, and she stared at her mother.

Rosa looked up. "Yes! This is a godsend for both of us, don't you see? Luisa needs someone to care for her, to cook and clean and take care of the new baby when it comes. And I'm good at all those things." She continued speaking as she climbed to her feet, "And they have plenty of space, and plenty of money, it looks like." She stooped and gathered up two pairs of shoes which she placed on the chair by the door. As she put the others neatly back, she went on. "And, besides, I've seen plenty of advertisements in the newspapers from English women who want Austrian housekeepers and maids. It seems that good help is hard to find in England these days, and everybody knows Germanic women are better workers than those lazy English girls! Why, I could find a good job anywhere! And for good pay! Don't you see, Hilde! I could make enough money there to pay off our debts and still have some left! This is just what I needed!"

"But . . . but what about me?" Hilde asked in a bewildered voice.

"Oh, pooh! You'll do fine. After all, you're *my* daughter! And haven't you supported us both like a grown woman for the last few years?" Rosa dragged out her heavy winter coat and examined the cuffs carefully.

"But Mama . . ." Hilde was in complete confusion. She felt suddenly abandoned and very young. "But Mama, you hardly know any English."

Rosa hmmphed, a superior expression on her face. "I'll study it while I live with Luisa. All of my family are wonderful with languages. Look at Johann and Richard. And you with your French. I'll speak English in no time."

Hilde turned uncertainly back and forth, wringing her hands. "You're just going to leave me?" she asked in a small voice.

"I'll miss you, of course, dear. But Luisa needs me far worse than you do now. And it's time you learned to stand on your own feet. Why, I was a wife *and* a medical student at your age, and with my husband gone to the war, as well. Besides, we have a few weeks left together. I have to get a passport and a visa, and straighten out all my business dealings."

Hilde fell onto the sofa, her stomach feeling hollow.

Rosa gestured to the chair by the door. "I'd like you to take those shoes to the cobbler tomorrow on your way to work, please. They need new heels. Go to the one on Obergasse; we don't owe them anything. Tell them I need them by Friday. Go put them in a bag now, so you won't forget." She draped her coat over her arm and pulled a light jacket from a hanger. Placing a cheerful kiss on Hilde's head, she went out the door and up the stairs.

Hilde could only sit and stare at the shoes. Her breaths were short and shaking. She heard her mother bustling around above. *Mama gone? Just like that? Good-bye. Luisa needs me worse than you do. You'll get along just fine by yourself. Well, I suppose I will. I've done practically everything for myself for a long time. But being all alone? I've never been alone before. Not all alone. Doesn't she even care about me?*

Hilde thought about what it would be like. The empty house every day. Every night. She shivered. But she could go to the library on the way home, instead of rushing to fix supper, and she could read in the evenings without interruption. And she wouldn't have to worry about Mama's moods. And when Ferdi came to visit, they wouldn't even have to think of Mama coming in and hogging the conversation. A little smile began to play at the corners of her mouth. She could have the girls from church over any time she wanted. In fact, she could have a swimming party of her own on the Danube for all the young people, just like Mama's. Only this time it would be *her* friends and *her* party. Hilde's heart began to beat faster as ideas and realizations began to crowd her mind. Mixed with them all were tiny qualms of trepidation. But she could do it. Maybe it wouldn't be so bad. Maybe not bad at all. In a month, as Hilde kissed her mother good-bye at the Westbahnhoff, she had accepted the idea with complacence.

❖ ❖ ❖

A year passed, and Hilde found herself enjoying her new freedom. She felt uninhibited to grow to be the woman she hoped to be. Mama wrote from England every two weeks or so. Luisa's baby had been a boy. Rosa ran her house with an iron hand until Tom couldn't take it anymore and asked her to leave. It was just as well. The following summer Rosa took a job as companion to an eccentric duchess who raised pigs for a hobby. That fall she was hired as head housekeeper for General Fuller, an important man in the British army, who had a busy house with a lot of entertaining. Rosa took it all in stride, and earned the respect of her employers.

But Hilde could tell from her letters that something had died in her mother's heart. She thought of her mother's absorbing work in the clinics of the medical school and the kitchens that helped prevent the starvation of hundreds. Surely Rosa must realize by now that there was a big difference between rubbing shoulders with those considered noble, and doing work which the heart considered noble. Hilde had to give her credit, though. Mama did her best and didn't complain.

In Vienna, Hilde found life peaceful, if not perfect. The highlight of every week was Sunday. Especially Sundays in summer. Hilde took a streetcar to Seidengasse, near the Westbahnhoff, where the Church rented several large rooms on an upper floor to serve as their chapel. The main room held sixty folding chairs, with a raised platform for a podium and a piano. A kindly old Jewish woman had long since volunteered to accompany the group simply for the joy of having an instrument to play. Eventually, she and her musician son joined the Church, and provided beautiful music for the branch's Sabbath worship.

After prayers and songs, the members were given the sacrament of the Lord's supper from silver trays and tiny glass cups. Then regular members of the congregation gave brief sermons on selected topics from scripture. Sometimes the missionaries gave talks, or they had special speakers from other LDS congregations. On infrequent and wonderful occasions, a visitor would come from the Church headquarters in Salt Lake City, in the United States.

Hilde had arrived early and in great anticipation on this particular day, because the speaker was to be an actual Apostle of the Church. There were twelve, of course, just as there had been in Christ's time. But each had to minister to so large a part of the world, that a visit from one of them was a rare and cherished event.

Hilde sat in the second row and watched eagerly as a small, slender man with wavy white hair stood before them. His slight frame was belied by a firm, resonant voice which spoke German with only a slight accent.

"My very dear brothers and sisters," Apostle John A. Widtsoe began. He expressed admiration for their faithfulness and dedication. He exhorted them to pray for and practice Christian virtues. He told a few amusing stories of his experiences in other countries, which made the members laugh with love and appreciation. Then his demeanor changed, and he looked quite serious.

"I have a special message for you young people," he said. There were less than a dozen in the Vienna branch, mostly girls. They sat straighter. "It is not easy remaining faithful to the Lord when you have not only your own temptations and weaknesses with which to contend, but must practice your faith in opposition to those you love the best. It was so in the early Christian church, and it is just as true today."

Hilde felt he must be speaking specifically to her. She thought of her own mother, of many dear friends, of all those in whose presence she could only be half of herself because the other half, the part that mattered most to her heart, was an object of boredom or humor, or even mockery.

Apostle Widtsoe continued. "One of the most bitter and unflagging sorrows that can come into the life of a true lover of Christ is being married to a person who either does not care for their beliefs, or is antagonistic to them."

Hilde looked down at her clutched hands as thoughts of Ferdi flickered through her mind.

The speaker opened his Bible. "The Apostle Paul, in his second epistle to the Corinthians, 6:14 has said, 'Be ye not unequally yoked together with unbelievers; for what fellowship hath righteousness with unrighteousness? and what communication hath light with darkness? . . . Wherefore come out from among them, and be ye separate, saith the Lord.' Now please, young people, understand that I am not calling your friends unrighteous or dark. The world is full of wonderful people who simply have no interest in eternal things. But I am telling you, as one who counsels brokenhearted people every single day, that your lives will be immeasurably happier, more fruitful and more peaceful, if you will seek a mate whose soul and spirit answer to your own. I can tell you for a fact that being forced to choose between loving Christ and loving your husband or wife is the most wrenching choice you could ever be forced to make."

As he spoke, a strange feeling came over Hilde. It began as a small warmth deep within and grew gradually until she felt filled with light and certainty. She knew with all her heart that what he was saying was the truth. She knew how much she cared about the concepts he portrayed. But . . . But . . . She thought of Ferdi's smiling face again. She did love him! But, oh! She loved Christ more! She *knew* she loved Christ more.

When the meeting ended, the people would not go home. They gathered around the Apostle for the next hour, smiling or teary eyed, asking him questions, shaking his hand, sending messages to friends he knew in Salt Lake City as Hilde watched. She felt a little shy, but was determined to say something, anything, to this dear, warm man. Finally she stood before him, told him her name, put her hand in his. He looked intently into her eyes for a long moment.

"Dear Sister Hildegard," he finally spoke quietly. "I feel there is something I must say just to you." He paused, his eyes searching her face as if trying to remember something long forgotten. "You are a very special spirit, very beloved of the Lord. He has plans for you which will not be easy for you to fulfill. But if you are to begin, there is something you must first do."

"What is that?" she breathed.

"You must go to the United States. You must seek there a righteous and faithful companion. The Lord will place angels round about you to clear your path." They looked a long time into each others' eyes. Hilde nodded gravely. Apostle Widtsoe smiled and placed his other hand over the one he had continued to hold. "You will do well," he promised.

Hilde left the branch with an odd, light feeling of remembering. Oma, too, had once promised that God would place angels round about her.

A week later Hilde paced nervously along the bank of the Danube beside her house. It had been so easy to decide to change the course of her whole life while she was looking into the eyes of Apostle Widtsoe. She had begun to collect the papers and instructions that would eventually lead to her emigration. Sometimes she quailed, and then reminded herself that there was nothing to fear in simply finding out what would have to be done in order to go. She was barely eighteen. There was no great rush, was there?

But there was. There was an earnestness, a pressure within her that would not go away, even when she grew afraid of the magnitude of such a decision. And now Ferdi was coming over to see her as he had a hundred other times. Could she pretend that everything was the same? Yes, she could do that. She could do that for months. Everything would be just as it had always been. They would have fun, and talk, and go boating, and kiss each other slowly and lovingly.

Hilde stopped pacing, miserable. She could pretend to Ferdi, but it would be a lie. It would be a matter of dishonor, and honor was very important to her. And he would be here any moment.

After he came, they walked hand-in-hand for an hour, Ferdi talking about excited letters from his friends still in Berlin, about Chancellor Hitler, and of that dynamic leader's plans for the country, for their race, their world. It was certain now that Ferdi's father would let him join the army, rather than seeking a practice in law. He was almost graduated and would be a commissioned officer right away—how would Hilde like that? At last he noticed Hilde's lack of attentiveness and expression.

"What is it, little brown eyes?" he asked, using one of his pet names. "You've hardly been listening to me. Is something bothering you?"

They stopped, and Hilde leaned against a tree with Ferdi before her. He held her hand and stroked it as she collected herself. When she looked up at him, she could feel her eyes moistening at what she knew she must say.

Ferdi's brow darkened. "Something's wrong. Tell me. Have

your mother's creditors been hounding you again? I wish you would let me . . . "

"No Ferdi," she interrupted gently. "I . . . I have something to tell you, and it's going to be difficult. And it's going to make me sad." Her voice caught on a little sob.

"Darling girl," he said, enfolding her, "nothing is so difficult we can't solve it together."

She pushed him gently away. "Yes, Ferdi, there is something too difficult. Oh, Ferdi, I do love you!" she burst out. "Please, please, remember that I love you when I tell you what I must. I've *never* loved anyone else."

Ferdi looked entirely perplexed and a little alarmed.

Hilde twisted her hands together and took a shaking breath. She looked up at him with eyes of misery. "Dear Ferdi, I've tried and tried to tell you how I feel about spiritual things. About God. About Eternity. About sacrifice and obedience and all those kinds of things. And I know you are a very, very good man. But . . . " she bit her lips and looked away before turning back. "There's something in me that needs more. That cries for more, Ferdi. That wants to devote my whole life to loving the Lord."

"But, Hilde . . . " he began. She interrupted him by raising her fingers to his lips.

"Please, let me finish, or I'll fall apart before I do." She took a deep breath. "Ferdi, I've learned something I didn't know before. My faith means more to me than anything in this world. Even . . . even you. I've made a decision to change my life so my faith can flower the way I want it to. I . . . " she faltered, then spoke more firmly, "I'm going to emigrate to the United States. I'm going to go where there are people who feel as strongly as I do. I'm going to try to find a . . . someone who feels the same commitments I feel . . . for a . . . a partner. Because I can't spend my life trying to pretend I don't care very much about this, when I care with all my heart." She searched his shocked eyes, pleading with her own for understanding or forgiveness, she wasn't sure which.

Ferdi had been holding his breath, and it gusted out as he stepped back, bewildered, hurt. "Hilde, I don't understand what you're saying. You're . . . you're leaving Austria? You're leaving *me*? For religion?" He whirled away and rubbed the back of his neck, then turned back. "For *religion*?" He sounded dumbfounded, amazed.

"It isn't just religion, Ferdi," she pleaded. "It's my whole heart! It's what I care about with my whole heart!"

"I thought you loved me!" He sounded abused. "How could you care more about a . . . pastime . . . fairy tales? I thought we . . . I thought . . ." His voice became bitter. "I guess I was wrong." His lips were a tight line. His eyes glistened.

Hilde couldn't think of a thing to say that would make anything better for either of them. Ferdi ran strong fingers through his hair, a gesture she loved. He looked at her, his eyes begging her to recant. She looked down.

"I guess I'd better go, then," he whispered. She didn't watch him walk away. She couldn't see through her tears.

❖ ❖ ❖

Madison, Wisconsin, 1937

*A*rthur Hasslem, who had once been a missionary in Vienna, was surprised to see a letter from that city on the hall table when he came home from school one evening. Now a young professor at the University of Wisconsin in Madison, he had acquired a kindly wife, two young children, and a respectable reputation. He opened the letter and read, walking toward the kitchen with the pages.

"Mary," he called. "Here's a letter from Hilde Edler, the little girl I baptized in Vienna." Mary was stirring a pot on the stove. "Yes, I saw it. Isn't she the one who mistook your companion for her father? A sweet girl. Her Christmas letters are always so nice."

"That's the one. She must be about seventeen or eighteen, now. Interesting family. Apparently her mother wasn't able to become a doctor, and has gone to live in England, so she's alone now. I told Hilde long ago that if she ever wanted to come to America I would be her sponsor. Hmmm." He continued reading. "She says here that Apostle Widtsoe visited the branch in Vienna, and told her she should come to this country and meet some good LDS men." He chuckled. "Well, there are certainly more here than she'll ever find over there."

Mary turned off the burner and looked at her husband, head cocked. "So she'd like to come here to us, would she?"

"Looks like it. Of course, she asks very nicely if I still mean what I said. I'd really like to help her out, honey, if you wouldn't mind. After all, she would only have to live with us for a few months. We'd just watch over her, make sure she has all her papers in order, things like that. Get her into school, help her find a job somewhere."

Mary thought about it as she carried the food to the table. "I've always liked her from her letters. And she's a pretty little thing in that picture she sent. I suppose we could work it out. Art, please call the children before the food gets cold."

As they ate, Mary became enthusiastic. "You know, Art, there are all kinds of single boys in the Utah-Idaho club. Ed West . . . um . . . Richard Galbraith . . . and who's that graduate student of yours? The one who's so diligent he squeaks?"

"Who, Harris Newell? Please!" Art laughed. "Listen, don't start matchmaking just yet. It'll take months and months for her to get her passport and visa and tickets and all that stuff, especially considering how things are developing in Europe. Ten to one it won't pan out, anyway."

❖ ❖ ❖

In England, Rosa opened a letter from Hilde, and read.

Dear Mama,

Everything is fine here. The house is holding up, but the garden misses you. My job at the cafeteria is much more interesting since I graduated to cashier, because I get to talk to people, and use some skill other than just peeling and dicing vegetables. There are such odd and interesting people in the world, and a great many of them come through my line.

But actually, the reason I wrote today (I'm sure you noticed it has only been a few days since my last letter) is because I need to explain something special about myself. Mama, you are a strong woman who has always tried to do good in the world. You have helped so many people in all kinds of ways. I admire those qualities in you. But I must admit that sometimes your very strength frightens me. I'm not strong like you, but I am trying to be. And part of trying to be strong, I think, is being brave enough to be myself, even if people I love don't agree with me sometimes.

So, because I'm trying to be brave and trying to be true to my own convictions, I want to confess something I have been holding back for two years. I'm sure you remember the Mormon church, and that you let me join it when I was eleven. You liked the people, and attended with me sometimes. But then when I went back to Notre Dame, you told me I would have to quit going if I wanted to stay in school.

Anyway, after I graduated, I met one of the members again, and she invited me to come back. I did, and I loved it there. Oh, Mama, it felt so good and right to me. But I never told you I was going to the LDS church again. I hid it from you because I didn't know if you would make me stop. You know I have always had strong religious feelings, like Uncle Johann and Oma. Really and truly, though, I have never been quite sure how you felt about God. I remember you helping me say my prayers when I was a little girl. I remember the way you looked at Mass, sometimes, as if you saw something above the altar that you cared about very much. And how very, very often you had long discussions with all kinds of people about theology. It surprised me how much you knew. But I have never known what was in your heart.

Mama, I want you to know how I feel about this important thing in my life, and not hide it from you anymore. This religion and my feelings for it mean a great deal to me. I intend to stay very involved in it. That's my confession. In fact, I wish you would find the Mormons there in London—my branch president says there is a congregation someplace called Hammersmith—and visit them again. They are such good people, whether you want to be a member or not. I know you don't have much of a social life, and I know you like to be around interesting people. It's an idea, anyway.

I mail this with a little trepidation. Will you still love me?

Your daughter,
Hilde

Rosa wrote back to Hilde with the next post.

Dear Hilde, you silly little girl!

I don't know whether to hug you to calm your fears, or slap you for being an idiot. What have I done to make you believe I'm some kind of atheistic monster? Of course I believe in God! I always have, even when all my prayers for my marriage to succeed and for my husband to be faithful failed utterly. I know God doesn't always choose to answer prayers the way we want.

I suppose, to be fair, that my feelings about religion never were very obvious. It is my nature to keep my deepest feelings private so people cannot mock them. So, as these English say, "I keep my cards close to my chest." (The staff

*here likes to play card games in their free time, and once I
learn a game, I can usually beat them at it. If you ever
come to visit me, I'll teach you to play poker. But this is all
quite beside the point.)*

*If you like the Mormon church, who am I to object? I
never thought it mattered a bit which church a person went
to, as long as they believed something that made them want
to be a better person. The only thing I have no tolerance for
is religious hypocrites, and I've found examples of those in
every church I've ever encountered.*

*I can't write any more now, I've got to go oversee din-
ner preparations. We're having a crowd tonight.*

Of course I love you, silly goose!
Mama

❖ ❖ ❖

The excitement was terrific in Vienna in March, 1938. Austria and Germany had united! Hitler himself was to parade in
triumph through the streets of Vienna!

During the past months Hilde had heard people talk about
the tensions leading up to the Austrian national vote for unifi-
cation, but had been far too busy to be more than marginally
interested. She did know, of course, that the ban on Nazism
had been removed earlier in the year, and that only last month,
in February, Austria's Chancellor von Schuschnigg had installed
the leader of the Austrian Nazi party into his cabinet. There
were bitter rumors that Hitler had used coercion on the Austrian Chancellor, but Hilde had heard so many conflicting stories
she considered it futile to guess at the truth. Still, she couldn't
help but feel the growing ferment among the populace. Half
the people who came into the cafeteria were buzzing with it,
one way or another.

An election was held on Sunday, March 13th, to allow all
Austrians over age twenty-four to vote on whether they wished
to freely join with Germany. Strict Austrian patriots had warned
for years that it would be the ruin of Austria. Supporters of a

United Germany insisted it would bring back the pride and prosperity they had known in the glory days of the Empire.

There had been riots in the streets. Three times the Spannegels had invited Hilde to stay with them in their flat over the cafeteria to avoid the danger of traveling alone to her home. Finally the vote was taken and, surprising to Hilde, was strongly in favor of Austria uniting with Germany. There had been great celebrating by many in Vienna, but grumbling and despair in others.

Regardless, the anticipation of Hitler's parade today was palpably infectious. Hilde wished she dared take a few minutes to run the two blocks to the parade route and catch a glimpse of whatever was passing by.

As time for the parade grew closer, the cafeteria became deserted. Through the front windows she watched people rushing in the direction of the parade route. Her pulse increased with everyone else's. Impulsively she made a decision. The Spannegels weren't here, and neither were any customers.

"Magda," she begged the only other employee there, "would you be a darling and cover for me just for a few minutes? There isn't any need for me at all right now, and I only want to rush down to the corner and take a quick look. I'll come back right away."

"Oh, go on ahead!" the other girl shrugged. "Everyone's crazy today. You might as well join them. But only be gone a few minutes. Promise?"

"Absolutely!" Hilde cried as she darted into the back room for her coat and hat. She was out the front door in an instant.

As she ran down a side street toward the parade route, she heard cheering, underlined with the stamping of many feet. On the main street there were mobs of people in front of her, and she was too small to see a thing. Bodies were so densely packed there was no hope of her squeezing between.

Glancing around, she saw a fire escape ladder attached to the wall of a building. It wouldn't be at all proper, but she would be able to see over the crowd if she climbed it. Did she dare?

Why not? This could be an important historic occasion! The shouting and cheering grew suddenly louder.

Hilde darted between other gathering onlookers. Giving her best leap, she grasped the bottom rung of the fire ladder, and pulled it down. In a moment she had scrambled up.

Endless columns of soldiers marched down the center of the main avenue. Each man looked strong and serious. Each lifted his leg in stiff uniformity. They were as perfect as the chorus line in a variety show.

The noise of the crowd increased to a deafening pitch as a dark, open car approached. Before and after it great red banners waved and undulated in the breeze, the white circle and black swastika appearing and disappearing. Smaller versions of the same flag were waved wildly by many in the crowd. A man inside the car was standing, turning from side to side, lifting his arm to the people.

Could this actually be him? Hilde stretched and strained to get a better view. Closer, closer came the car. As it passed, Hilde's view was brief but clear. Smiling under his dark mustache, he was lifting his hand, nodding to the screaming crowds. He was gone in a few seconds, followed by more flags and marching soldiers.

"I'd better get back," she mumbled, climbing down the ladder. The people were laughing and milling about as if this were a holiday. She paused on the bottom rung, estimating her jump down to the sidewalk.

"Just a moment, Fräulein," called a cheerful young man. "I'll help you down! But you must hold this, first, and let me take a photo of you and my friend." He thrust a large red flag up into her hand, and told his grinning friend to stand close. In an instant he had snapped a picture, given the flag back to his friend, and lifted Hilde to the sidewalk. "A day to remember, eh!" he exclaimed, grinning. Then they were gone, leaving Hilde feeling disconcerted.

❖ ❖ ❖

For six months Hilde had been cashier at the cafeteria; she knew all the regular customers by sight, and some by name. Here was Herr Apfel, whose shiny bald head and ruddy complexion matched his name. He worked in finance, and always read the latest stock reports over his unvarying bratwurst and sauerkraut. He nodded and wished her good afternoon. And now the pretty, dark-haired girl about her own age who always had a too-serious expression on her face. But today the girl was smiling engagingly.

"You look happy today," remarked Hilde, ringing up her coffee and roll and bowl of knoedel.

"Yes, things are fine," she replied brightly. "Do you know," she added, "I see you every day, but I'm not sure of your name. Don't they call you Hilde?"

"That's me. Hilde Edler."

"Were you named Hildegard, or Hilde?" she asked, handing over her money.

"Hildegard, actually. I like it better, but everyone else seems to prefer Hilde." Hilde counted the change into her palm.

The girl looked interested. "Are you Viennese, or were you born somewhere in the countryside?"

"Oh, Vienna has always been my home," smiled Hilde. "What's your name?"

The girl looked surprised a moment. "M-Maria. Maria Schmidt." She smiled again, and walked to a table.

The old gentleman behind her also smiled as he glanced between them. "You two look enough alike to be sisters," he remarked. "Very pretty sisters."

Just then Frau Spannegel touched her shoulder. "Time for your own lunch, dear. I'll take over. Try the noodles with sour cream and meatballs. Excellent, if I say so myself."

Hilde ate from a tray in the back room with her boss, Herr Spannegel, who enthusiastically discussed the imminent opening of a new branch of the cafeteria.

"We've got all the seating delivered now, and are just about ready to begin hiring," he announced. "My wife and I will have to supervise the place ourselves for the first little while, of course, even though it's much smaller than this. But we have plans! Plans for *you*, Hilde!"

"For me?"

"Yes indeed, my dear. Frau Spannegel and I would be blind not to see you're the best, hardest-working employee we have. So," he raised his fork like a maestro about to begin conducting an orchestra, "we have decided to let *you* manage *this* cafeteria for a few months, while we get things established in the new one!" He emphasized each of the next words with a stab of his fork. "Complete with a pay raise! What do you think of that?" he grinned.

"I think that's wonderful! I think that's an answer to my prayers! I need . . . I really *need* to earn extra money right now."

He scowled. "Not to keep on paying for your mother's debts, I hope."

"No, no! Those are almost all paid off. Mother's actually been sending *me* money to pay on them for some time." She smiled with shy excitement. "I'm saving for something special. But I won't tell you what, yet."

Emigrating was more complicated than Hilde had thought. She had to show several forms of identification in order to get a passport, including her birth certificate and baptismal records. And after that, a visa from the American embassy, with letters from her sponsors, as well as proof that she had pre-paid for transportation.

Her morning and evening prayers became more urgent. *Help me Heavenly Father, please. I don't have any idea what I'm doing, and sometimes I'm so afraid. But I'm willing to do thy will, if you'll just keep me pointed in the right direction. Please, oh, please don't let me feel alone now. Stay with me!*

And often, in response, would come a peaceful feeling, and

the memory of Elder Widtsoe, saying "The Lord will place angels round about you to clear your path."

With her mother gone, Hilde had no idea where to find important documents. She looked through all her mother's boxes and trunks without success. Where would Mama have put such things? Hilde couldn't write to ask; she didn't want Mama to know she was leaving until everything was certain. Mama was always trying to rearrange her life. At least she had been able to tell Mama about the Church. That had been step one in leading up to why she had to go.

Maybe she could ask Grandmother Edler. She must have been at the christening. And of course, Hilde would have to tell *her* she was going to America, even if she hadn't yet confessed it to anyone else but Oma and Ferdi. A little hollow pain settled somewhere beneath her breastbone as she thought of Grandmother Edler's apartment above her sewing school. If only she could see Papa once more. In all the years since he had gone, she had never stopped missing him. Yes. She would go see Grandmother.

Charlotte Edler was regally gratified to see her granddaughter. "My dear! What a lovely surprise! And how you've blossomed, even in just the last half year."

Hilde kissed her powdered, scented cheek. Grandmother was still elegant and beautiful. She was to be married again, after years of widowhood, and it was no wonder. An attractive woman with a comfortable income and a respected reputation was always desirable, even in her mature years. Grandmother Edler ordered refreshments, and they enjoyed little cakes with their superficial chit-chat.

Finally Hilde emboldened herself for her task. "Grandmother, I'm always glad to see you, even if I don't get a chance to visit very often. But today I came because I need some special advice. You can probably tell me what to do."

Charlotte raised her eyebrows inquiringly.

Hilde went on, "I've decided to go abroad. That is, I'm

actually planning to emigrate. To America." She explained her plans, and finished, "and I can't find my birth certificate, and I don't know where I was christened or anything. Can you please help me?"

"You take my breath away," her grandmother replied. "But I cannot say I don't see wisdom in your desire to go to America, things being what they are here. Don't they call it 'The Land of Opportunity?'" She smiled slightly. "And *of course* I can tell you how to obtain identification if you can't find the originals. You simply go to the Bureau of Records for the county of your birth, which is in Vienna, in your case. There they keep copies of every citizen's birth certificate. I had to obtain duplicates for your father's schooling and military service. You need only go and ask for a copy, and they'll give you one for a little fee. And your christening, as I remember, was at St. Michael's. It was your parents' favorite church. Do you remember it from when you were little? Very beautiful. I was there at your christening, of course, with your Aunt Margit, even though we are Protestants. Did you know I made and embroidered your christening gown myself? I believe your mother pawned it. "

Hilde looked down at her hands for a few moments, then raised her eyes to the older woman. "Grandmother, there's something else, too. Could you . . . ? would it be all right . . . ? Oh dear. What I mean is that I want my father to know I'm leaving. I know he's been a forbidden subject all these years. I don't know why. You love him, and I do, too. Oh, I love him so very much, Grandmother." She felt her throat constrict. "I don't care what happened between him and Mama all those years ago. I . . . I just want to be able to say good-bye. And I don't even know where he is . . ." her voice choked, and she had to stop.

Her grandmother put out a well-shaped hand and touched Hilde's knee. Her smile was sympathetic. "Don't worry about that, my dear. I'll see what can be done."

It was two weeks before Hilde could go to the Bureau of Records during her lunch break. The day was cold and blustery, and Hilde clutched her hat to keep it from blowing away. She waited twenty minutes in a long line at the records counter. She gave the clerk her information. The woman wrote it down, then walked into another room. Hilde fidgeted impatiently. Finally the clerk returned, looked with a puzzled expression from one paper to another in her hands, and then shrugged. With flowing script she filled out a new birth certificate, copying from the original and affixing a stamp. "There you are," she said finally. "But it's rather unusual needing two new birth certificates in one month." In a hurry to get back to work, Hilde gave little attention to the odd statement.

Yet another week, and she was able to go to St. Michael's. An assistant to the priest looked through large record books until he found the entry for her christening, and copied out a certificate for her.

Hilde was surprised when she arrived at work a few days later. Frau Spannegel greeted her with raised eyebrows. "Your so-elegant grandmother called on the telephone this morning before you got here. She asked if you could come by her apartment tomorrow evening about eight o'clock. She did not say why."

Hilde's breath came faster. Could it be? She mustn't get her hopes up.

When she rang the bell outside the Edler apartment, she was as nervous as she had ever been in her life. A maid opened the door, smiled in greeting, and led her to the parlor. Hilde went in, holding her breath.

A tall slim man in uniform rose from the brocaded sofa. He had a crisp, narrow mustache, and the hair at his temples was touched with gray. His smile was gentle and questioning.

Hilde swallowed. "Papa?" she could only whisper.

He walked toward her. She could see that his eyes were moist. His voice was exactly the way she remembered when he said, "Can this very beautiful young woman be my own little Hilde?'

Without another thought, Hilde flung herself into her father's arms and burst into tears. He held her to him gently, crooning endearments.

"Papa, I missed you so much," she sobbed. "Oh, Papa!"

He led her to the couch, and held her close, saying nothing while her tears raged and then passed. He kept his arms around her.

"Darling girl," he said in a voice cracked by emotion. "I have been a desperate, stupid fool not to find you sooner. Seeing you now . . ." He released her and moved back, but kept one hand on her shoulder, "I realize what a terrible thing I've done to both of us. It's useless for me to give you excuses."

"Hush, Papa, hush. I don't want this spoiled by old grievances. I just want to be with you for a little while. Tell me what you're doing now. You're wearing a uniform."

"I've been all kinds of things in the last ten years, little Hilde. And I've been all kinds of places. Right now it looks like the military is the best place to be for steady pay and a possible future. Things are better in Austria, but they're far from wonderful. So, I'm a soldier again." He chuckled. "As usual, I'm a soldier in front of typewriters and adding machines. But I'm a captain in charge of a platoon of them this time,"

"I'm glad!" she hugged him "I prefer safe soldiers to endangered ones."

"Women!" he laughed, then continued conversationally. "My mother has kept me informed of the highlights of your life. Usually by mail. But she didn't tell me how pretty you are. Do you have dozens of beaus?"

"Not likely, working in a cafeteria. There have been a few boys I liked. Only one, really, that I cared about." Her face sobered.

"And you're leaving him behind, is that it?" he asked.

"Yes. It's a matter of principle. I have to do what my heart and my conscience require."

"You're like your mother in that. She knew what she wanted, and went after it with fire in her eyes."

They talked for hours, their hearts fitting together as if only a few months had passed, instead of years. When she finally had to leave, Hans reached for a package on the table beside him.

"I have a couple of things for you." He handed her the flat parcel, which she thought might be a book. "Oh!" she exclaimed as she pulled it from its wrappings. "This is perfect! What a wonderful photograph of you! You couldn't have given me anything dearer to take with me. How handsome you look in your officer's uniform!"

"I hope the frame isn't too heavy. You won't have much extra space in your luggage if you're taking all your worldly goods."

"This is most impressive! You ought to be a general, at least, in a frame this large and beautiful. I love it!"

He sobered. "There's something else, too, which may become very important to you, Hilde. Do you follow politics very much?"

"Only superficially, I'm afraid. I can't afford newspapers, and I don't have a wireless. But I read what people leave at the restaurant. And Ferd . . . I have friends who like to talk politics a lot."

"What do you know about Adolf Hitler and his plans for this United Germany?"

"I've heard a lot about *that!*" She smiled crookedly.

"He's a powerful man, Hilde. More powerful, I think, than anyone imagines. I've been around career military men all my life. This man is unique. He has an ability to sway people above and beyond anything I have seen in all my experience. Not many people have read his book, *Mein Kampf,* but I have. He speaks more conservatively in public right now than he does in his book. But Hilde, I believe he means to take over the world someday, if he can do it. I don't know if there will be anyone who can stand in his way."

"Are you a Nazi, then, Papa?"

"No, just a career officer who knows where the action is going to be, and wants to be on the right side when it happens. I believe any other position will be futile. Anyway," he said as he turned back to the table and picked up a small black booklet, "the time will come when you may need to prove your ancestry, that you have no Jewish blood." He handed the booklet to her. "This is an Ahnenpass, an official record book that gives your certified genealogy back for six generations. Proof of Aryan purity. I had to have one for my commission in the military, and I arranged for a copy for you. Hold onto it. It could be very valuable."

❖ ❖ ❖

A week later, in an envelope clutched under her arm, Hilde carried all her forms, photos, and identification to the passport office. A long line stretched out the office door and down the hall. She hadn't imagined so many people wanted to leave the country. Did they only want to travel, or, like her, were they seeking new lives far away? When she finally reached the counter, she handed her papers to the clerk. The woman checked them over, pulled out yet other forms, and began copying information. At a certain point she bent to take something from a card file on her desk. Suddenly she stopped and glanced up quickly at Hilde. She licked her lips and looked down again. Her eyes didn't quite meet Hilde's when she straightened and spoke.

"There's a slight irregularity here. I'm sure it's nothing, but it will take a few minutes to correct. Could you please step around the end of the counter and follow me?"

Hilde followed the woman through a bustling office and into a room containing a table and half a dozen chairs. "Please," Hilde said, "I'm on my lunch break, and must get back. Will this take long?

The woman averted her eyes and answered, "I . . . I really don't know. I'm sure we'll be as quick as possible. Please take a seat." She gestured to the chairs surrounding the table, and closed the door as she left.

Hilde pulled out a chair and sat. After a few minutes she tapped the table with her fingertips. She glanced around the plain room, and then at the clock on the wall. *What can they be doing? This is taking much too long.* She rearranged herself twice in her chair. The clerk had kept her papers and there was nothing to do but wonder what was irregular about them and feel nervous about what the other employees back at the cafeteria would do if their manager didn't get back when she was supposed to. She couldn't bear for the Spannegels to think her irresponsible; they had put such trust in her. After fifteen minutes she could no longer wait. She would come back another day if she had to.

She rose to go to the door, but before her fingers touched the handle, it was opened from the other side, and two black-coated men came in. They looked grim. Hilde stepped back a pace.

"Hildegard Edler?" asked the taller one with a Berliner accent. He was carrying her envelope of application materials.

"Yes."

"Sit down." His tones were peremptory, and Hilde felt taken aback. Trained to obedience, she returned to her seat. He sat across from her. The other man closed the door and stood before it.

The man eyed her narrowly, then spoke abruptly. "You are not Hildegard Edler. You are Miriam Feldman, an enemy of the state!"

"What?" said Hilde, startled at the accusation, and bewildered at the man's demeanor.

"We know who you are. You are the daughter of Ruven Feldman who was arrested for writing and speaking against the Nazi party and the Fuhrer."

Hilde sat stunned and gape-mouthed.

The man raised his voice. "You cannot deny it!"

"But . . . no! I . . . I *am* Hildegard. I . . . I . . . " Utterly confused and beginning to be frightened, Hilde shook her head and tried to find words. He spoke over her protests.

"We received a tip that you are trying to leave the country

with a false passport, with stolen identification belonging to the *real* Hildegard Edler! We *know* this! The file of Hildegard Edler was marked weeks ago and the clerks warned to watch for you. You have been discovered, Fräulein Feldman! You may come with us willingly, or we can forcibly assist you."

"Please," she begged, heart thumping fast, "what are you talking about? I don't understand you. Of course I'm Hildegard Edler, I have my . . . *you* have my documents right there."

"These are false documents! We have already checked with the Bureau of Records, and they report giving out two birth certificates in this name during the last month!"

Hilde shook her head, trying to capture a memory. "But who could . . . I remember the clerk said something about two birth certificates. What is going on?" She looked up, fighting down her fear, trying to think how her mother would act if someone said these things to her. She sat straighter. "Who are you? What right do you have to make these accusations?"

The man took a wallet from inside the breast of his coat, and flipped it open to reveal a badge. "Gestapo. You will come with us!" the man stood.

Hilde's mind worked wildly, trying to grasp the situation, trying to think of a way to make them believe her. This could not be happening! But she knew she must answer them, now! "No! I really *am* Hildegard Edler! I can prove it! I have a hundred friends who will vouch for me. My employer! She is the sister of my Catholic school teacher who has known me since I was in first grade. Uh . . . my neighbors . . . They will tell you who I am." Her face lighted with hope. "Yes! Yes, in this very building! Judge Rupert Graff! He has known me and my mother for years. His home is on the Danube, a little ways from ours. Ask *him*! He must be in the building now! Please, can we go and see him? Now?"

The tall man exchanged a long look with his partner by the door, then glared back at Hilde. The silence drew out. Beneath the table Hilde's clenched hands were ice.

"We will see who is the real Hildegard Edler, Fräulein. You will receive a summons to appear for a hearing within a few days. You will not leave town upon pain of severe penalty. You will bring your witnesses and any other documents of proof to the hearing." He tapped the envelope "We will keep this until that time." Piercing her with a last threatening glare he turned, and the two men stalked from the room.

Hilde tried to swallow, but her throat was dry and tight. Suddenly she began to shake uncontrollably. She felt an overwhelming urge to cry, but struggled to master it. "Oh, dear God," she murmured, half prayer, half fear. "Oh, help me." When the trembling abated, she stood on rubbery legs and left the office. Embarrassed and shamed, she was sure all the people in the office must be looking at her with suspicion.

Now she would *have* to tell the Spannegels about leaving Austria. They might be upset, but she knew she could count on them to be witnesses of her identity. And Judge Graff? Dared she ask him, an important man? How would he feel toward her after she had rejected Ferdi?

The Spannegels were surprised and shocked that she would want to leave Vienna, and begged her to change her mind. But when she told them about her passport and the Gestapo, they were deeply incensed. How dare those hooligans threaten the little girl who was practically a daughter to them! Of course they would accompany her to the hearing. "As if anyone could think *you* an enemy of the state! These Nazis are gaining too much power when they can accuse and terrorize a born Austrian on nothing more than some crazy hearsay!"

Hilde obtained a letter from Notre Dame testifying of her identity, but preferred not to announce her situation nor her intentions to her neighbors. With feelings of immense gratitude she clasped to her breast the Ahnenpass her father had given her. What better proof than a document from the government attesting her true ancestry?

The summons came two weeks later. She assumed they had

used the time to locate the other girl who pretended to be Hilde-gard Edler. Thank heavens the girl hadn't left the country already!

All her prayers the night before were for courage at the trial, and justice to be done.

The hearing was held in a large room with one table for the judge, and two others for the contending parties. Chairs were placed around the room's periphery. She and the Spannegels sat behind one table. No one else was there yet except a skinny policeman who was adjusting some kind of writing machine.

The opposite door opened, and a tall man from the Gesta-po escorted a young woman into the room. Hilde gasped and half rose when she saw the girl. "Maria . . . Maria Schmidt," she murmured.

"You know her, Hilde?" Frau Spannegel looked more close-ly. "Why, yes! I've seen her. At the cafeteria."

They were all ordered to stand for the judge. He entered, sat, and ordered the commencement of the hearing. The charg-es and counter charges were read from a file on the table in front of him.

Hilde was asked to testify first. Her Ahnenpass was power-ful proof, reinforced by letters she had from her mother, and the lease on their property. Those were bolstered by the Span-negels' testimony. When the other girl rose, fists clenched, there was obviously nothing she could say to defend her case, but she spoke up passionately.

"Yes, I am Miriam Feldman, and I did impersonate Hilde-gard Edler in order to get out of this country. And with good cause! There is no longer any measure of freedom here, and no safety even for loyal Austrians! Austria is just as much caught now in the Nazi trap of oppression and lies as Germany is! I am guilty of *nothing* but being the daughter of my father. And he was guilty of nothing but daring to speak the truth! But these Nazis are so afraid of people hearing the truth . . ." The Gestapo agent leaped to his feet, and she stepped out of his reach. ". . . that they must arrest and persecute even the innocent families of those who are courageous enough to speak out!"

"You will be silent," roared the agent of the Reich, grasping her arm.

"You will both be seated!" spoke the judge sternly. "This courtroom is neither a soap box, nor a possession of the Nazi party!" He looked pointedly over his wire-rimmed glasses at the Gestapo agent. "This is a hearing to determine correct identity. Miriam Feldman, you are found guilty of impersonation. Crimes against the state are not part of this hearing, and will be judged by some other tribunal." He turned to Hilde's group. "Fräulein Edler, you are free to leave. You will receive your passport as soon as it is correctly processed."

Thank you, dear Lord! Thank you!

❖ ❖ ❖

In England, Rosa read the newspapers. She also watched the newsreel films at the cinema. There she had seen snatches of speeches by Chancellor Hitler of Germany more and more frequently throughout 1937, and had heard even more about him through letters from home. But she wasn't sure she wanted her country swallowed up in a "greater" Germany. Yes, yes, Hitler promised all of them increased national pride and prosperity, but she had heard those speeches before from every politician who sought office. Still, she was here in England, and secure for once in her life. The distance between herself and her native land buffered her concerns.

But in March of 1938, the annexation of Austria to Germany had been approved. Hitler had moved into Austria, and the newsreels showed cheering crowds waving the new flag. Suddenly the Austrian army was absorbed into the German army. That meant her brother Richard and her countrymen now looked to Herr Hitler as their supreme commander.

Rosa felt distaste. Of *course* she knew Germanic people were superior. All one had to do was look around at scientific advances, inventions, discipline, cleanliness, music, and whatever

other standard one may choose. But that vulgar, shouting, ges-
ticulating man who called himself "Fuhrer "—even if he *had*
been born Austrian, he had no class at all.

But distaste became fury when she was informed, along with
the rest of the Austrians in Great Britain, that they were required to go and have their passports re-stamped with the label,
"German Citizen," and a large swastika.

"I am an Austrian!" exclaimed Rosa to several of her fellow
employees. "I neither want nor need to be changed into a German. And especially I don't need to be identified with a swastika.
I'm not a Nazi! Not all German and Austrian citizens are Nazis!
That's a political party, not a nationality. I'm not going!"

The butler was a German, and very proud of his nation's
escalating importance. He also prided himself on being the highest ranking person on the domestic staff at the home of General
Fuller, where they were all employed. "Mrs. Edler," he said coldly,
peering down his nose at her, "you may object all you like. But
let me remind you that if you do not have your passport changed,
you will be a woman without a country. Austria no longer exists
as a country. And when the British government reexamines your
papers at the beginning of the new year, you will be required to
leave England if you don't have a valid passport." He gave a
smug smile. "And, not having changed your passport, you will
have no country to return to."

Rosa glared at him and left the room.

She did, of course, have her passport restamped, although
on the last possible day. And she felt a shade more dislike toward Herr Hitler.

❖ ❖ ❖

Now that Hilde had her passport, she could apply at the
American Embassy in Vienna for a visa to the United States.
She was not alone in her quest. In recent weeks the Fuhrer had
made it easier for Germanic citizens to leave the country. Some
said he wanted to be rid of malcontents. Others believed he

wanted plenty of Germans living in countries which might not politically agree with him, sure that expatriates would encourage good relations between their new countries and the land of their birth. Whatever the reason, Hilde received a surprise the first time she approached the American Embassy during her afternoon break.

Three blocks from her destination, she began to see people hurrying forward. Around the corner a crowd was gathering. No, not a crowd; it was a line of people. A double line. And more stepping forward from every direction to swell the ranks.

"What is this?" she asked a woman who had just joined one of the lines.

"The queue for the American Embassy, of course," she replied.

"But the Embassy is blocks away."

"Right you are. Is that where you're headed? You'd better get in line, then. We may not make it to the door before it closes, even at this distance."

"Per . . . perhaps I had better come back on another day," Hilde stammered in dismay.

"Believe me," the woman said, "it doesn't get better. If you want to try another day, I suggest that you be here very early in the morning."

Hilde went away, discouraged. What could she do but try some other time?

The Spannegels were sympathetic to her needs, but explained that they couldn't spare their new manager for an entire day. Not now that people seemed able to afford to eat out more, and business was picking up. It must be true that the Fuhrer had increased prosperity.

On various afternoons during the next few weeks, Hilde again tried the embassy lines. But she was seldom able to move more than a block closer than when she had arrived. Even when she took half a day off, she never made it near the doors before closing.

"Please, Frau Spannegel," she begged. "The embassy isn't open on Saturday. Can't you somehow give me a whole week-day off? It's been a month, and I'm beginning to panic. I still have so much to do before I'm ready to go, and I *can't* go without a visa."

The older woman clucked and complained, but in the end consented to come in and take over herself while Hilde did what had to be done.

Joining the lines at daybreak, the girl's chagrin was enormous when she finally made it inside the embassy, only to learn that all she could do that day was collect the forms and instructions needed for application. She was told to bring everything back later to complete her processing.

Winter slush turned to the tender leaves of spring, and the chestnuts bloomed on the riverside. Hilde had collected and filled out and filed and received proofs and letters and receipts. But she had not yet taken the frightening final step of turning them all in at the American Embassy. She would have to prove sincere intent to emigrate by actually purchasing her travel accommodations. After many prayers for heavenly support, she gathered all her faith and all the money she had saved in the world, and bought a ticket to the United States on the German steamship, *Hansa*. She would sail to England in August, and then after a month of visiting and touring, go on to America.

It was July, and the lines at the embassy were longer than ever. Even another full day of waiting didn't get her into the door.

Trembling at the memory of the unforeseen trouble with the passport office, she prayed, "Please, please, find a way for me. You told me to go. Now make it possible. You know I believe, Lord, but 'help thou my unbelief.'"

She managed a morning off the following week, and traveled by streetcar to the center of Vienna at four o'clock in the morning. Appalled, she saw that crowds of people had actually slept on the sidewalks in front of the embassy through the previous night. The line seemed as long as ever. As the sun crawled toward

zenith, and the space between herself and the door grew shorter, Hilde became tense, wondering whether she could possibly
make it in. Closer, closer. Perhaps only twenty people were in
front of her when the uniformed young men at the doors began
to pull them closed. A groan went up from the crowd. Despair
washed over Hilde in a drowning wave, and she felt her eyes fill
with tears. *No, no, not again! It will take hours more, and I can't
stay all day. Frau Spannegel is growing angry with me, and besides,
I need to earn every bit of money I can before I leave.*

She knew she was going to break down right there in front of
the embassy. It was all so hopeless! Holding herself together with
rigid effort, and trying through her watering eyes to see a private place she could reach in a hurry, she stepped from the line.
A little gardened walk at the side of the Embassy seemed deserted. Head down, she hurried quickly until she was out of sight
of the crowds in front. Sinking down onto a wooden planter
box, and groping blindly in her purse for a handkerchief, she
burst into tears. With the tiny piece of fabric over her face, she
sobbed. *Whatever will I do? I've got to leave in a few weeks! Nothing is working! How am I going to get my visa? Oh, Lord, don't you
care what's happening to me? Can't you see?*

Her sobs increased, and she bowed under despair.

"Fräulein?" a timid hand touched her shoulder, and Hilde
jerked upright, embarrassed.

An old man stood beside her in blue shirt and trousers, carrying a full wastebasket. His face was distressed. "Fräulein, what
is the matter? Is there some way I can help you?"

Hilde tried to control herself, but her voice broke and her
tears continued to stream as she explained.

"No one can help me. I'll never make it now! I've been waiting in this line for weeks and weeks trying to get a visa, and I
never even make it to the door! And my boat is going to leave in
two weeks, and a whole year's savings will be wasted because I
won't be able to get on it, and I just don't know what to do-hoo-
hoo." She wept into her handkerchief again.

The man beside her stood quietly, absently rubbing his free hand up and down his pant leg.

"Now, Fräulein, stop crying. I think I have an idea. Yes, I think I know what we can do."

"You?" she looked up, not daring to hope.

He smiled. "Yes, I. Even an old man may sometimes rescue a young maiden in distress. Now, dry yourself off, and powder your nose, and come with me."

"I don't have any powder," she said inanely, mopping her face.

"My wife always has powder. But that's no matter. There, are you better?"

"I guess so. Who are you?"

"Oh, nobody. Just the janitor. Just the man who sweeps the floors and empties the wastebaskets." He nodded at the one in his hand. "One moment while I put this in the bin, then we'll go inside."

"Go inside?"

The old man lifted the lid of a large bin, and emptied the trash into it. Closing the lid he came to her side and took her elbow. "Yes. You see, I can go in the back door." He guided her to that portal, and held it open while she went before him. An American soldier stood guard, and looked surprised when the old man appeared with a young girl. Before he could say a word, the old man put a finger to his lips, and gave the soldier an exaggerated wink. The soldier grinned.

"Just come this way," the man spoke softly, putting down the wastebasket.

He led her through one passage and another until they were in the stately front hall Hilde had entered on her first visit. "Do you have all your papers with you?" he asked.

Bewildered, Hilde nodded, and showed him her folder. He smiled and patted her hand.

Then he reached for the front door and opened it.

"Now, Fräulein," he said loudly as he led her out onto the steps. "You cannot wait inside. You will have to wait out here with the others until the embassy staff has finished eating. But don't worry, you'll be the first one in when they're done. It will only be a few minutes more." In an instant he was gone and the door was closed.

Hilde's heart swelled within her, and she swallowed twice to keep from shedding more tears. *Thank you, Lord. Forgive my unbelief. Thank you for sending an angel to deliver me. Please, please bless him for his kindness.*

❖ ❖ ❖

Vienna and London,
August–September, 1937

*H*ilde waited apprehensively for her mother's reaction to her announcement that she was leaving Austria forever. One never knew how Mama would react. With mixed relief and dismay she read the letter that came only a week later.

Dearest Hilde,

What splendid news! I can hardly wait to see you! My head has been so busy with plans all night, I've barely slept.

First of all, I can see plenty of wisdom in your wanting to get out of Austria now. The English here are bursting with concern of all kinds about the United Germany, certain that the German people want war. The idiots! Why would we want another war? We were the ones who suffered the worst and the longest with the last one. I, at least, am reassured by what you say, that Hitler promises his intentions are only peaceful. But the British press is known for printing anything that will upset people and sell newspapers. Still, this is a nervous time to be in Europe, and I applaud your decision.

But you know, my dear, you really don't have to go to America. You could stay right here with me in England. In fact, the news of your leaving couldn't have come at a more perfect time. Although I like my job well enough, being housekeeper for General Fuller, I have always thought I would be happier working for myself, being independent, and not having someone else telling me what to do. And only a couple of weeks ago I passed a little dress shop that had a "for sale" sign in the window. The woman who owns it is also German. She says the shop has consistently done very well, selling a little ready-to-wear, as well as having a good clientele for made-to-order and alterations. Just the thing for both of us! Think how well we could do together, and how free we would be! I'm going to go talk to the woman today.

I'll also write to my mother and ask if she can loan us some money if my plans for the shop look as though they might work out. I wish we had more than a month before you leave. It's going to be a tight squeeze to arrange everything. You'll stop in St. Pölten on your way, of course, and I'll ask Oma to give you whatever money she can spare at that time.

I won't say anything to the General and Mrs. Fuller yet, until I'm sure what's going to happen. But I will ask a month's leave for the time you're going to be here. They owe me more than that, and they're going to be out of town the whole time, anyway. I can get a little flat for us to stay in so we can be right in the heart of London and come and go when we like. We'll have a glorious time!

I'm afraid I would *have* been worried about my house on the Danube, but the friends you say will rent it sound like a good, reliable little family. A couple with two children will not want to be up and moving away in times like these. And since you tell me she is an excellent housekeeper *and he is handy with repairs, I feel comfortable about what you have done. I could have hoped for higher rent, but must believe what you say about the going rate.*

Heavens! It just occurs to me, now that I re-read your letter, that if the German government has forbidden people to take money out of Austria, that a perfect solution to one problem is to have the renters pay their rent directly to my mother, and what they send her will pay off whatever she loans to me. Better and better! But how are you going to get her *money out of Austria* now? *Oh, dear! You had better think of some good, secure hiding place. They aren't actually searching people, are they? You must be very careful!*

I really have to post this now. I hope I've covered everything. There won't be time for more than one more exchange of letters before you leave. If anything else occurs to me (I'm sure it will!) I'll send another letter tomorrow.

Oh, it will be so good to see you again! We're going to have such a wonderful time!

Love,

Mama

Hilde folded the letter. *How exactly like Mama, to have arranged an entirely different life for me, in spite of all I've said.* She sat with the mail in her lap on the outside stairway, letting the late afternoon sun soak her. The only other letter of the day had been dropped through the slot with no postage and no return address; only her name on the outside. As she tore it open, her mind was still on her mother. *But I'm strong now,* she assured herself. *I won't let her bully me any more.*

She opened the single half sheet from the second envelope. Her eyes widened, and her heart began to thump.

I must come to see you this evening.
Please be there for me.
   Ferdi

After months of silence? What could he want to say to her now, after ignoring half a dozen notes from her, begging him to talk to her, for them to part as friends? Words of love or words of reproach would be equally painful. And it was already evening. He might be here any moment! She raced up the stairs to her room. With shaking hands she straightened her hair and wondered if she would look too brazen if she put on some of the new lip color she had bought for her trip. It was a light pink, perhaps she might dab on a *bit*. There. She stood back from the mirror. Yes, better, but not too obvious. She tucked in her blouse more neatly and smoothed her skirt.

She went back to sit on the stairs, trying to look relaxed. She had seldom been more nervous. And she waited.

She jumped when he finally spoke her name from behind.

"Oh, Ferdi! You startled me! I . . . I expected you to come from the road. You must have rowed over in your kayak." He looked so handsome with that sun-blond strand of hair falling down, constantly having to be pushed out of his eyes. He wore pants and a shirt instead of his uniform.

"Yes, I rowed." He seemed as nervous as she. There was a long pause.

They both spoke at once to break the silence:

"You wanted to talk to . . . "

"I had to see you before . . . "

They both laughed nervously and looked shyly at each other.

"Come with me," Ferdi said holding out his hand. "Let's sit in the boat on the water and pretend it's last summer, and that I haven't acted like a stupid lout."

She put out her hand timidly, and he helped her to her feet.

They had become expert at getting into the narrow craft without tipping themselves over. Both moved automatically from experience together. Both of them wielded their paddles, and they glided out onto the tributary stream, floating gently awhile until they reached a still place in the shade of a willow.

It was peaceful there. A sense of suspended time surrounded

the little backwater and they sat quietly, enjoying the sounds of evening.

"When are you leaving?" Ferdi asked.

"August 1st. I'll take the midnight train to St. Pölten to see Oma. Then on to Hamburg. We board my ship in Cuxhaven on the 3rd, and sail from there to Southampton." She laughed nervously. "I've never seen the sea before."

"Are you frightened, Hilde? This is such an enormous step."

"I'm scared to death."

He took her hands in his. She didn't resist.

"I'm such an idiot to have wasted the last half year acting like a spoiled brat who didn't get his way for once. That's what it was, you know. I'm so used to getting what I want, somehow or other. I should have known you had too much principle and pride to come running back to me. You tried for years to tell me how you felt, and I brushed you off like a fly." She had been looking at their hands as he spoke, and he tugged on them until she looked up into his eyes. "Hilde, I'm sorry."

She couldn't speak, just squeezed his hands by way of forgiveness. Finally she managed, "Are you in Vienna for long?"

"No, only a few days. Then I'm being transferred to Baden."

"Baden." She repeated.

"My mother has been furious at me ever since I stomped off and refused to answer your notes. She really likes you."

"I really like her, Ferdi. Your parents are wonderful people."

"She asked me if you had anyone to take you to the station when you leave."

"No, I was just going to take the streetcar. I only have two suitcases and a big bag."

"You're going to haul two suitcases across Vienna in the middle of the night, all alone?"

She nodded.

"No you aren't. Mother is going to come with the car, and personally deliver you to the station. She told me to tell you not to argue, because she insists."

Hilde felt her throat tightening. "She's such a dear thing."

"Then that's settled. Now tell me about where you're going in America, and let me be sure I have your address."

Hilde felt more animated as she described her plans, and laughingly told him of her mother's letter, remaking all those plans. He told her of his experiences in the army. They carefully avoided discussing religion or politics. Dusk was descending, and they paddled back to her house. He helped her to the bank.

"I'm so glad we talked, Hilde. I feel a lot better, now."

"So do I, Ferdi. Thank you for coming. I really needed that. And thank your mother with all my heart for taking me to the station. I'll feel a lot braver with her there."

"You know I would take you myself if I were here, don't you?"

She smiled and nodded.

"Just one more thing." He reached into the pocket of his shirt, where she had noticed an irregular bulge. He removed a square of blue silk folded into a thin package and fastened together with a pearl corsage pin. He gazed down on it a moment, then handed it to her. "Open it carefully, or they'll fall out."

Curious, she slipped the pin out and unfolded the silk. Nestled within were four small, white flowers, each shaped like a many pointed star. Their petals were thick and felted. One or two leaves clung to each stem.

"Edelweiss," she whispered, touching one with her finger. She looked up at him questioning.

"I picked them myself, in the mountains. For you. You know what they mean."

"That . . . that one would risk his life to reach these little flowers that only grow in the highest crevices of the rock. For . . . someone he loves."

"For someone he will *always* love," he corrected.

As he circled her with his arms, she held the flowers carefully. With all her heart she returned his long kiss.

"Maybe someday you'll come back," he whispered.

❖ ❖ ❖

Uncle Johann had written to say he would come to Vienna two days before Hilde was to leave, to personally tell her good-bye. Throughout the morning she had glanced eagerly through the window, hoping to see him striding down their little lane. Finally he was there, and she flew out the door and down the path to meet him. He wrapped his arms around her and held her for several minutes while she talked into his jacket.

"Uncle Johann, I'm so glad you came. I couldn't bear to think of leaving without seeing you, and I didn't have a minute to come to St. Polten. Thank you so much for coming to me."

He pressed her away to arm's length, keeping his hands on her shoulders and looking down smiling into her eyes.

"So, my little one. You're really going."

"Yes. At last. And I'm so excited and scared; I hardly know what I feel. I've been through the most awful things. But I really believe it's the Lord who has helped me make it through."

Johann turned her toward the house, and with one arm over her shoulder, walked back with her. "Yes, Mother has told me. She read me your letters." He shook his head. "I don't know what to think of the way the country is going. Perhaps you are wiser than we think to leave at this time." He opened the door for her, and they went inside. Hilde served him a piece of kuchen. Together they talked through the afternoon. As the shadows began to lengthen, he reluctantly rose to start back to the train station.

Again he held her for a long moment. "I'll miss you so much, Hilde. You are special to me in so many ways. Nobody will ever take your place in my heart."

"Nor yours in my heart," she replied. He took her hands in his and looked deep into her eyes. "I want you to know that I am very proud of you, Hilde. This has been a hard thing for so young a girl. It would be hard for anybody. I'm proud of what you are willing to do for what you believe in."

Hilde brought his hands to her lips and kissed them. "Thank you, Uncle Johann. I'm so glad that you, especially, are pleased with me. And I have something I want to give to you." She reached over to the lamp table beside the sofa and picked up a black book. "Uncle Johann, I want you to have this. I want you to read it. For me?" The last was a question.

"This is your Book of Mormon. I know it means a great deal to you. Are you sure you want to give it to me?"

"Yes, dear Uncle. Because *you* mean a great deal to me. Will you read it?"

He weighed it in his hand in silence for a moment, then opened the cover to read the inscription inside from Sister Negrini. After a few moments of thought he answered, "Perhaps I will. Perhaps I will."

❖ ❖ ❖

Aunt Steffie pouted, "Well, *Hilde*! Of all things! *I* would have taken you to the station! I'm such an imbecile, I didn't give it a thought! Why don't you let me do it, anyway," Aunt Steffie pouted.

"No, dear Aunt Steffie. It would seem that I was rejecting Frau Graff's kindness. And I suspect that Ferdi would never have come to say good-bye if she hadn't badgered him. She's a wonderful lady."

"Yes, then, I suppose she must be the one. Oh, you and your mother! All my best friends are running away from me! Why, do you know I tried to keep your mother from leaving Austria by offering her an excellent job? I was going to buy a farm, as she suggested, and let her manage it for me. Do you remember when she suggested that?" she chuckled, "The day that terrible bill collector came and she made me hide in the wardrobe. But she wouldn't even stay if I bought her a farm. Oh, dear . . ." She sighed sadly, and then brightened. "But finish up your dessert, because I have a little present for you to take with you."

"Oh, no! Not something else, Aunt Steffie! The luggage you gave me is wonderful, and more than I can ever thank you for."

"Ach, this is just a little thing. Now hurry up."

Hilde lifted the last bite of Sachertorte to her mouth, and groaned sumptuously. "Mmmmm. This was the most delicious meal I've ever had in my life. Thanks for the dinner, Aunt Steffie. I've never been in such a luxurious restaurant."

As tuxedo-clad waiters whisked away their dessert plates, Steffie placed a beautifully wrapped package on the table. "Open it now. And read what it says inside."

Hilde was careful not to tear the ornate paper. Within was an elegant bound leather book full of lined pages, all of them empty. Written in Steffie's scrawled hand on the inside cover was a message:

> *The pages are empty now, but you will fill them with an exciting new life. Don't let a single memory slip away.*
> *All my love to my "almost" daughter,*
> *Aunt Steffie*

"Oh, Aunt Steffie! A journal! I've always wanted to keep a journal, but I didn't have anything to write about before." Her eyes sparkled. "Oh, I'll write *everything* down!" She threw her arms around this dear woman who had, indeed, been like another mother to her for many years. There was so much she was leaving behind. How could she bear it! And the life ahead? She trembled with mixed emotions.

❖ ❖ ❖

1 August 1938
Vienna. Westbahnhoff:
The first entry in this new journal. The first page of my new life.
I'm sitting on the train in the station, nervous and waiting for it to leave. Although it is nearly midnight, all around is noise, people shouting, everyone running back and forth, crowding each other, anxious for a place by the window. Mrs. Graff accompanied me to my compartment,

and kissed me good-bye when she left. I was very happy that some people from the branch came to see me off, even though it was the middle of the night. Elder Watkins made me promise that I would visit him if I ever came to Utah.

The companions in my compartment are a nice lady with a twelve-year-old son, two foreign women from somewhere unknown, and a gentleman in his "best years," who is sitting next to me, and finally a girl from Germany, blond, blue eyes, strong, full of energy, very helpful. She is also going to England on the Hansa. *Oh my Vienna, when will I see you again? I cannot think about anything except Ferdi. What might have been? But one must make choices, sometimes very painful.*

Aunt Steffie gave me a large bag to carry over my shoulder at all times. In it are my important papers, my photograph of Papa, and the things I will need while I am on the train. And you, journal.

❖ ❖ ❖

It was after 1:00 in the morning when the train made a ten-minute stop in St. Pölten. Hilde rushed from the steps into the waiting arms of Oma.

"Oh, my darling, darling girl!" murmured the old woman into her granddaughter's hair. "How I will miss you! But you will write me often, won't you?"

"Oma, dearest! You are the most beloved person in the world to me! Of course, I will write every chance I get. I promise!"

"Now, now, we haven't time for tears. Here is the envelope with money for your mother. Tell her it was all I could get, and with all the restrictions, there is *no* way I can send more later. She will have to make do in other ways. How are you going to hide it?"

"I have a good place, I think. Look." She took from her shoulder bag the framed photograph of her father. "Here on the back I can remove the cardboard, and look here! It's such a deep frame there was plenty of space behind the photo once I took out the cardboard padding. Here's all my money, and I'll slip yours in with it. See, it fits just fine. And then I put the cardboard back on."

"That will work if they aren't too nosy," Oma worried. She paused and took Hilde's shoulders in her hands. "Now there's something I must say to you, dearest, and we haven't much time." Her wrinkled lips pursed, hesitating over words. "Your mother is a good woman. She works very hard, and really cares about doing what she believes is best for herself and others. She *does* care about others. But you know that oft-times she is so busy with the big picture that she doesn't pay attention to details. Without really meaning to, she can run right over people who stand between herself and the goal. You know?" Hilde's one-sided smile showed that she knew very well.

"She has all these big plans," Oma continued, "and I can see she intends for you to be part of them. What I'm telling you, Hilde, is 'stand your ground!' I know you've been raised to obey without question. But sometimes you must think things through carefully, and do what *you* think is best for yourself."

"Thank you, Oma. It will be easier because you understand."

The train whistle blew, calling passengers aboard. No time to talk longer.

"Now, liebchen, I have some strudel here, and a big bar of chocolate so you won't have to buy food on the train. Just tuck them into your bag. God go with you, my dearest! I'll pray for you every minute."

A hard hug, desperate with love, and a quick kiss, and Hilde was aboard again, waving through her window as the train pulled away.

She felt too high-strung to relax for the first hour. Then sleepiness hit hard. She had been up most of the previous night with last-minute details, and hadn't slept more than three hours. The two foreign women were still talking animatedly as they had done since they left Vienna. The young boy and his mother were sleeping against each other. In his corner, the middle-aged man snored softly while the German girl read. Finally the two talkative women, noticing their sleeping companions, rose and went into the hall. Hilde gratefully stretched out across their vacated seats and drifted into fitful slumber.

Used to early rising, Hilde woke before the others. The sky was barely graying into dawn. She looked at her watch. 6:00 A.M. Yawning and stretching, she felt stiff in odd places. The two women, who must have been up all night talking and wandering about the train, chose that moment to reenter the compartment, waking the others.

❖ ❖ ❖

2 August, 1938

At sunrise I went into the hallway of the train to look out the windows on the other side. There was a pilot standing there who told me that he was on his way to Baden. Why always the same thought? Why do I see a connection to Baden in everything? Is it still the reaction from saying good-bye?

Soon we came through my homeland's largest industrial area. Factories, workshops, labs, warehouses, chimneys and all the signs of our world-famous industrial complexes. I thought, "Here is proof of the worth of the German people. Here they prove their diligence. Who in this world hasn't heard of German machines, chemicals, and techniques?" I feel very proud of my people, even while I am leaving them.

Then we were in the area of Luenburger Heide. What a beautiful sight! Heath, all over the soft rambling hills. Such colors! From the fullest red to the palest purple. I have never seen that much heath in free nature, and I do so love heath flowers.

Our train was running late, and I knew we would never make the connection to Hamburg as planned. So we (the lady with the boy and I) left the train in Leipzig to do a little sightseeing. Without a doubt, Leipzig possessed the most beautiful and grand station in Europe! There was uninterrupted traffic, life, and noise. I can hardly describe it. Yet, everything proceeds with a certain air of elegance and nobility. The porters are immediately ready and nobody seems frantic. And the station! Super modern and elegant, full of light, everything made of glass, tracks beyond number, water fountains to drink from.

The luggage carts are motorized instead of having to be pushed as they are in Vienna. I had the urge to stand on one and drive it around! There are information offices, elevators, restaurants, travel bureaus, a post office, everything to make traveling very comfortable.

The three of us toured the city by bus. What a beautiful, memorable place. We agreed that we would never regret the hours we spent there. And tomorrow we will visit Hamburg, my last day on German soil. I am frightened. I am excited. I am worried. I don't know what I am. With all my heart I pray that the Lord will be with me.

✤ ✤ ✤

Hamburg was shrouded in rain, fog, and finally hail. This was not the way Hilde had wanted it to be when she said goodbye to her homeland, her people, her old life. The city was full of rushing vehicles, soldiers, and chaos. She took a bus tour of the city, but bad weather made visibility impossible, and she wished she had stayed at her hotel. A nebulous anxiety was floating within her like the fog outside.

She repacked her suitcases and bag again that night, wondering about her hiding place for the money. If they found it, they would confiscate the money, possibly arrest her. Perhaps she should try the suitcase lining? No, she had seen that in too many moving pictures. Not inside her shoe, either. Her shoe would probably fall off. Inside the wrapper of the chocolate bar? No, not enough space.

She picked up her father's photograph and smiled at it. "Well, Papa. I'll just have to trust you to guard my money for me." *And you, Heavenly Father. Please protect me. Are you bored with my constant begging? Please don't be. I need you so.*

❖ ❖ ❖

And here she was at last, at the seaport in Cuxhaven. The ship which would bear her to a new life was less than a hundred meters away. But between herself and the ship stood the inspectors and the Gestapo guards. Their presence hadn't seemed so great a threat last night as she repacked her things. But after watching them haul away the man who had hidden money in his socks, they looked terrifying. She knew she had licked off all her pink lipstick, and hoped she didn't look as pale and frightened as she felt.

How had she come to this point? Because she missed her Papa so, she had opened her door to the missionary who looked like him. The first step into a whole new life. Softly she whispered the promise made to her by Elder Widtsoe, "'The Lord will place angels round about you to clear your path.'" *Heavenly Father, if ever you have sent angels, send them now. Be with me. I need You. I love You.* She took a deep breath and stepped to the front of the line.

The inspector motioned to the table. "Put your bags here, please."

Hilde swallowed and tried to look unconcerned. Deliberately she slowed her breathing as the officer opened her first suitcase. He followed the same procedure as with all the other luggage: side and bottom lining, between the clothes.

What will I do if he finds the money? Will they take it away? Will they take me away? Dear Lord, please, please, make him blind!

She felt a guard pause just behind her. He was so close she could feel his body heat. His breath prickled the hairs on her neck as he leaned over her shoulder to watch the inspector's search. She wished she could push him away or look at him angrily to shame his for his rudeness. But she dared not draw his attention at all.

The second suitcase was similarly searched. Hilde blushed as the inspector patted her brassieres and underpants and was furious with embarrassment as the soldier behind her snickered at her discomfort.

"Your shoulder bag, Fräulein." He closed the second suitcase and pushed it away.

If he takes all of Oma's savings, Mama will be furious and blame me. Oh, please, Heavenly Father! And I would have nothing to pay for food and transportation in America, either!

The officer took each of her books and fanned the pages. He was like a machine that had done this a thousand, thousand times. He pressed the wrapper of the chocolate bar as though his fingers could see what lay within. He palpitated her extra sweater from top to bottom, laid it aside, and took out the Ahnenpass.

"Ah!" he murmured pleasantly as he flipped quickly through the pages. "Here is a *loyal* German citizen." He looked directly at her for the first time and nodded with a little smile of approval. Next came the picture of her papa, and his smile increased as he compared the features in the photo to the girl before him. "Your father?"

"Yes."

"An officer in our glorious Fuhrer's army! You are to be congratulated." He quickly replaced the contents of the bag, courteously put it back into her hands, and clicked his heels together smartly. "Heil Hitler," he raised his arm in salute.

Hilde smiled at him brightly as she lifted her suitcases. "Heil!" she returned, and walked toward the pier, her legs wobbling only slightly.

❖ ❖ ❖

August 3, 1938,
On the ship Hansa:
Thanks be to heaven that I got past the checkpoints without crisis! I thought I would faint on my way up the gangplank.

But when I set foot on the ship, and looked back, I felt suddenly desolate and frightened. Will I ever see my homeland again? I fought the tears when the ship left the harbor amidst sirens and other loud noises. How could I be so excited and so sad at the same time?

But my emotions changed completely when, a few hours later, I was leaning over the railing with an absolutely horrible feeling in my stomach! I fought like anything against becoming seasick, but it was hopeless! The ship was leaning and rolling all over the place.

To add to my humiliation, my roommate, who is the blond German girl from the train, remained quite unaffected and said our sea cruise was "magical." If that was magic, I was under an evil spell in the darkest dungeon, sure my last hours had come. I went to bed and was lucky to be able to sleep the whole afternoon and throughout the night. Late that evening, when my roommate came in to announce that the buffet supper had been magnificent, I silently hoped she would fall off the ship.

The next morning, August 4th, I woke up and felt quite well. I dressed and went outside to find a slight breeze, and the sun brightly shining. The storm which had caused the tossing last night had decreased and the ocean was deep green with white breakers tipping the waves. After watching this beautiful sight awhile, I went down to the writing room to pen a message to Oma, and write in this journal. Now I am going to go have a big breakfast because I am very hungry!

Evening:
After breakfast, when I went to explore the decks of the ship, I came upon a very quiet spot shielded from the wind where the motion is not so noticeable. There I sat all morning, and looked out across the ocean. A gong called me out of my dreams at about 1:00 P.M., and I went to have lunch. For the first time I could enjoy the never-ending menu of international cuisine. In the afternoon, we entered the English Channel from the North. Everything was calm, and I could clearly see the French and British coasts on either side.

*About 4:00 in the afternoon we reached Southamp-
ton. But large ocean liners cannot go directly into the harbor,
so our ship stayed far out in the deep water while passengers
and luggage were placed on smaller boats and taken to the
city. I felt a little frightened to be leaving familiar German
territory.*

*On land at last, we all lined up in front of a passport
check in a huge hall. It seemed very strange. Everyone there
spoke only English.*

*The London-bound passengers were taken by train to
Waterloo station. Mama was waiting, and we went directly to a little flat she has rented in a section called Woodgreen.
There are no woods, and it is not green. Mama asked me
right away about the money from Oma, and was very upset that there wasn't more.*

*Then we went to see the sights. I was astonished at the
very wide and comfortable underground train system with
the longest escalators I have ever seen! They are similar to
those in the Prater in Vienna, but everyone here is so serious and disciplined! Mother thought I was silly, but I just
had to ride up and down the long escalators several times.*

*As I waited for Mama to buy tickets to the underground
(which the British call the "tube"), I saw for the first time
Scottish military men. How funny it is to see members of
the stronger sex wearing skirts and long socks, with crossed
strings on the legs. They also wear caps with ribbons hanging down, and other strange things. I am told that, like so
much in England, all this is tradition!*

*The women run around in full "war paint" which I
found very bold and forward. But even more shocking, in
this country the men do not seem to mind taking out their
small infants in a baby carriage, even when their dear wives
are not present. No one seems to mind, but I don't know
what to think! Even shopping bags are carried by the men,
not the women!*

*The English love nothing more than what is easy. There
are no garbage cans in the streets or in London's many parks.*

(I was surprised at how very many parks they have right in the city!) So people throw garbage and papers on the ground wherever they might be. But then, what a strange contrast in standards I saw next! Every morning, each housewife sprays her front steps with water, and then paints them white with chalk. Mama says a woman would be shunned and looked down on by other women if she did not! And the doors here have round knobs to open them, instead of handles.

Mama says that everything one wants is delivered from the stores: meat, milk, eggs, vegetables. So the women don't need to go shopping every day. And things are very inexpensive, so they save a lot of money, which they then spend on makeup.

The Englishmen possess unbelievable discipline, particularly in traffic, and I heard it said that there are very few accidents in London because of the attention the pedestrians and drivers pay to each other. Small children run around in groups without adult supervision and no one seems to mind. I have to say that they must all have guardian angels since nothing happens to them, even in traffic!

The drinking water here tastes awful. Compared to our Vienna spring water, it's nothing! But it is available at every corner for free! There are fountains everywhere like the ones at European spas. One is curious what they do for the citizens in winter—perhaps free ice cream?

✢ ✢ ✢

After walking among wonders all day, Hilde was exhausted. Mama took her arm. "Just one more thing, Hilde, and then we can go home. I want to take you by the dress shop so you can see what a marvelous opportunity it is!

"Mama, do we have to see the shop tonight? Couldn't we go some other day? Or in the morning? It must be closed now, and I'm so tired."

"I've been waiting for closing time. I want to show it to you while no one is there so the owner won't see us gawking through the windows. If Mrs. Shenk knows we're interested, she might raise the price."

The shop wasn't far from the apartment in Woodgreen, and Hilde admitted it looked pleasant from the outside. The late sun shone through sparkling clean windows and revealed neat racks of ready-to-wear dresses, three-way mirrors, and doors opening into a couple of dressing rooms.

As they walked home, Rosa enumerated the benefits of their owning such a store. Hilde let her talk, knowing a confrontation must come soon, but not up to facing it just now.

"So you see," Rosa continued as they put down their shopping bags inside her flat and took off their hats, "there's everything to gain, and no great risk that I can see. But the problem is that even with my savings and my mother's loan, there simply is not enough money. We must think of a way!" She sank down into a chair, and looked out the window with furrowed brow.

Hilde took a deep breath, and reminded herself that she was not being a disobedient daughter to feel as she did. She was of an age to arrange her own life. She sat opposite her mother, on the edge of her chair, and leaned forward.

"Mama? Your plans are good plans. I can see that the dress shop might be a wonderful idea. It looks good. It really does. But Mama, I hope you won't be angry at me . . . working in a shop, staying in England . . . that isn't what I want to do with my life. I told you why I was going to America, and I haven't changed my mind. I have everything arranged. My tickets are bought. I have a job and a home and friends waiting for me. I love you, Mama, but I'm not going to stay in London. I'm going on to America at the end of August, as I planned."

Rosa looked surprised, then hurt, then determined. "But Hilde, you don't *have* to go to America. Or, at least, you don't have to go *now*. This shop . . . Besides, I *want* you to stay here with me. You're my daughter. We have to help each other. The problem is that you just can't see what a wonderful opportunity it will be for both of us. With my skills and both of us working hard, there's no telling how far we could go! Expansion! Perhaps another shop or two in time! Really, you must understand that I have more experience in the world than you. You must trust your mother, dear."

Hilde's hands were clenched in her lap. "Mama, listen to me, please. I *do* trust you. I have all kinds of faith in you. I know you can make your shop work perfectly well without me. But I am not staying in England. I am going to America, Mama."

Rosa huffed as though she were talking with a dense child. "Hilde, I'm proud of you for your adventurous spirit, and your determination. You are quite grown up, and quite a bit more strong willed than you used to be." Her eyes glinted. "But please don't make up your mind just yet. Think about it. There is no hurry about going to America."

Hilde sighed and leaned back, looking at her mother. *She doesn't hear me. She still doesn't hear me. She will refuse to believe I have any mind or plans of my own that don't depend upon her, until she sees me leaving on the ship. It's useless to discuss. I'd best just keep my mouth shut and do what I must do.*

When her daughter didn't reply, Rosa smiled. Hilde knew her mother was sure she had won her point as she always had.

Rosa jumped up brightly. "Well, then! Let's make supper. I'm starved from all that walking."

Sunday:
I was completely surprised and pleased when Mama announced this morning that she was taking me to the LDS church. I had no idea she even knew where it was. Apparently she has gone several times, and even made some friends.

The spirit in the service calmed my heart about our disagreement the other day, that it was right for me to refuse to stay with Mama and her dress shop. I felt inspired yet again to go to America as planned, come what may.

Afterwards, a family named Wilmuth invited us to dinner, and were very kind in every way. They are good people, and Sister Wilmuth is quite cultured. I can see that Mama considers them pretty much her equals. I'm very glad she has some friends here. It is a terrible thing to be without people one can count on. Although I have kind acquaintances in America, they really aren't friends yet, the kind with whom I can be anything at all, and they will stand by me. If I didn't have my Heavenly Friend always with me, I would be very much afraid.

Interesting here in London is also the world famous wax museum of Madam Toussoud. Every great personality of world history is carved in wax and looks perfectly alive. After our visit there, we went to a lovely park in the city where everyone is allowed to walk and lie down on the grass. One may rent a lawn chair for a penny for the whole day. People place their chairs in the sunshine and take off almost all their clothes to bask in the sun. Quite shocking! Any liberty is permitted in such a park—exercising, and all kinds of sports. (On windy days, flying kites.) Mother says there is one park that has a whole zoo with deer, kangaroos, rabbits, guinea pigs, rare birds, canaries, and many others.

My mother and I seem much more like friends here than we ever did at home. It must be that I am a woman now, and we see each other with different eyes. But ever so often she puts me back in the place of a child, and acts as if I can't even decide what flavor of ice cream to choose.

❖ ❖ ❖

Rosa left Hilde at home writing postcards and letters, and went shopping by herself. She paid little attention to the scene around her as her thoughts skipped from her daughter to her situation and back. *That girl has become so stubborn! It's as if she hasn't heard a thing I've said. This dress shop would be a godsend for both of us,—isn't that obvious? Oh, blast! If Mama had just been able to send more money! I have no collateral for a loan. The only possibility I can think of now is to borrow Hilde's ticket and pawn it for a little while. But the way she has become, she would be sure to throw an enormous tantrum, even if it would only cause a temporary delay in her plans! I don't know what has come over her, being left alone without my direction so long. She seems to have no respect or discipline anymore. But it wouldn't be as if I were* taking away *her chances to go to America.*

Rosa stopped to wait for a light to change, then continued across the street. *If she would stay with me only a few months we would earn more than enough to get the ticket back, and then if it's all that important, she could make new reservations and be on her way. It's simply stubborn and selfish of her not to be willing to sacrifice a few weeks of her own life to help insure the future and comfort of her own mother. Besides, I am absolutely positive that once she spent a little time here, and saw our fortunes rise, that she would see that England is every bit as good as America.*

A stop at the butcher's for pork chops (which were very cheap just now), suspended Rosa's train of thought for only a few minutes. As she walked out the door, her mind returned to the question, darting between every conceivable course of action. *In the last analysis, perhaps the only thing I can do is present her with a* fait accompli, *and put up with her storms until she comes to her senses. It would only be temporary.*

A needle of guilt pricked her as she envisioned herself secretly taking the ticket to a pawn shop. She crushed the pang resolutely. One had to do what was necessary, even if it were unpleasant. Heaven knew she had been required to do many things she would rather not have done in order to survive.

But of course I won't do it unless I absolutely cannot think of any other way, she promised herself. Suddenly she brightened. *Well, of course! The first alternative is to see if the owner, Mrs. Shenk, will take what I already have as down payment, and let me pay her the rest in installments.* Rosa felt the tightness within herself relaxing. *What a fool I am! Why didn't I think to ask about that before?* She turned her footsteps in the direction of the dress shop.

The door tinkled as Rosa stepped inside. Mrs. Schenk was

helping a customer, but nodded and smiled at Rosa. Patiently, nervously, Rosa glanced through a rack of dresses. Soon the patron left, and Mrs. Schenk greeted Rosa warmly.

"I'm so glad you've come back to see the shop again, Mrs. Edler." Mrs. Schenk was an attractive, plump woman with mousy reddish hair. "I've a strong feeling you're just the woman to make a success of my little enterprise. I have some very interesting reports to show you that I think will help you make a decision."

She led Rosa into the rear office. "I'm a very methodical person, as I gather you are, Mrs. Edler. I keep good records. And here are last year's reports of the profits from the shop. See here, in these columns? And here. You can see the earnings from month to month. If you're as good a designer and seamstress as your experience looks to be, there isn't any reason why you shouldn't make as much, or maybe more than I have. If my husband wasn't so sick that I'm going to have to take care of him full time, I couldn't possibly give up such a good business."

Rosa could see the impressive figures well enough, and her determination strengthened that this shop was her best plan for a successful future.

"Mrs. Schenk, I am very impressed with all you show me. And I have been investigating avenues to buy your shop. But the fact that you need to sell so quickly hasn't given me as many options for raising the money as I'd like. I have well over half the price you've asked already. But I cannot see how I can come up with the rest right away. Here's my own proposition: if you'll let me pay what I can now, I believe I can pay the rest in installments within the next six months.

Mrs. Schenk's brow furrowed. She pursed her lips and looked worried. Slowly she shook her head. "Mrs. Edler, from the first moment I met you I thought how perfect it would be to sell my shop to a countrywoman. And I am frankly impressed with you. But I'm afraid your idea is impossible. I *must* sell within the next two weeks and then clear out my personal things as quickly as possible. I'll be honest with you. Even though I'd prefer to sell to you, I've been approached by another buyer." She looked keenly into Rosa's eyes. "I really have no choice but to sell it to the first person who has the purchase price."

Rosa returned her look with tight-pressed lips.

"But," continued the owner, "if it is a matter of financial difficulty, I might possibly offer you a counter proposal. Processing checks and loans and things costs money and takes time I don't have to give. If you would be willing to give me payment in cash, I would be willing to knock a hundred pounds off the price."

A hundred pounds! Rosa calculated quickly. *If I had the price of Hilde's ticket, the cost of the shop would be within reach and we'd still have a bit left over for unexpected expenses.*

Mrs. Schenk continued. "But if I am going to give you such a break, I really want to have the whole business taken care of within a week. Otherwise . . ." she shrugged and left it dangling.

Rosa knew she mustn't let this chance slip away. Boldly she replied. "Very well. If you will have the legal papers ready to sign next Friday, I will bring the purchase price in cash."

Mrs. Schenk smiled warmly. "Oh, wonderful! I'm so glad! I'll have all the papers and everything ready and waiting. We can take care of the signing right here. You can bring witnesses, or I can furnish them, if you like. We'll want all of this to be perfectly legal."

For an instant Rosa considered asking Hilde to witness, but banished the thought just as quickly. "Your witnesses will be fine."

Two days later, the Wilmuths took Hilde to the Royal Museum while Rosa pleaded a headache and stayed behind.

Rosa found Hilde's steamship ticket easily in her envelope of important papers. It required less than two hours for her to get the best deal from one of several pawn shops she had seen. It was a good deal. There was enough for the shop, and extra to spare. Success was in sight! Then why did she tremble so much inside? Feeling oddly afraid of her daughter for the first time in her life, Rosa thought it best not to mention what she had done until the shop was in her hands.

❖ ❖ ❖

London, August 1938

It was a week later while Rosa was fixing an early supper that she began to hear the bureau drawers being opened and closed repeatedly and with increasing loudness. "Hilde, what are you doing?" she asked.

Her daughter's voice was tense. "Mama, I can't find my steamship ticket. I know it's here somewhere. I put it in the top drawer with my important papers, I'm sure, but I can't find it."

"Why do you need your ticket right now?"

"I was just checking the departure time on the itinerary letter, and I'm positive I clipped the two of them together." Hilde paused in the doorway with a paper in her hand and a worried look on her face. "I found the itinerary but it wasn't with the ticket." Her voice was edged with panic, and she went back to the bureau to slide the drawers in and out again.

"Calm down, Hilde. The food is ready. Let's eat first, and then we can take care of the problem." Rosa's stomach felt distinctly unsettled.

"I can't, Mama. Just give me a few minutes. I know it's here someplace." She went through a stack of papers and looked in envelopes, examining each carefully.

"Well I'm going to eat now." Rosa set out dishes, glasses, and silverware, served herself, and sat down with her napkin while Hilde turned to look in the pockets of the clothes in the wardrobe, and then in the suitcase compartments.

"Oh, Mama! What am I going to do? I saw it Sunday before last when I got out my address book. But I've searched every-where twice. Do you think," she looked up, alarmed, "that someone could have gotten into the apartment and stolen it? Should I talk to the landlady? Maybe she's seen someone in the building. I'll just run down right now and . . ."

"Hilde, stop!" Rosa's firm voice drew her daughter's eyes. "You don't need to do that. Your ticket isn't lost." She took a deliberate bite of the suddenly tasteless food.

Hilde looked at her blankly. "What?"

Rosa lifted her chin and looked levelly at her daughter. "I said your ticket isn't lost. I know exactly where it is."

"Wh . . . why didn't you tell me? You can see I've been worried sick! Where is it?"

Rosa chewed and swallowed. "It is, for the moment, at a shop on Fleet Street." She took another bite.

It took Hilde a few moments for the information to regis-ter. Her eyes grew wide in horror. "Oh, no! Oh, Mama! You didn't pawn it! Tell me you didn't pawn my ticket! No!"

"Hilde, for goodness sake, get hold of yourself! I *borrowed* your ticket for a little while, that's all. You'll get it back very soon, and with interest, I assure you."

"But why? Mama, how could you? I'm supposed to leave in only six days!" The girl was trembling with emotion, her voice near tears.

"Hilde, this isn't some major tragedy. I learned that I could get the dress shop for a hundred pounds less if I would pay for it this week, and the only way I could do that was to borrow your ticket. The papers for the shop are already signed. It is legally ours. We will take ownership in two weeks. Now stop worrying so much. Sit down and eat your dinner. What differ-ence will a couple of months make?"

Hilde stood stock still for a long moment. Then she an-swered in a hard voice Rosa had never heard before. "The difference it will make is a matter of horrible rudeness and inconvenience to several people who have broken their backs to get me to the United States on a particular day! The difference is that you *took* that ticket without so much as asking me, and I have worked for *two years* to save my own money to buy it, as well as giving a great deal of my own money to pay off your debts!"

"How dare you speak to me in that way!" Rosa leaped to her feet.

"The difference is that taking things without asking people is dishonest! The difference is that I am no longer a child you can bully into doing what you want!"

"Hilde! I am your mother, and you will respect me!" Rosa shouted over her daughter's litany.

Hilde stopped, and met her mother's eye with a glance so steely Rosa took a step backwards. The younger woman spoke softly. "Mother, if you do not go to that shop tomorrow and get back the money for my ticket, I will go there myself."

Rosa was aghast. "Don't you dare! How could you humiliate me so? Even if I wanted to, I doubt it would be legally possible now the papers are signed."

"You go, Mother, or I go."

"Hilde, you must be mad! You've never behaved so badly in your life!"

"You go, Mother, or I go" she repeated. "And if it is necessary, I will tell them why I have come."

Rosa felt thoroughly backed into a corner. It was a most unusual and unsettling feeling. She was furious at the girl, but guilty and afraid, too. She lifted her chin and threw down her napkin. "I do *not* have to tolerate such verbal abuse from my own daughter!" Turning, Rosa stalked out the door without even her hat or handbag, and slammed it behind her.

Down the stairs and out the door she marched. She strode down one street and up another without stopping or seeing, until she grew tired. With every step she struggled to push down the nagging voice of conscience. "It was for the best," she kept insisting aloud. "I am her mother, and I know what is best for her!"

Unbidden pictures entered her mind of her daughter remaining in Austria and paying off more than three quarters the debts Rosa had accrued for years. "I have supported her all her life," Rosa exclaimed to no one in particular. "She owed me those debts!" But she knew in her heart it was a lie. The majority of the debts were a result of her infernal obsession with social climbing, not for feeding or clothing her daughter. She blocked the thought as quickly as she could, searching for memories that would fuel enough resentment to hold self-condemnation at bay.

Against her will, quick calculations came of the deprivations Hilde must have endured to save enough for the expensive ticket. "I'm her mother! I gave her her very life! How can she ever repay me for that?" Then Rosa remembered the dismay, resentment, and shame she had felt at the accident of her pregnancy with Hilde. That memory was followed immediately by the subversive challenge, "And how did *you* repay your *own* mother for *your* life?" Rosa gritted her teeth in frustration that her analytical mind always, automatically, presented her with both sides of every issue.

A knot grew in Rosa's stomach, and a painful lump in her throat. Wilful self-deception was becoming increasingly difficult to maintain. "Well, I can't do anything about it now! Even if I wanted to!" she said out loud. A man passing her on the darkening street glanced at her, startled.

She entered a little park at the center of a crescent of three-story houses, and sank onto a bench. Her defenses were dropping as her weariness mounted. For the first time she looked with undisguised clarity at what she had done. She had stolen from her daughter to fulfil her own intense desires. Her promise to buy back the ticket once they got established did not change that fact.

But how desperately she had wanted the shop! *Needed* it! How she dreaded going back to work as someone else's servant! She'd *had* to take the ticket, hadn't she? There was really no other way to get the shop. She supposed Hilde had *tried* to tell her she had no interest in staying in England. But staying hadn't been a *bad* idea, had it? No, the idea was perfectly sound. The shop actually *could* make them financially independent. Except . . . except that Hilde had said from the beginning that she didn't want anything to do with it.

Street lamps came on as night descended. Traffic on the streets around her dwindled to an occasional cab or bicyclist until they were as empty as Rosa's heart. Over and over she saw herself opening the drawer. Taking the ticket. She remembered her perfect knowledge at that moment that what she was doing was completely wrong. And she remembered the rapidity with which she buried the feeling as deep as she could. Rosa sunk her head into her hands.

"I'm a thief," she whispered. "No matter how I wrap it up, I have become a simple crook." Her throat ached terribly, and her eyes burned. "What have I done? Have I come to such a point that I can convince myself wrong is right?"

She did not want to think these thoughts! The pain of self-realization would not allow her to sit. She had to walk! Walk away from the searing inside. Walk as quickly and as far as she could.

Rosa hurried from one street to another for hours until her feet hurt. She heard a bell toll somewhere. Was it once or twice? The heaviness in her heart only increased until she felt more wretched and abandoned than she ever remembered feeling in her life. Her rushed steps became a blind plodding. As she slowed, she began to feel the chill of the night, and wrapped her arms around herself. *I should go home,* she thought. But she kept walking.

Even when Hans left me, it wasn't this bad. It was he who did wrong then. I had my own self-respect, at least. But who can I blame when I've abandoned honor? Where can I run when I suddenly realize I loathe what I have become? I cannot stand myself! I cannot stand this pain! She felt something on her cheek and reached up. It was wet. She looked at her fingertips glistening beneath a streetlight, and the shame she thought could grow no worse deepened. *I've never cried! Never! Weeping is for weaklings! Tears are for those who have no pride!*

Half a block away she saw a large man leaning against a doorway, the dim light barely showing his shabby clothes and stubbled face. A tiny glow came from the tip of a cigarette drooping from his mouth. Her pace never checked as she walked toward him. *He looks dangerous*, she thought dully. *I should go another way.* But she felt nothing, and kept walking.

The man pushed himself away from the door as she came nearer, and cast his cigarette to the sidewalk. She stopped two paces from him, her eyes burning directly and defiantly into his. She spoke in hard quiet tones. "What can you do to me that I would care about?" At that moment the thought of death promised relief. She smiled bitterly into his face. He uttered a curse and stepped through the doorway behind him.

Rosa laughed shortly with an unexpected burst of humor. "Even the thugs don't want me. I'd better go home."

And what will I possibly say when I get there? And what will I do? "Oh God!" half groan, half prayer, "What can I do? Is there any hope for me? Any? I don't want to be this way anymore! Oh, God! Please! Are you there? Are you *anywhere?*" She heard no reply, but there was an infinitesimal lifting of the pain.

❖ ❖ ❖

Hilde had spent the evening wrestling with her own bitter anger and resentment. How could her mother *do* this to her? All her life she had been obedient and dutiful. And all her life it had been her *mother's* desires, needs, and obsessions that had come first. She remembered how the scholarship to the University had been snatched away so her mother could go back to medical school. A laughably abortive plan! She thought of the years of debts and hiding from bill collectors. For what? So her mother could throw away their earnings, basking in the decaying glow of the erstwhile elegant, the tattered talented, the impoverished intellectual. And now she had stormed out, furious for having at last been brought up short by the daughter she was used to running over.

Well, let her fume! Tomorrow one of them *would* go to the shop and demand their money back.

But if she forces me to do it, thought Hilde, *it will be the end of our relationship.*

Evening darkened into night, and Hilde's innate honesty began to soften the edges of her indignation. She had to acknowledge that Mama had indeed given up several years of full-time attendance at medical school to pay for part of her tuition at Notre Dame. Mama had worked at three or sometimes four poorly paying jobs every day to keep food on the table after Papa left. Mama had taught her to cook and sew with inventiveness, and exemplified what courage could be in the face of defeats which would have destroyed lesser women.

But Mama had no right to take my ticket! Hilde's thoughts chased each other around her brain from resentment to rationalization, and back again. She tried to pray for the Lord's help in getting back her money, but felt her prayers fall lifeless from her lips, a certain sign that she was out of tune with the Spirit. Part of her knew she must forgive.

But not until that ticket is back in my hand!

When bells from the nearby church struck midnight, Hilde began to worry. *Mama should be back by now. Surely she can't be so angry or humiliated that she would stay out this late. How typically inconsiderate!* Hilde got ready for bed, and waited by the window, looking down on the street for the familiar figure.

The bells tolled one. *What if...? What if something bad has happened to her? London is so big and strange, and this is not the best part of town.* Apprehension began to twist in Hilde's stomach, and grew over the next hour into full-blown fear.

What will I do if she doesn't come home? How can I find out whether she's in trouble. I know so little English; how could I get to the police or the hospitals when I don't even know where the police or the hospitals are, and can scarcely ask? Oh, Mama, please come home! Oh, Lord, please make sure she's all right. Where can she be? Why is she letting me worry this way? She must know I'd be scared sick by this time. Maybe this is her way of punishing me.

The final reflection turned her fear again into anger. She got under the covers and tried to sleep. Turning from side to side, she punched the pillow and tried to empty her mind. But visions of her mother lying injured or dead insisted on replaying themselves in her brain until she was again at the window, agonized.

By the time the palest of pre-dawn light began to dilute the blackness, Hilde lay in bed, exhausted and wretched. *If Mama will only come home, I'll try to forgive her. We can work something out.*

Over and over Hilde murmured, "Please, Lord, oh, please bring her home safe."

When at last she heard the turning of the knob, relief flooded her with such intensity she almost wept. She sat up in bed, straining to see through the dimness.

"Mama! Is that you? Are you all right?"

"I'm safe. You shouldn't have worried." The older woman came to Hilde's bed and sat beside her. Hilde sensed a difference in her, but couldn't identify it. A softness of voice? A strangeness in the tone? Something in the way she held her body?

Rosa's hand reached out toward her, hesitated, and drew back. "Hilde. . . " The strange tone again. "I . . . I have been thinking a great deal. And walking. I. . . . "

Hilde sensed that she wanted urgently to say something, but couldn't force the words. She watched her mother wring her hands, listened as she stumbled with short breaths for sentences she couldn't utter. Rosa's head turned toward the window for a moment, and Hilde was astonished to see the reflection of a dried iridescent line running down her cheek.

Her mother reached out again, and again withdrew her hand

without touching before she said softly, "I'll go to the shop to-morrow and get your money back."

❖ ❖ ❖

Rosa entered the shop late the next morning. A saleswoman she had not met was arranging dresses on a wall rack, and turned at the bell. "Hello. May I help you?" she asked pleasantly.

Rosa glanced around. "I'm looking for the owner, Mrs. Schenk."

The other woman looked blank for a moment. "I'm sorry, Mrs. Schenk used to be the *manager*, but she quit last week. *I'm* the owner, Mrs. Rowley."

Rosa was dumbfounded. For a full minute she could only stare, trying to connect this woman with the events of the previous weeks.

"Is something the matter?" asked Mrs. Rowley.

"How can you . . . be the owner? Mrs. Schenk is the owner. She had the papers, the deed, everything. I looked carefully at all the documents. They were authentic, I know." Confusion crowded her brain.

Mrs. Rowley's eyes narrowed. "What are you talking about? What has Mrs. Schenk done?"

"She sold this shop to me, with all its contents. A week ago. I bought this shop last week. There were witnesses. The Spanish couple who run the restaurant next door signed as witnesses. Look, I have the papers here." With shaking hands, Rosa opened the document envelope she carried, and held out the papers to the other woman.

Mrs. Rowley looked through them with growing astonishment and anger. "Why that filthy thief! That wretched criminal! I leave her in charge of my store for a few months, and she tries to *sell* it! No wonder she was in such a hurry to resign the day I returned!" She looked up at Rosa. "Oh, the *forms* are authentic, right enough. Anyone can get them from a lawyer or court-house. But the information is false! The signatures have no validity! *I* have been the legal owner for fifteen years! What day did you say this happened?"

Rosa could not speak. Darkness grew and blurred her vision, and Mrs. Rowley's voice came from a distance. She felt herself pushed into a chair. "Put your head down," said Mrs. Rowley, sharply. Gradually Rosa's sight cleared but the heaviness within her was unbearable.

"I'd faint, too! Well! That also explains why I can't seem to make my inventory match the invoice sheets. That dirty little crook pinched my clothes! Are you going to be all right now? I'm ringing up the police!" She walked toward the office.

"Wait, please," Rosa called out. "Before you do, do you have an address for her? A telephone number?"

"Of course. What are you going to do?"

Rosa followed her into the office. "I'm going straight there, this minute. I'm not waiting for the police to come with all their sirens and scare her away before I have a chance at her."

"I don't think they do that in real life. You ought to wait and let them do their job." She paused and shrugged. "But if you want it . . . " she pulled a handwritten list of phone numbers off the wall, "that's it, right there. Third one down." She turned to the telephone.

Half an hour later, Rosa stood grimly on the street of the address, a slip of paper in hand, scanning the numbers over the doors. She trembled with black anger. She had never before desired to kill someone with her bare hands! There it was!

The street door, when she tried it, was locked. She pressed the electric bell button hard, and held it down. There was banging within, and a voice called out muffled profanity. The door jerked open. A skinny, bald man with a mustache stood before her dressed only in trousers and an undershirt.

"What! Whatcher doin' ringin' the bloody bell ofen ther wall!"

"I want to see Mrs. Schenk."

"Oh, yer does, does yer! The bleedin' sow. Ah'd like ta' see 'er maself, ah would! And wring 'er skinny neck! Run off middle o' ther night a week ago! Bleedin' Jerry! Owed me six month's rent! What'd she do you fer, eh?"

"*What?*"

"Y'heard me! Filthy cheat run off last week. Yer wanner see 'er room?"

"Yes, I would."

"Foller me, 'en. Y'aint the first to come lookin' fer 'er." They climbed to the upper floor. He pushed a key into the lock and swung the door open.

The apartment had that look of abandonment even furnished rooms have when all living has ceased within. Papers and trash on the floor. Wardrobe standing open, nothing inside but a few bent hangars. Bathroom cabinet empty, sinks and tub with a few red hairs stuck to the rims. There were some half empty packages of food: flour, cornstarch, salt. A dying plant drooped on the window sill.

Footsteps mounted the stairs, and two men in suits walked through the door. "Police," they said, flashing badges.

"'Baht time. Called yer days ago."

"You're Mr. Murphy, the landlord?" A nod.

He turned. "You're Mrs. Edler? We got your name from a Mrs. Rowley at a dress shop. She said you might be here. Might want to make a statement."

❖ ❖ ❖

It was three hours later when Rosa walked up the block to the little flat she shared with Hilde. It seemed like three years. She was drained, dead inside. Everything gone. She was past fearing Hilde's reaction. What more could the girl do to her than had already been done?

Hilde wept tears and cried recriminations, and Rosa recovered from her numb trance long enough to shake her daughter out of hysteria. What good would shouting and crying do? Rosa had lost far more than a stupid boat ticket. She had lost everything! Everything! There was *nothing* to be done! Apparently the filthy woman had taken money and jewelry from a number of friends and departed by night for Germany. The passenger lists would be checked, of course. But how could they find a woman who was a week gone, and nobody knew where?

The two women finally sank exhausted and despairing into bed. Rosa put the pillow over her head to muffle the sound of Hilde's weeping.

❖ ❖ ❖

Late that night, after Hilde felt sure her mother slept, she rose and crept into the small bathroom. She locked the door and switched on the light. Her face in the mirror was red and swollen, and she splashed it repeatedly with cold water before drying it. She knelt before an ancient four-legged bathtub and sank her head onto her hands. A bathroom was an unlikely place to pray, but Hilde had never needed it more desperately.

"Oh, my Father," she whispered, and felt the tears well up again. Resolutely she fought them down, and took a few deep breaths. "Father, what am I going to do now? I've pinned all my work and my hopes on Elder Widtsoe's counsel to me. I've felt so inspired and blessed to go to America. And I've seen the miracles you've sent to get me my tickets, my passport and visa, and to distract the guards at the checkpoint in Germany. I know this is thy will! I know it's what you want me to do! So why did this happen? Why?"

She couldn't restrain the tears that flowed again, and grabbed a towel to muffle her sobs. Sitting on the floor with the towel against her face she wept and pled with the Lord for help and direction. As she prayed, a barely perceptible calm began to descend upon her. Her sobs stilled, and her whispered words became steady.

"Lord, I don't know what you have in mind. But you do. I know you do. All I can do is trust you. And I do. I know you'll find a way for me, somehow, some time. And if it isn't now . . .

if this is another trial I need to endure, please give me the strength to get through it. And please, give me the heart to forgive my mother for this. Please soften her heart; not just that she will understand me, but that she'll be able to let go of all the pain and suffering which have made her so hard and miserable that she would sink to this terrible level."

Suddenly, unbidden, understanding seemed to flow into Hilde, and it was as if she could see her mother through God's eyes. She could see all the years of disappointment and betrayal. The dreams of her career shattered twice. An adored husband who abandoned her, cheapened her love, and left them both to years of poverty and semi-starvation. She saw also the hundreds of times Rosa had come to the rescue of other people less able or resourceful than herself. No, Mama had not been gentle, or kindly, or tactful in her methods, but her compassion was real, if badly expressed. Hilde understood that the bitterness and selfishness had developed over the years like calluses grown to shield a tender heart from unendurable pain. Hilde saw these things with an understanding which was not her own, and then she wept tears for her mother.

"I'm sorry, Lord!" she murmured. "I'm sorry for only thinking of my own pain. She's lost everything, hasn't she? And she's lost it over and over again. She probably did think the dress shop would be a solution to my problems as well as her own. And, typically," Hilde gave a watery laugh, "she saw the quickest way to a solution, and took the shortest path, without giving a thought to anybody else. That's the trouble with terribly intelligent people. They're so used to being correct, that they can't tell when they aren't."

Hilde sighed deeply, peace in her heart. "Oh, Lord, what will we do now? I know you have a way. I know you can see all the paths to get us where you want us to go. I don't! All I can do is trust you. Show me what you want me to do, and I'll do it. And I know I'll be afraid again, and cry again, and pray again. Please don't give up on me. Please comfort and strengthen me

again. Help me to hold this peace, and to trust you. I love you.
And I pray this all in Christ's name. Amen."

Hilde inhaled so deeply it was as if her lungs had no bottom. She got up, washed her face again in cold water, and hung the towel on the rack. Turning out the light before she opened the door, she crept quietly back to her bed.

❖ ❖ ❖

Rosa had not been asleep. She heard her daughter go into the bathroom; heard the muffled sobs. The self-discovery of the previous night only heightened her feelings of distress and despair.

With sickness thick in her stomach she finally whispered, "Dear God, how can I make it up to her now? And what am *I* going to do, now that all *I* had is also lost. Oh, God," she continued to murmur softly, "I don't pray very often. Not nearly often enough. I don't know what to do now. And I don't know how to tell her . . . "she had to pause. It was impossible even to whisper the words she had never learned to say; she could barely think them in her mind. *How to say I'm sorry.* "Oh, what can we do now, God? What can we do?"

Rosa was finally on the edge of a troubled sleep when she heard Hilde slide into her bed.

❖ ❖ ❖

Both women were subdued in the morning. They didn't speak much, but the few words were gentle and free from recriminations. Plans would have to be made about what to do next. The lease on the apartment would be up in a week. There was still the money that hadn't been spent on the shop, the money left over from the sale of Hilde's ticket. But it wouldn't last long. Rosa had the option of going back to her job with Mrs. Fuller; how fortunate that she had not resigned. But Hilde would have to find work and a place to live. They would buy a newspaper and tramp the streets to see what was available. That had to be the first step.

Together they walked down an avenue, speaking in the soft-ened German which identifies the Viennese.

"But, Mama, I'm not trained for *anything* except cooking and food service. What else *can* I do?"

"Well, you were a manager for six months, weren't you? That ought to be good for something."

"When I can barely speak English?" They stopped on a cor-ner to wait for a light. "I don't know more than a few hundred words. No one can understand me. What about working in the kitchen at the general's home, with you?"

"The staff is full. That's no good."

The corner on which they waited was in an area of very exclusive shops. Two meters away stood a woman dressed in a beautifully cut suit which Rosa recognized as raw silk. The wom-an was looking in a window at a gown which would have cost Rosa a year's wages.

"Is there any chance the general's wife knows other big homes that might need . . ."

Hilde got no further. The woman in front of the store had turned around and was looking at them with wonder on her face. She interrupted the girl with a cry. "Vienna! Oh, Vienna! You are both from my beautiful home! Oh, dear ladies, forgive my rudeness, but you *must* understand! The music of my lan-guage is a drink to my thirsty soul!"

She, too, spoke the Viennese dialect of Rosa and Hilde. Af-ter looks of bewildered surprise, both of them had to smile at the blonde woman's effusive appreciation.

"Yes, we are Viennese, too," said Rosa. "May I guess that you haven't been here very long, and are missing home?"

"Oh, I've been here too long! Too, *too* long! And yet not long enough to learn this ghastly language the English speak. Any time away from the City of Song is an eternity! I haven't spoken intelligently to anyone but my husband for months, and he isn't interested in *anything*! Oh, you must think I am insane! Absolutely crazy! But I'm going to ask you a very dear, very special favor. It's almost noon. Won't you please come with me, as my guests, and let me give you luncheon? There's a lovely little French restaurant just around the corner. And you could talk to me, and I could understand you! Oh, *please* say you will!"

Rosa and Hilde glanced at each other. "We would be delighted," Rosa answered. At least they could save the price of one meal.

As they walked around the corner and down the street, Rosa had the strange feeling she had seen this woman before. Mrs. Frazier, she had introduced herself. Could she have been connected with the Karitarsocialis kitchen? No, Rosa would have remembered her from the duty rosters. Perhaps it was the easy, carefree acceptance of wealth this woman had in common with some of Rosa's old friends.

The restaurant was a study of understated luxury, and the food was delicious with delicate sauces and rich pastries. They chatted about England and laughed over the strange customs of the British. They reminisced on the beauties of Vienna. Mrs. Frazier's diamonds sparkled on fingers and wrists as she fluttered and sighed over how she missed this and that.

As the conversation progressed, Rosa mentioned her management of the food kitchen at the Cathedral, and was delighted when she and Mrs. Frazier discovered they had a number of acquaintances in common.

"Perhaps that's where I have seen you before, Mrs. Edler. I have this feeling we've met somewhere. A party at this place or that?"

"I've been wondering the same thing, and searching all my memories of Vienna," confessed Rosa.

"Well, I'm not really from Vienna," said the loquacious blond, "but I never tell anybody that. Just a little town nearby, St. Pölten."

Rosa gasped. "St. Pölten! So am I! I was born and grew up there!"

"No, it can't be! What was your name?"

"Oh, you never would have known me. I was just little Rosa Reiner, then. Nobody at all."

The woman's brow furrowed in thought and her lips felt over the name. Then her eyes widened and her mouth dropped. "I don't believe it! Rosa Reiner? Rosa, of course! Don't you remember me? I'm Marta Goldstein! My silly big sister, Sophie, used to bribe you to do her schoolwork! She could never do it herself!"

It was Rosa's turn to be dumbfounded. She could only shake her head in astonishment. "Of course! I see you now, Marta, hiding behind your woman's face!"

There was laughter and even more talk, reminiscences and life histories exchanged. Rosa dwelt only on the brightest parts of her past: her medical schooling, no, still not quite finished, the depression had forced her to come to England. But she had been a companion to a Duchess here, and General Fuller and his wife declared her invaluable as their housekeeper.

Marta rattled on in turn about her marriage, her politician husband who advised the British war department on the real situation in Austria and Germany. Her face grew sober. "We had to leave Austria when Hitler came in, of course. He hates Jews, although I don't know why. Half the scientists and musicians and *everybody* are Jews." She threw up her hands. "But I don't want to talk about that! Too gloomy! So! Since that time we've just traveled and traveled. Everywhere! Why, only a month ago we were in America."

Rosa felt the same constricting rope of jealousy that had tortured her heart as a girl in the presence of this rich schoolmate. All the talk of parties and famous people, beautiful dresses bought in Paris, and travel, travel!

"America? Really?" Rosa asked brightly. "Why Hilde is sailing there on the *Hansa* in only a few days!"

"The *Hansa*!" Marta reached out and touched Hilde's hand. "Oh, darling, you'll love it! We traveled on the *Hansa* last year, and it was marvelous! And you're leaving right away?"

Hilde, who had been quiet during all the voluble exchange, spoke up boldly. "Yes, I had planned to. But unfortunately we've suffered some serious problems, and have had to pawn my ticket. If we can't think of some way to get it back, I'm afraid I won't be going after all."

Rosa was scarlet with mortification. What must Marta think! How could Hilde have embarrassed her in public this way! In front of *this* one of *all* women! Was this her daughter's revenge?

Marta's eyes clung to Hilde in sympathy. "Oh, you poor darling! You must *not* let that happen. Oh, this dreadful situation in Europe! I know *hundreds* of people whose investments have just gone bust! I mean, their whole life *savings*!" She turned to Rosa. "That's it, isn't it! I know! You *shouldn't* be embarrassed, *really*."

"I'm afraid you're right," Rosa said looking at her lap. "Our investments were not as sound as we had thought. What can one do?" she shrugged.

"Well, for one thing, Hilde *must* have her trip! My husband and I are certainly well enough off to make a little loan to one of my dear childhood friends. You'll take it, won't you? I'll be so hurt if you don't!"

Hilde spoke quickly. "Yes, thank you. You are very kind! I can see why my mother is so fond of you." Rosa looked at her daughter, startled at her uncharacteristic presumption.

Marta rushed on with travel advice for the young girl, and took them past her bank after lunch. She was about to hand the cash to Rosa when Hilde exclaimed, "Why I've never seen British money in these denominations. Isn't it pretty?" and took the money into her own hands.

"*I've* never thought so. I think Austrian bills are much more beautifully designed. But I suppose novelty makes things interesting." She put her arm through Rosa's and declared that they must get together again very soon.

Hilde put the bills into her own purse. She carefully copied down Mrs. Frazier's address, solemnly promising her to repay the money from America as quickly as she could.

❖ ❖ ❖

Rosa was very quiet as they traveled by train to Southampton three days later. Hilde couldn't decide if her mother were sad, angry, or preoccupied by the griefs that forced her to go back to work at the general's house the next day.

I've never understood my mother, she thought. *And she has never known me at all. We might be from different planets.* A sudden impulse of tenderness enveloped the girl, and she put an arm around the older woman.

"Mama," she said, laying her cheek against her mother's. "I truly do love you." She couldn't think of anything else to say, but maintained the embrace. In a little while Rosa turned her head and placed a wordless kiss on her daughter's cheek.

Rosa rode with Hilde on one of the small steamers that took passengers out to the big ship in deeper waters. Together they went on board for a little tour, and to say farewell.

"We're on German territory, again," Hilde said.

"It has been years for me," replied Rosa, gently running her hand along a brass railing and smiling a little. "Listen to everyone chattering away in German. A sound I haven't heard for so long it seems almost strange. Come. Let's find your cabin. You have the ship's map?"

They put Hilde's bags on her bunk, locked her cabin, and went up to the top deck to look at the view. The day was clean and crisp. Whitecaps crested and tossed against the ship, while gulls screeched and wheeled against bright scudding clouds.

In a short while a blast from the horn announced visitor departure.

"I have to go now, dear," said Rosa. But she didn't move. She squirmed and looked uncomfortable. Her lips worked nervously as she tried to say more. "But before . . . About what happened, I want to . . . I don't . . . When I took . . ." She stammered to a halt and her head hung miserably. Hilde had to lean close to hear her mother's whisper. "Hilde, what . . . what I did was wrong. Not honest. I'm . . . I'm . . ." She gulped.

Mama had never managed a direct apology in her life, and Hilde felt pity, seeing her struggle so. "It all worked out, Mama." She squeezed her mother's arm, but was unable to concede more. "I'll write to you. I promise."

The two women held each other close for a long moment. "Hilde, don't come down with me, please. Stay up here so I can see you from the boat as I go back." They kissed, and Rosa went to the stairway.

Hilde saw her walk onto the boat far below, and turn to wave. She waved back. The great ship moved out as the smaller craft continued toward land. Hilde watched until the little boat had blended into the haze of the city beyond.

Turning, she looked toward the prow of the ship surging forward through great whitecapped waves which were the still-powerful remnants of a hurricane half an ocean away. Some of them seemed enormous, as if they could turn back the craft by their very size. And yet somehow the ship cut through them, spewing foam and water as high as the lower decks. The ship was large enough that the force of the wind and the waves sent only a reduced shudder to her on the high deck. Enough to remind her of the awesome power far below.

It's like life, she thought. There is always another wave, a bigger one, one that seems insurmountable this time; one that shakes the very foundation of existence and faith. And yet somehow the ship passes through. The ship may tremble and be drenched, but it passes through.

Like the ship pressing into the waves, Hilde's thoughts pressed into the future. What lay ahead? What unknown waves would shake and drench her? She breathed deeply, half exhilarated, half frightened, and remembered the words to one of her favorite hymns, *Jesus, Savior, Pilot Me.*

❖ ❖ ❖

Madison, Wisconsin, 1938

The clean, concrete room at the university medical school was large. Although it was called a laboratory, it was really a kennel room for the dogs who were being examined and tested. A young man sat on the floor dressed in a stained, threadbare lab coat. He was laughing, playing with a mongrel bitch who growled and tried to pull a towel away from him. The dog's red-blond curls indicated some cocker spaniel ancestry, but she was much too large. The man yanked the towel away, balled it up, and threw it hard to the other end of the room. Scrambling, the dog clawed against the slippery floor, dashing for the towel. She brought it back, prancing, grinning, just out of the man's reach; flirting, daring him to fight her for it again.

"I'll bet you've got some retriever in you, too, Venus," he told her as he grabbed for the towel.

"For crying out loud, Harris. Are you playing with those dang dogs again! And *Venus*—what kind of name is *that* for a mutt?"

"Hi, Dr. Hasslem! I call her Venus because she has hair the color of that Titian painting, 'Venus Rising from the Sea.' And playing with her is scientifically sound, because when she trusts and likes me, she cooperates when I have to draw blood."

"Oh, brother! I'm sure that's *exactly* why you haul them all out and get them worked up all the time." They grinned at each other, and Harris nuzzled the dog as he lifted her back into her cage.

"Anyhow," continued Arthur Hasslem, "Dr. Gammon wants those renal results from last week's tests, if you have them compiled yet." Harris handed him a sheaf of papers. "Right. Thanks. I bet you had them done before you went home last Friday."

Harris shrugged.

"You going to the game this weekend?" the older man asked, leafing through the report. "Isn't official season yet, but we'll beat the socks off Ohio anyway, and scare 'em good for when it counts."

"I could, I guess. But I really think I'd better brush up on my biochem. You and your wife going?"

"Wouldn't miss it! Wouldn't miss it! Why don't you pull your nose out of your books and find a nice girl to take?"

"Maybe," Harris replied as he opened the next cage and filled the food dish. "Hi there, Woola." He scratched the bulldog's furrowed brow.

"Woola? What's that, some other painting?"

"Nah! Burroughs! Didn't you ever read Edgar Rice Burroughs? There's this man who gets transported to Mars and has an ugly Martian watchdog named Woola. She just reminds me of that."

Hasslem shook his head and cast his eyes to the ceiling. "Gads!" He walked out with the report.

Back in the office he picked up the phone and called his wife.

"Hi, honey, any word from Hilde yet?"

"Yes, Art. I got a letter in the mail this morning. She's in New York with your sister for a few days, and will be here on schedule on September 24th. She sounds very excited about being here. I am too. Edna told her about our new baby, and she says she'd be thrilled to stay here with us and help take care of me and the kids for a while. I couldn't be gladder!"

"I don't think that's a word."

"Sure it is! Sad, sadder, glad, gladder!"

"You win. Listen, I gotta run. Be home about 6:30, okay?"

"Hugs and kisses!"

"Same to you."

❖ ❖ ❖

On Sunday, October 2nd, Harris Newell walked into the back of the chapel and looked around. The LDS branch on campus was larger this year. There must have been sixty or seventy people: the usual single students from last year, plus a few new ones. Half a dozen professors and their families, young people who worked in town, but wanted to socialize with other Mormons, and student couples with their inevitable babies. The piano played hymns while the members found seats, shook hands, and greeted each other with more enthusiasm than reverence.

The first service of every month was special. Each of the members would have fasted for the previous twenty-four hours, and donated the money they saved to feed the poor. It helped people remember how much they were blessed, and allowed them to share what they had with others. Then, during this one service, members were free to stand as they felt moved, to express thanks for the blessings of God and to bear their witness of gospel truths.

Harris took a seat on the second row from the back next to Wanda Peterson who had three squirming preschoolers, and whose husband was in the branch presidency and had to sit on the stand. She always had her hands full with the kids, and he sat near her to help keep them entertained and quiet. He smiled as he thought of his own eight younger brothers and sisters, filling an entire pew in faraway Utah. One parent would be at each end of the row to discourage escapees.

"Thank goodness, the cavalry arrives," Wanda murmured as Harris sat down.

"Will you draw me a picture?" asked Susan, crawling into his lap.

He took a paper from his coat pocket, and began to draw animals of various kinds. Billy stood on the seat and draped himself over Harris's shoulder to watch. The room filled and the singing began. Harris had a baritone voice, and loved to harmonize. He held Susan's arms gently folded during the prayer.

When the time came for expressing thanks and testimony,

Harris was paying only partial attention. Wanda was trying to hold her baby in one arm and with the other retrieve toys from a diaper bag under her seat. A couple of people spoke of their blessings and gratitude. Finally Susan and Billy were busy with books, and Harris relaxed and began to listen more intently.

Close to the front a young woman stood up. She turned to face the greater part of the congregation, and Harris saw a sweet, piquant face with large brown eyes. A crown of glossy black hair was covered by a tiny hat of netting. He had never seen her before; she must be new. There was something unusual about her hair and her clothes, but he couldn't quite put his finger on it. It took a moment for her to begin, as she seemed to search for words. When she spoke, Harris realized why she seemed different. Her musical voice was heavily accented with German. She was so small and ardent, his heart constricted in his chest.

"My brothers and my sisters, how glad to be here . . . I have come. My home has been Vienna, in Austria, but the Lord . . . I have followed to this very large new land."

As she struggled with words Harris was captivated. A young man in front of him poked another with his elbow, and Harris frowned.

"These dear people, Arthur Hasslem and Mary have to their home taken me. So many danger . . . hard things . . . it was to come to here . . . " her voice broke; she paused and struggled to regain her composure. Harris wanted to reach out and comfort her. "But the Lord have to me help and protect as . . . as with angels has . . . around me b-been."

The boys who had nudged each other were smiling slightly as the young woman struggled. Harris's breath quickened. *If they laugh at her, so help me, I'll knock them down.*

"I thank the Lord in much love. In Christ I thank him. Amen"

She sat, sinking from view behind other heads. But the sight of her lingered in his mind.

After the meeting, a small crowd clustered around the Hasslems, greeting them and being introduced to their pretty guest. Harris hadn't realized how tiny she was until he stood beside her; she was barely more than five feet tall, slender and shapely. A phrase from a book popped into his head, "a pocket-Venus." He smiled at the thought.

"And let me introduce you to Harris Newell, one of the graduate students who works with me," Dr. Hasslem was saying.

"Wie geht's!" Harris spoke to her in German. "I am very glad to meet you. By your words today I was touched."

"Oh, how do you come to speak German?" she asked in that language.

"It is the language of Doctoral I have to study chosen. No doubt I badly speak. And with an accent wrong."

She dimpled. "Well, it cannot be worse than my English."

Arthur broke in. "It is far worse than your English, Hilde."

The girl turned to her sponsor. "Brother Hasslem, please, I would like to be Hildegard, now. Not Hilde, anymore. That's the name from an old life, and this is a new one."

Harris spoke in English, "Then Miss Hildegard, may I please call you this week?"

"Call me?" she asked perplexed.

Arthur interpreted, "He means he wants to talk to you on the telephone, Hilde . . . Hildegard. Go right ahead, Harris. Now get out of here so some of these other young men can have a chance to meet her."

Harris wandered over to the lab to feed and water the dogs. In a bit of a daze he informed some of them that if they impartially considered it, shining black hair was probably the most beautiful kind, in spite of fairy tales and Hollywood.

❖ ❖ ❖

Mary was bathing the children when the phone rang, and called out for Hildegard to get it. Arthur was in his study preparing a lecture.

"Hello," the girl answered, sure she could manage the call if she only needed to take a message for her hosts. She understood far more English than she could speak.

"Hello, is this Hildegard?"

"Yes."

"Good evening, Hildegard. This is Harris Newell; we met last week at church. Do you remember me?"

"I am sorry, no. There . . . so many were. Do you wish to Dr. Hasslem to speak?"

"No, I want to talk to you."

Hildegard began to panic. "What do you want to talk about?" she asked.

"I want to ask you if you will go out with me."

"Go out of what, please?"

"'Go out' means that you will come with me and we will go together to eat, or perhaps see a movie."

"Oh!" she brightened. "This is a 'date' that it is called?"

"That's right. I want you to go on a date with me."

At that moment Arthur came into the room. "Who's the phone for?"

Hildegard held the phone away and answered happily, "It's for me. A date!"

"That was fast. Who is it?"

"I don't know. The names are so strange, I forgot it."

"Well, ask him."

"Hello? I am very sorry, but your name . . . I forget."

"That's all right, Hildegard," Harris answered slowly and distinctly. "You met many people on Sunday. Tell Dr. Hasslem that it is Harris Newell, and ask him if it is okay for you to go on a date with me."

This time Hildegard put her hand over the mouthpiece and spoke in German. "He says his name is Harris Newell and he met me on Sunday; but I can't remember who he is. He said I should ask you if he is safe to go out with, or something."

"Harris, huh? He's the one who tried to speak German to you. Yes, he's as safe as Fort Knox." She looked confused. "Uh, never mind. Just an expression. Yes, he's a decent young man. He works with me at school."

"Hello. Dr. Hasslem says I may go on a date with you. Where will we go?"

"Would you like to go to the football game on Saturday? It's a very American thing."

She turned from the phone. "Dr. Hasslem, would I like to go to the football game?"

"Oh yes! Definitely! Football is the greatest thing in America! You'll love it!"

"Hello. Dr. Hasslem says I will love it. Okay. Is this the correct word to say?"

"Yes! 'Okay' is *exactly* the correct word to say! I'll come and get you on Saturday at 3:00. Dr. Hasslem's house isn't far from the stadium, so we can walk there. Thank you very much for going with me."

Hildegard hung up the phone and smiled at Arthur. "I am going to have a date! This is very American, is it not?"

❖ ❖ ❖

"I do not think I understand, " Hildegard sounded bewildered. "All the crowd is screaming and happy, but the man on the grass has been badly injured. Why did all of the other men jump on his body."

"Watch for a minute," Harris said. "Look, he's getting up. You see the helmet on his head, and the padding on his shoulders and body? These things help him not to be hurt, even when other men jump on him."

Hildegard looked up at her partner, "But now they stand and talk and talk. If they wish to carry the ball to the sticks . . . the . . . "

"Goal posts," he supplied.

"Goal posts. If this is important, why do they not pick up the ball immediately and continue to run?"

"Ahhh. That's a good question. This game is a little like a

war. The teams must have a plan. Each time a man is knocked down or drops the ball, it's like an army going into a new country to fight. The players must get together and talk about a new plan for how they will fight."

She considered a moment. "You tell me things very clearly. And you speak slowly. You are a good teacher, I think." She smiled at him.

A feeling of enormous joy welled through Harris at the simple words. He suddenly wanted to be the best teacher in the world and spend his life explaining things to please her.

After the game, they walked around the campus, talking.

"Football is very strange to me," said Hildegard. "All of the people in one minute are shouting and happy, in another minute in anger they are shouting. They clap the hands and jump up, and shake the fist and scream to the man who is a judge that he is many bad things. This behavior is not known in Vienna."

"They don't have sports in Vienna?"

"Of course there is sport. Many kinds. But not with many people screaming. This is not done. Do you think also that football is the best thing in America, as Brother Hasslem has said?"

Harris laughed. "No, I'm not a sports nut." He saw her puzzle at the last word. "*Nut* is what one is called when he likes something very, very much."

Her face lighted. "Oh! I think I am a music nut. I am a Chopin nut very much."

Harris smiled and began to whistle the melody from his favorite Chopin Nocturne.

"Oh! You know this music! This is a very good thing!" She put her arm through his and squeezed it happily.

Harris thought he would stop breathing. He thought he could fly!

They walked and talked until after sunset. She told him as well as she could, sometimes having to switch to German, about her life in Austria, and her conversion to the Church. He told her about his youth, growing up in the hot red mountains of southern Utah, riding horses and caring for sheep.

"This is like a cowboy, I think," she remarked.

"Yes, a little. But not like in the movies. Not exciting or dangerous. Just hard work all through the year. But that wasn't our whole life. My father was the president of a small college there. I was expected to be the best in my school because I was his son."

"Did you go to college in your father's school?"

"No. When Dad realized all his children would soon need higher education, he took a position (that's a job) at Brigham Young University. He is the head of the Chemistry Department there. We moved to Provo so all of us could go to the university."

Harris went on to describe his six sisters and two brothers. She was astonished at the idea of such a large family. People in Europe certainly did *not* have so many children!

"My brother is studying to be a veterinarian. A doctor for animals."

Hildegard was silent for a few moments. "My mother wanted very much to be a doctor for people. She worked hard, oh, many, many years."

"Is she a doctor now?" Harris was impressed. In his heart he had longed to be a doctor, but there had never been the money for it.

"No. It was so many, many years, her schooling took, when she was done, all her knowledge too old was. The old knowledge was not right. They said she would again many classes have to take. This she could not do. It was the thing to break her heart. So to England she went away. But it is not the life she wanted. This thing makes me sad."

Harris was struck with powerful empathy for the simply told story. "Oh, the poor woman! That would kill me!"

"It killed her heart, I think. But my mother is strong. She is now—what do you call the boss of a big house with many servants? *Oberhaushaelterin*"

"Uh, house manager? Oh, probably the housekeeper."

"Yes, housekeeper. For a big general in England. She does not like so much to do this."

Harris's mind began instantly to calculate. He wished he could find some way to help the mother in order to please the daughter. He knew most of the medical faculty. It wouldn't hurt to ask.

"I think we must go home." Hildegard shivered. "The cold is becoming more."

"I'm an idiot! All you have is a sweater. Here, put on my jacket."

She tried to refuse, but he insisted, arranging the sleeves, thrilling as he touched her arms, her shoulders. When they said good night on Hasslem's porch, Harris knew he was hopelessly in love. He would do anything for this tiny, exquisite being. Why didn't they have white horses and quests anymore? Why couldn't he carry a ribbon or her scarf as a token to die for, to live for!

He walked two blocks past his own apartment house before he realized where he was and turned back.

❖ ❖ ❖

Mary was washing dishes when Hildegard came into the kitchen that evening. "Well, Hildegard, how was your date?"

The girl smiled at inward thoughts. "It was a nice date. I think the football game was very strange. I don't think I like football so much as Dr. Hasslem does."

"Nobody likes football as much as Dr. Hasslem does."

"He is a 'nut,' yes?"

Mary was startled, then laughed. "Where did you learn that? Yes, Art is an absolute nut for football. Oh, here comes the nut now."

"Who's calling me a nut? Hello, Hildegard, how did it go?"

"The football was very noisy and confusing, but we had a good walk, and talked very much until now. This man, Harris Newell is very nice. Very kind to me. And he speaks slowly so I can understand."

"Well, yes." Arthur poured himself a glass of milk from the fridge, and sat down. "He's very nice, Hildegard, but there are plenty of fish in the sea." Seeing her perplexity, he clarified. "Many men who will date you. You need to get to know a lot of them."

"I like this one very much."

"He's nice enough. In fact he is so *very* nice, and works so *very* hard, and is so *very* dutiful, and so *very* religious, he makes me a little nervous."

Hildegard was taken aback. "Is it not a good thing to be *very much* all of these things?"

Art gave a frustrated sigh, and looked around, considering. "How can I say it? It is good to be all these things. But moderation is good, too. *Mit Mass.* Harris works too hard at everything. And although he is worthy in every way you can think of, there has to be more to life than that. His drive is more for gaining knowledge than for using it to get ahead. He's nice enough to date, and he has a superb mind. But you're very pretty, Hilde. You can do better than that. He will probably never hold a high position, or be rich or nationally known. He's just so terribly. . . good."

Slightly offended, Hildegard asked, "Is it possible for a person to be too much good?"

"Well. . . no. But it makes other people feel uncomfortable, that's all."

Hildegard bid the Hasslems good night and went to her room. She curled up in a chair by the window with her lights off, gazing out at the moon-washed street. There it was again, but she never would have expected it here! It reminded her of Ferdi, who thought religion itself was excessive, and of her mother, to whom position was all-important. Too good? Should one deliberately be less than one's best to make others feel comfortable? To obtain a high position? Perhaps she *was* strange, even among these kind people whom she had thought felt as she did.

During the next weeks, the Hasslem's introduced Hildegard

to many young people of whom they approved. Hildegard sat
with the Hasslem family and their guests at the dining room
table during a small dinner party. The young man who was speaking, Richard Galbraith, was very handsome and charming. He
was telling a story about a professor whose demonstration animal, a wild raccoon, had suddenly revived from the anesthetic
and escaped, staggering into the crowded lecture hall. Everybody was laughing. He spoke quickly, and Hildegard missed a
few words, but was still able to catch the gist. He was one of the
five students the Hasslems had invited to help her expand and
solidify new friendships. They were all very nice. One of the
girls seemed a little silly and shallow, but was pretty. The other,
Sally Bach, was delightful, and would make a good friend. Sally
was a convert to the church, the outgoing daughter of a German
family who ran a farm in Northern Wisconsin. Hildegard was
delighted to meet someone her age who spoke thoroughly com-
petent German.

Both Richard and another of the men, Clark, had paid her
special attention. She had been on dates with both of them (Richard twice), and had enjoyed herself.

But on the advice of her sponsors, she had put Harris Newell off since their first date. Everybody respected him, she could
see that; even though Clark had called him a square (whatever
that was). She had a feeling that meant Harris was considered a
bit of an outsider. For some reason, that saddened her. Harris
was such a wonderfully kind and interesting man. Very likely,
she too was a "square."

Hildegard was surprised at how her heart leaped when she
received a call the following day from Harris.

"What are you doing?" he asked her.

"I have been studying my English. Often Mary helps me to
learn, but today she has to the doctor taken the baby. So I am
studying only what the book is saying."

"Hildegard, how would you like me to help you with your
English study? I would be very happy to come to your house."

"Oh, I would like so much for your help to me!" She paused. "But I would like for your help at another place, I think. The children are noisy very much." She felt a little sheepish for making an excuse, when really she was just too big a coward to risk disappointing Art and Mary by encouraging Harris. But she *did* need to study her English, after all. And it *was* her own life. Besides, studying was not a date. "I will be in the afternoon able to go away, when Mary is again home."

"Wonderful! There are dozens of quiet places where we can study. What time shall I come and get you?"

"I think 4:00?"

"Great! I'll see you then."

Hildegard felt fluttery as she waited for Harris to arrive. Mary hadn't said anything when she told her where she was going, thank goodness. Her books were ready, and she had chosen her prettiest daytime dress and a warm jacket.

When Harris arrived, she eagerly opened the door. He stood before her, smiling hugely, as if seeing her were the happiest event of his life. His light-brown hair ruffled in the breeze, and his gold-flecked green eyes glowed. He was really very nice looking. Suddenly a thought popped wholly formed into her mind: *This is the man I will marry.* It was a simple, matter-of-fact statement, but stunned her so that she could not move, only look astonished at Harris. A lot of time seemed to pass, but Harris appeared quite content to stand and gaze at her.

Suddenly embarrassed, Hildegard jerked back into reality. "Oh, I'm sorry . . . I have in my room forgotten a thing. I will . . . please wait." She turned and dashed up the stairs, leaving him on the porch in front of an open door.

She darted into her room, closed the door and leaned against it, hands held to her hot cheeks. *This is ridiculous. That was just a silly thought, it didn't mean anything. I don't even know this man! Maybe I should stay home. But he's down there on the porch; what could I tell him? Hildegard, get hold of yourself, you're acting like a ninny! Go back down there and be grateful someone who speaks clearly is going to help you with your English. Quit behaving like an idiot! Random thoughts are not prophesies!*

She breathed deeply, smoothed her skirt, and looked around for something to pretend she had come for. Ah, yes. A scarf. The wind might come up and get chilly.

Calmly she returned down the stairs, picked up her books, and went out on Harris's arm.

They found a bench in a sunny, protected spot, and there she learned that if Harris said they were going to study English, that is precisely what they would do. He was a very good and patient teacher. It helped that he could speak a little German and clarify many things in the book. Carefully explaining, he demonstrated how to place her tongue and her lips so the sounds came out with a better accent. They were both so engrossed they didn't realize the time until the sun had left their sheltered grove and they began shivering.

"Come on," he suggested, standing and holding out a hand. "Let's go up to my lab and keep working. You're doing too well to stop now. Unless you're tired?"

"Oh, no! This is very good." She put her hand into his. It was a warm, comfortable hand, so she left hers there as they walked across campus.

She was amused as Harris introduced her by name to several of the dogs. He told her clearly how he and Dr. Gammon were doing original research which would explain the function of the kidney to the world.

"This is where I spend most of my time. I even study here because that way I can save on my electric bill at home. And it has a phone, which is nice. The work we are doing here has never been done before. Up until now, the anatomy (the exact form and parts) of the kidney was not understood accurately. And the physiology (that is how it works) has been a mystery. But once we publish our findings, medical science will be able to solve all kinds of problems, help cure diseases, and make patients feel better. There is no end to the good that can come of this."

Hildegard smiled at his enthusiasm. "My mother would like very much to talk with you about these things. She, too, is a nut about medical things of the body."

Harris laughed when she used the word he had taught her, and she felt warm inside. He was such a nice friend.

❖ ❖ ❖

Mary called up the stairway, "Are you ready, Hildegard? The baby tender is here."

Hildegard turned around once again and looked with approval in the mirror. She descended the stairs regally, staging an "entrance."

"Oh, you look lovely! You're quite a little seamstress. And those flowers tucked in your hair are perfect! Look Art, doesn't Hildegard look wonderful?"

"My, yes! You'll break hearts tonight!"

"You are both kind, but I think I'm just ordinary." She put on an evening coat Mary had loaned her. "Where is to be this dance for the coming home?"

"It's 'homecoming,' A special occasion this year! The 50th anniversary of the University of Wisconsin. Alumni are here from all over the country. There will be two ballrooms in the Memorial Union building, with orchestras and everything. Art and I are chaperones for one of them. There will be lots of men who are there stag, and you will have all the partners you want."

"What is 'stag?'" Hildegard asked, thinking of deer.

"It means men who don't bring their own dates, but like to take turns dancing with lots of different girls."

Art took one woman on each arm as they walked over to campus in the crisp evening air. "What a wonderful night!" he exclaimed. "After a *wonderful* day! Didn't we just beat the socks off old Indiana for our Golden Jubilee! And now a little cuddling on the dance floor. Didn't you tell me you learned dancing in your girl's school, Hildegard?"

"Of course! Young ladies in high station must dance often

in society. I would never be in society, of course, but I was taught to dance, anyway. I very much like the dancing."

She found it totally delightful to whirl around the floor in various arms. Life after Notre Dame had not afforded her much chance for such pleasure. But it was obvious that dancing was not formally taught in America as a social skill. Some partners were wonderful, leading her in imaginative steps. Some were positively plodding, unable to even hear the beat of the music. With those, Hildegard could have screamed!

As she was returned to the side of the room after one such partner, a man appeared at the microphone wearing a cowboy hat with his suit. "Okay, all you Westerners!" he cried. "Grab yourself a little filly and form sets for a square dance! Yaahooo!"

Hildegard looked around apprehensively for Mary and Arthur, but couldn't see them. Couples were grinning, dashing for the floor, forming in clusters of eight. The music strummed out, bold and loud, and Hildegard realized this was her cue to find a place to sit and watch. Chairs and couches bordered the room, and she sat on a plaid sofa.

"Honor your partner with a bow; turn to your corner any-how! Allemande left with your left hand; back you go in a right-'n-left-grand." Hildegard couldn't help but tap her foot as the man in the hat cried out words half in speech, half in song, with a strange accent. She had no idea what he was saying, but the dancers seemed to understand. He was calling instructions for them to move in intricate figures. Occasionally some of the dancers would get it wrong and crash into each other with gales of laughter. How very interesting and strange! Someone sat down next to her, and she glanced over.

"Harris! Oh, I am glad to see you! Tell me what this dance is. I have never seen such a thing before."

Over the music, laughter, and occasional shouts, Harris explained this form of American folk dance. "Would you like to try it?" he asked.

"Oh, no! Only I wish to watch it. Do you like to dance?"

"I would like to dance with you. Will you let me write my name on your program?"

From her wrist she detached the silken cord which held a card and a tiny pencil and gave them to him. He found a blank line and penciled in his name. Later, as he held her in his arms for the waltz he had spoken for, she recognized that although he was not a great dancer, he kept good time and didn't step on her feet. Oddly, she felt very comfortable in his arms. She glanced up at him, and found him gazing down at her.

She thought, *I believe Harris likes me very much.* A little imp of fun tickled her fancy, and she turned her eyes demurely toward his, a quick flutter, then let her lashes fall to brush against her cheek. Ferdi used to like that. What would it make Harris do? She heard his intake of breath, and felt his arms tighten around her. A little thrill ran through her. For the rest of the dance she gave him tiny smiles, fell against him gently as if she had lost her balance for a moment, and ran an occasional fingertip across his shoulder. She was delighted that when he delivered her back to Mary, he looked properly dazed.

As Harris left for his next partner, Mary leaned close. "You are a very naughty girl, Hildegard. I saw how you were tormenting poor Harris."

Conscience stricken, Hildegard looked up. "Oh, I did not mean to *torment*. Truly. Just a little bit I flirt."

"Well, I don't think Harris is used to girls flirting with him, so you had better take it easy. Especially since there are several other very nice young men here who are equally smitten by you."

In bed that night, Hildegard thought about many things. But her mind kept returning to Harris. *He is so awfully nice. So very kind and good. He's sincere about everything—that's plain to see. He makes me feel comfortable and happy. And yet . . . and yet. Mary and Art have been so good to me—they give me a place to live, food, and money for helping in the house so I can repay the price of my ticket—and they know Harris so much better than I do.*

If they think he isn't right for me, perhaps they know best. But all the other men seem superficial when I compare them to Harris. Oh, Richard is much handsomer. And Greg is an enchanting dancer. And Andrew makes me laugh with his stories and impersonations. But Harris makes me feel good inside.

She accepted a date with Harris the next weekend to see the movie *The Sister,* a story of the 1906 San Francisco Earthquake. It was very exciting, but Hildegard could not understand all the words. So they stayed to see it again, Harris whispering commentary that made it all much more enjoyable.

It was the beginning of November, but the evening was not terribly cold, and there was no breeze. So they walked again, glove in glove, and talked. Up the street toward campus, over to the lab so Harris could pick up a letter he had left there, across the crisp frost on the brown lawns. The moon was waning, but lamp posts throughout campus cast a moonlike glow around the dark shadows of trees.

Beneath an enormous pine was a hollow space like a cave, carpeted with half a century of soft needles.

"This makes me remember the woods near St. Pölten," said Hildegard. "Big trees like this, with soft ground on which nothing is growing." They stopped and looked up through the branches where stars could be seen blinking between the needles. It seemed so natural that while she looked up, Harris would gently lower his lips to hers, would circle her in his arms. His face, his arms, were so warm on this cold night. The warmth spread through her heart to her limbs, and outward. A sense of light swelled with the sweetness of the kiss. As his lips lingered on hers, emotions of a depth and power she had never known before swept away all other thought. She trembled in the wonder of it; hungering to stay in his arms forever, longing for the kiss to never end.

"Hildegard," he breathed against her lips. "I love you. I love you."

Her reply flowed as naturally as the warmth and the light

and the trembling joy. "I love you, too, Harris."

He held her gently and looked long into her eyes. She saw worship, comfort, safety, adoration, home. Home. It did not seem at all strange that he then asked her to marry him. It did not seem odd that they had known each other such a brief time.

"Oh, yes," she whispered. "Oh, yes."

❖ ❖ ❖

"Oh, no!" Mary cried. "Oh, no! Hildegard, what are you saying? You *didn't* tell Harris Newell you would marry him! Oh, my dear, you haven't known him eight weeks!"

Hildegard was distressed at such a reception of her joyous news. "But Mary, I love him. Truly, I do! Never have I felt more right about a thing in my life."

"Arthur!" Mary called down the hall to her husband's study. "Arthur, you have to come out here and talk some sense into Hildegard. She's gotten engaged to Harris Newell!"

The couple pleaded and reasoned with Hildegard that she couldn't possibly be in love on so short an acquaintance. Confused, and beginning to doubt herself, Hildegard tearfully repeated that she was sure she loved Harris. And she did, didn't she? How could his kiss have moved her so deeply if this weren't love? The Hasslems insisted she open her eyes for a moment and use good sense. Certainly they considered Harris a fine young man, but reminded her of the difficult life she would have married to a poverty stricken graduate student at this point. And on only a few week's acquaintance! She mustn't confuse gratitude and pleasant acquaintance with love. They begged her not to let the passion or drama of one moment overcome her rational thought and the sensible planning of her future.

All night, memories of their discussion echoed in her mind. Her pillow was moist with tears of indecision. Their last argument beat on her brain like a drum: "If it's really love, it will wait. If it's really right, it will still be right in six months. Give it time. Give it time. Give it time."

So the next morning she called Harris at the lab, and asked him to meet her on the bench where they had studied English together.

Her lips trembled, and her swollen eyes stung. She couldn't bear the look of concerned sympathy on Harris's face before she had even spoken a word. She poured it all out in broken English and broken German. All the arguments, and the rationale, all the doubts they had raked up in her fearful heart.

He held her against his chest and comforted her like a child. "Hush, hush. It's all right. Everything will be all right. Hush."

She finally quieted, too spent to think any longer. "What shall we do?" she asked, looking up. His face looked haggard and gray. She was shocked.

"Hildegard, dearest. You must answer one question. Then we'll know what to do. Last night you said you loved me. I have never been so happy. But I need to know whether it was the circumstances that made you say that, or if you still feel it now?"

She looked down miserably. "I don't know."

With his hands on her shoulders, he thought for a few moments. Finally, "It would be wrong for you to tell me you love me or to agree to marry me if it was just an impulse." He paused a long time. "I cannot take advantage of you if you didn't really mean it." He dropped his hands. "Maybe the Hasslems are right. Maybe you need to wait and see how you feel in a few months."

"Harris, do you know how *you* really feel?" She spoke in a very small voice.

He laughed briefly, silently. "Oh yes. I know how I really feel."

Hildegard had never felt so lost and miserable in her life.

"Come on." Harris raised her to her feet. "Let me take you home. Give yourself some time if you need it. Date other men if you want. In fact, you should." Suddenly his voice broke, "Oh, Hildegard, if . . . if you can be happier with someone else, that's what you should choose."

She clutched his hand a little harder and held her lower lip between her teeth so it wouldn't tremble. Could this man be real? She could see his heart was breaking, but it was breaking for *her!* She reached up to touch his cheek, but his hand caught hers.

"Don't do that, please." He paused. "Let's just try to go back to last week. I don't want you to feel embarrassed or strange around me. Let's be friends. Real friends."

They walked home in silence, and in silence parted.

The Hasslems breathed a sigh of relief when she told them, and put forth unprecedented efforts to help Hilde have a good time and meet a variety of people. They introduced her to men whom they thought might provide an impressive and prosperous future for the young woman they had come to love. Mary bought Hilde two pretty new dresses, and fixed her hair in a modern American style. Within the next two weeks she was invited to attended a dinner party, a dance, a play, and a concert. Her English improved rapidly, and she tried very hard to appear charming and cheerful.

❖ ❖ ❖

Madison, Wisconsin, Fall–Winter, 1938

In the outer office of the director of admissions for the University of Wisconsin Medical school, two women sat at their desks. The one with graying hair rose to file a stack of folders in the drawers behind her. The younger one placed a paper in her typewriter and cranked it into place. She was very pretty, with curly auburn hair and a voluptuous figure. When she spoke it was with a decided southern drawl, which everyone had told her was quite charming.

"Norma," the redhead said, "Ah think mah real problem has been that Ah'm just always excited by the wrong kind of men. Dangerous ones, you know? They just seem so fast and daring it gives me a thrillin' feelin' right in the pit of my stomach. You know what Ah mean?"

"Frankly, Dixie, I've never known any dangerous men. All I've ever had is Verl, and he's a million miles from dangerous or exciting. But he's a good husband. I knew he was a good man when I met him. No violins playing or anything. I just knew he would be good to me."

Dixie typed a sentence and paused, her brow furrowed. "You know, Ah've been thinkin' a lot about that very thing since Ah got away from Tom. Oh, mah! When Ah met Tom Ah just fell for 'im like a ton of bricks. So tall and handsome! He used to narrow his eyes and look at me, and not say a word. Then he'd smile kinda slow. Oooh! Ah couldn't resist him!" Her face darkened at that point, and she slammed the carriage return. After banging out a few sentences copied from the steno pad beside her, she stopped again. "But he sure enough was *not* good to me! How was *Ah* to know he was a hitter? How was *Ah* to know that after he married me he'd quit work and expect me to support him and his gamblin'? Oh! Ah tell you, Ah have had the *worst luck* in men!"

Norma closed the file drawer and asked, "What was your first husband like?"

"Handsome, of course. Oh, *so* handsome." Her voice turned sarcastic. "Handsome enough to attract all the girls in town. What *Ah* can't figure out is how come he had to *sleep* with all of them. Ah mean, *look* at me? Am Ah lackin' in looks? Ah was the purtiest girl in town, high school homecomin' queen, first runner up to Miss Texas! An' *plenty* willin' in bed. Why'd he have to cheat? And *he* was a hitter, *too*! Why do Ah *always* attract the hitters?"

"Dixie, what man *don't* you attract?"

"Well, that's what got me to thinkin', mah bad luck an' all. This time around Ah'm goin' ta let mah *head* lead mah *heart*. Ah'm goin' to find me a *good* man. And, by dang," when she smiled, two delightful dimples appeared on her cheeks, "he's goin' ta be a *rich* man, too! Which is why Ah asked for a transfer to *this* office."

Norma shook her head. "Well, Dixie, you ought to know that the men who come through this office aren't doctors yet, except the old fogies who teach. In fact, medical students must be the most poverty stricken boys on campus."

"Maybe. But they won't be poor for long," the girl went back to her typing, pausing after a few seconds. "Ah figure: choose 'em from a wide selection, get 'em before they've got a big head an' then train 'em up in the way they should go. Ah've already got my eyes on a few of 'em."

The door to the office opened, and Harris Newell stepped in, smiling. "Hi, Norma, Dixie. How's everything?"

Both women greeted Harris warmly, and Dixie added, "If you were lookin' for Dr. Gammon, he left 'bout five minutes ago."

"No, I hoped to see the director for a moment or two. I don't have an appointment, but I was in the building, and wanted to talk to him about some plans I'm trying to hatch. I can come back later if he's busy."

Dixie rose. "Well, just let me check. He might be free right now." She stepped into the director's office, and returned a moment later, smiling. "Y'all are in luck. Go right in."

Dixie sighed as the door closed behind Harris. "Now *that's* the kind of man I mean. Isn't he just the *sweetest* thing? An' so cute Ah could put 'im in my pocket and carry him home. Kinda churchy, though, so Ah hear. Too bad he isn't a medical student."

Norma dropped some paper clips in the drawer and answered. "It wouldn't do you any good. Everybody knows Harris is crazy about that little foreign girl who lives with Art and Mary Hasslem. I heard he asked her to marry him."

Dixie wriggled in a feminine way, a smug smile on her lips. "Well, maybe so. But it's like you Wisconsiner's say about ice hockey—'Jus' cause there's a goalie, don't mean the opposition cain't score.'"

"Dixie! Don't you dare!" Norma's expression was disapproving. "Harris is too fine a man for you to play your tricks on. You leave him alone."

"You needn't give it a thought, sugar. Ah *said* it was too bad he wasn't a med student. What good is it to have a *good* man who's a *poor* man?"

Fifteen minutes later Harris left the director's office and approached Dixie's desk. "Dix, Dr. Jenowski said you could give me an application packet for medical school, if you'd be so kind."

Dixie held still for a moment of surprise. Then her lips rounded into a pretty "o", and she gazed at Harris speculatively. "Why, Harris! Don't tell me you-all are leavin' organic chemistry to try medicine?" Her eyes sparkled.

Harris smiled and raised a finger to his lips. "What I'm doing is a secret, Miss Dixie. So don't you mention it to a soul. Promise?"

"Oh, Harris, I wouldn't tell *anyone* your secret." She rose and turned to her filing cabinet, bending over in such a way that she knew her tiny waist and rounded hips displayed to advantage. She handed the packet to him with a full dimpled smile. "There y'are. Y'all bring 'em back to me when they're done, and I'll pass 'em on to Dr. Jenowski." She let her hand brush against Harris's as he took the packet.

After Harris left, Dixie went cheerily back to work, but finally noticed Norma's stony stare. She raised innocent eyes to her friend. "Well? What're *you* lookin' at?"

❖ ❖ ❖

Hildegard sat before the dressing table in her room, brushing her hair into clusters of fashionable curls. She hoped tonight's date would be better than her last one. She was really trying to have a good time. Really. Carl Wilson was a little older, probably twenty-eight or nine. She had met him only once. Art and Mary had arranged the date, saying Carl was a terribly eligible bachelor, up-and-coming in the world of finance, a man of culture and refinement whose tastes would match her own.

She hoped so! Her previous date, Ted Boris, had taken her to a "jitterbug" dance last week, and she had hardly known what to think! The music was catchy enough, but had been raucous and noisy to her ears. Ted had been an impatient teacher, and left her feeling inept and confused by all the strange steps. In answer to the beat, some boys were throwing girls around like rag dolls. One girl had flipped right over her partner's back, showing her underpants for anyone to see, and shocking Hildegard speechless. Tonight would be a concert of selections from Wagner. Wagner wasn't her favorite, but at least the words were German, and she would understand them.

Carl was charming and elegant, and gave her a very warm welcome when she came down the stairs to meet him. He had intelligent things to say about the music during the intermission. In fact, he had intelligent things to say about everything. They went out afterwards for a late dinner, and he explained all about his business, the financial state of the U.S. and Europe, the reasons why the economy would improve now that it looked like Europe would need American-made goods to support the growing situation with Hitler, and quite an impressive number of other topics. Occasionally he would allow Hildegard to make a reply or a comment. He listened as she spoke, smiled, and then went right on as if she hadn't said anything at all. She found herself thinking, *I wonder if he actually knows I'm here? Would he notice if I vanished?* She also tried very hard not to think of Harris and how carefully he listened to everything she had to say.

The following weekend, Mary and Hildegard sat at the dining room table with cookbooks spread around them. Mary was
leafing through a book of appetizers as she spoke.

"It isn't going to be an actual Christmas party. It's more of a
last chance for a decent departmental get-together before the
final exams start and all the students get so busy they aren't
worth a thing before they go home for Christmas break. But
Art and I like to dress it up and make it look festive. Some of
the students are so broke it's the last good meal they'll have
before they start living on coffee and all night study sessions."

"Do you like very much to give parties?" Hildegard asked.

"Well, I must admit it's getting harder with three kids, and
the baby up half the night. But it's important to Art to make a
good impression. We are inviting some influential faculty members—men who will have a say in making Art a full professor.
It's his dream to make department head before he's forty. And,
of course, we'll have all the usual graduate students. You've met
most of them." She showed a recipe page to Hildegard. "What
do you think about these canapés? Cream cheese and shrimp.
But where on earth would we get shrimp in Wisconsin in the
winter?"

Hildegard thought a moment, and then brightened. "I have
from my mother a very good thing of this kind. It costs little,
and looks pretty. Many vegetables, cooked tender and cut small
into pieces. With mayonnaise and spices stir all together into a
salad. We must cook special bread in a tin can so it is round,
and put the salad on very thin slices of this bread. Then make
curls of cheese and ham in designs like flowers. On the top.
So?" She made little motions with her fingers.*

"Sounds like a lot of work, but if you're willing, by all means
go to it!"

Hildegard didn't like to ask outright, but wondered if Harris Newell would be among the guests. He had gone out of his
way to make her feel comfortable when they met, speaking to
her pleasantly and without strain. She still thought of him often

* See appendix for recipie

with both longing and guilt. But she had determined to give herself the test of time.

The evening of the party arrived. Pine boughs tied together with red ribbons decked the mantle and sent a festive aroma throughout the house. The buffet table was set and the food placed on covered trays or in the oven to stay warm. Mary had asked Hildegard to put the baby to bed so she could dress for the party. Hildegard sat in a rocker in the children's room, holding the infant in her arms and singing softly. The older children were already in their pajamas downstairs with Art. He would bring them up to bed after the baby was well asleep. With the door closed, the muted bustle below seemed a world away. The doorbell rang, but it was too early to be guests.

"Naomi," Hildegard murmured to the little thing in her arms. "Such a pretty name for such a pretty baby. And so soft." She stroked a rounded cheek while the child regarded her with drooping eyes. "Is there anything as beautiful and pure as you, Naomi? Do you still remember heaven? How lucky your mama is to have you, so soft and warm." The girl bowed her head to press a kiss onto the soft fluff of hair, and inhaled the lovely, milky smell. For a moment she pretended that this baby was her own, and snuggled it closer. How sweet and precious to have something so beautiful who needed you and depended on you. She smiled and closed her own eyes in a little surge of joy, and hummed a lullaby her Oma had sung to her.

Below, she thought she heard men's voices, and wondered if the guests were arriving. Rising, she placed the sleeping bundle into its deep oval basket, and left the room to go downstairs. The previous noise of children running about and chattering had hushed, and a man's quiet voice spoke something she couldn't hear. Arthur appeared on the stairway below her and shrugged as he came up.

"An early guest. I put him to work. I'll get my jacket, and Mary and I will be down in a minute."

As Hildegard entered the living room, her heart quickened.

On the couch sat Harris, both children seated on his lap. He had his arms around them, and was reading from a large picture book. He glanced up and flashed a brief smile, but didn't stop reading. She sat down to listen.

"The four little bunnies ran across the garden and popped through the hole in the fence. Behind them they could hear the farmer shouting, 'Stop! Stop! You can't eat my carrots!' The first little bunny was puffing and panting as she said, 'We had better hurry home before Mama finds out we're gone.'"

Hildegard smiled as she heard Harris read. His voice boomed deeply as he spoke the farmer's lines. It squeaked as he imitated the bunnies. It popped and squawked as he imitated rocks hitting a fence or rusty hinges. His tones and facial expressions mirrored fear, outrage, surprise and merriment with all the conviction of a good actor. The children were enthralled, and Hildegard laughed in quiet delight at the scenario. Apparently Harris was more involved with the children than he was concerned about her presence. She liked that. He would make a good father.

She cocked her head and regarded him. Odd, wasn't it, how some people kept getting better looking the longer you knew them, and others whom you had thought at first were quite handsome came to look routine? The lamp beside the couch shone on Harris's brown hair, picking out golden-red highlights above a clear, intelligent forehead. His lashes as he looked down at the book were as thick as her own. She liked the changeable green of his eyes and the quick smile that lighted up a room. His voice was beautiful and resonant. Most of all she liked his interest in all things and his enthusiasm for life. Yes, he was a very attractive man.

Mary entered the room as Harris finished the story.

"All right, children, time for bed. No, No! No more stories; and whining will do you no good. Hildegard will take you up to bed now, and don't you dare wake the baby! Harris, thank you so much for reading to them. You ought to be on the radio."

The doorbell halted any further conversation, and Hildegard smiled shyly at Harris as she shepherded the children up the stairs.

As the dinner got underway, everyone served themselves informally and then sat on chairs or around cardtables in various parts of the room. Hildegard had come back down to help serve the guests. By the time she finally filled her own plate, the only vacant chair was in a cramped corner beside Harris at one of the cardtables. Harris merely smiled at her and moved his chair slightly to give her more leg room. On his other side sat Sally Bach, her German-speaking friend.

"Hildegard!" said Sally. "These little sandwiches are delicious! I've had four already." There were murmurs of agreement from others nearby, and Hildegard felt a glow of satisfaction.

Several conversations were going on at once. Like the rest of her extended family, Hildegard was quick at learning languages. She had studied her English diligently, and listened intently to the radio and to people's conversations. By now she understood most of what she heard, but was not as fluent in speaking. She was quite content with the role of observant listener at this party.

An older professor whom she had met before, one of Arthur's superiors, was holding forth on the discovery of fossilized humanoid bones found in Africa.

"I think it is perfectly obvious that Raymond Dart's discoveries in the last two decades show a clear link between the ape and more recent hominids. Archaeologists have accelerated their digging in the Tanganyika area and will no doubt find numerous other skeletons to bear out the fact that man's earliest evolution came about in Africa. It's certain proof. Proof which cannot be denied."

Beside Hildegard, Harris's voice replied with calm interest. "Don't you think, Dr. Eldridge, that a few bones fall a little short of certain proof? The theory of organic evolution, however brilliantly conceived, is still pretty scantily supported by evidence."

"Nonsense!" the older man replied. "Anyone who has any credibility as a scientist accepts Darwin as fact. It's only a technicality that Darwin's postulates are even called a 'theory' anymore."

There were a few nods of agreement, but one skinny young man with a freckled complexion smiled and nudged his neighbor, murmuring, "Watch Newell in action here."

For her part, Hildegard was astonished and nonplused. How did Harris, a mere graduate student, have the *effrontery* to argue with a professor! This sort of thing was utterly unheard of in Europe. Any professor was an undisputed master, not to be questioned, let alone contradicted! Yet everyone here acted as relaxed as if it were the usual thing. Could one get away with such boldness in America? Revolutionary thought! And what was that skinny boy grinning about?

Harris had a slight but pleasant smile on his face as he replied. "Dr. Eldridge, are you familiar with the laws of thermodynamics?"

Cheerfully the professor replied, "Don't be insulting, Harris. Of course I am."

"Well, do you feel that Darwin's postulates are as unvarying and indisputable as the laws of thermodynamics?"

Hildegard understood most of what he was saying. She had studied both concepts in school, but wondered what connection he was going to make.

The professor replied to Harris, "Well, Darwin's principles aren't indisputable yet. Not enough work has been done. But it *will* be done as time goes on. Science always takes time. Nevertheless, the postulates are accepted as being as good as fact to the entire scientific community."

Harris persisted. "But the laws of thermodynamics—do you accept them as being *thoroughly* proven? That they really *are* laws, and cannot be broken, no matter what?"

The professor folded his arms across his chest. His eyes gleamed as if he were enjoying this challenge from an upstart youth. "Of course," he said.

Most of the others in the room were avidly listening now. The grinning young man said, "I'd watch out for that scheming look in Harris's eyes, Professor."

"Don't worry about me, Murdock," the professor replied. "What do you have in mind, Harris."

"Could you quote the second law of thermodynamics for me?"

"Not exactly. That isn't my field. But it's the law of entropy, that anything that's organized will, over time, degrade, become disorganized, eventually disintegrate."

"Yes," Harris agreed. "Everything degrades. Everything runs down. Everything becomes less and less complex with time in a process that *cannot* be reversed. *Always! Never* failing! If this law is true, then don't you think it astonishing that by some cosmic accident one protein molecule somewhere turned into a simple cell, and that the cell was able to carry on myriad complex functions, including to reproduce itself? Isn't it remarkable that this amazing, fantastic, cosmic accident continued to occur and occur *billions* of times? Wouldn't each and every occurrence break the unbreakable second law of thermodynamics? And yet biological scientists currently support the claim that each accident led to a greater and more complex entity."

Dr. Eldridge showed the beginnings of irritation. "What are you trying to say, Harris? That the law of entropy is false? That there are no real laws in the universe?"

"On the contrary. I say that entropy *is* a real law, and that it proves that accidental organic evolution is utterly impossible, regardless of how many trillions of years we suppose it took, or how fashionable it is for the scientific community to accept Darwin."

"Then how do you propose that all these very orderly differences in the kingdoms and phyla and species came about?"

Harris's smile was still pleasant and non-challenging. "By the activities and plans of a very proficient gardener. An expert biologist. A superb geneticist. The best scientist in the universe. God."

"Oh, *please!*" The professor said with the aggressiveness of having been caught without a good answer. "Some bearded old man in a white nightgown who says, 'Let there be light?'"

"No nightgown. But complete knowledge of the sciences of the universe, yes. Don't you suppose that if there is a God that he is at least as well informed as most of the science professors in today's universities? I think that a being of supreme knowledge who directs the whole show is the only rational way to account for both the orderliness of life, and the laws of thermodynamics."

The professor cast his eyes heavenward, as if exasperated at a child of slow understanding. "Don't tell me we're going to be talking about *religion* now?" He sneered slightly.

Art Hasslem rose to his feet, a cheery smile pasted on his face. Firmly he announced, "No! We aren't! We're going to go to the dining room where my lovely wife has prepared a scrumptious dessert, and we're going to talk about Christmases yet to come." There were several voices of agreement, and a number of people went into the dining room.

Sally Bach, seated on Harris's other side, punched him gently in the arm. "Harris, you scoundrel, how could you start such a thing? Poor Dr. Hasslem was nearly having a heart attack over such a confrontation with his sacrosanct boss."

Harris smiled and replied. "I did it simply from the demands of logic; Eldridge's blind acceptance of illogic is wrong."

"Illogical or not, you were defying a currently sacred cow to a currently powerful man."

"I guess I was."

Sally stood up with a crooked smile. "Well, although I happen to agree with you, Harris, you'll never catch me rocking the boat about it." The girl turned and walked to the dining room.

Harris glanced toward Hildegard, a look of question on his face. "Did I do wrong?" he asked.

She looked at him a moment before replying. "I have not thought before of the things you said. My mind and my heart believe them. I think you did right to rock his boat."

❖ ❖ ❖

Hildegard was delighted when Sally Bach called to ask her if she wanted to join her for Christmas shopping on Saturday.

"Yes, Sally, I would love this! There are gifts I must make in secret for the Hasslems. I did not know how I would get the things I need."

"Good!" Sally replied. We can take a bus and spend the whole day chattering in German. I know that will be easier for you, and prepare me to spend the holidays with my family."

Hildegard answered in German, "Oh, Sally, what a relief that will be. I learn more English all the time, but I get so *tired* of speaking it and listening to it! Sometimes I want to scream. What a joy not to have to think before I speak! What a refreshment to understand precisely what you are saying! How wonderful not to sound like a moron for a whole day!"

The girls walked slowly the entire length of the stores on State Street, and returned up the other side, exclaiming over the decorated and lighted shop windows. Bundled to their chins against the cold, they delighted in the color and excitement of the season. They bought little gifts for their families at Woolworth, and sat at the soda fountain at Walgreens for lunch. All the time they talked and laughed and enjoyed each other.

"I'm so impressed," said Hildegard, "that you're actually going to be a hospital laboratory assistant. That sounds so important! So interesting!"

"Well, it's far from as important as being a doctor, but rather more pleasant, I think, than being a nurse. Besides, I'm more fascinated with tests and experiments and diagnoses than with emptying bedpans and soothing fevered brows. I make my meager living right now doing blood tests on dogs, and really find it interesting."

"Oh, do you work with Harris Newell? I thought you just knew him from church."

Sally gave her a nudge. "Harris Newell, huh? Funny you should bring him up. Now, don't go blushing on me. I know the two of you were seeing each other. I don't know what happened, and you don't have to tell me. But yes, we're working on the same project—dog kidneys. He draws blood and tests it for chemical composition, while I look at the blood under a microscope and count a dozen types of cells. Harris is a good man."

Hilde stammered a little as she asked, "Do you . . . do you like him, Sally?"

"Like him? Sure? He's nice. He's sharp as a tack, too! You saw him tackle Eldridge at the party. But *like* like him, uh-uh. He's all yours. No, Hildegard, I don't want anything to do with men right now. I have a goal to achieve, and nothing is going to stand in my way." There was a thoughtful silence, and Sally continued. "Hildegard, I grew up in a family of thirteen children on a dairy farm where all we did was work and work and then work some more. My father worked and worried about the mortgage and the animals eighteen hours of every day. We children worked from before sunrise until after sunset through the whole year. All my mother ever did was slave over the family and agonize about how we were going to make ends meet. I hardly ever saw her smile. I decided early on that I didn't want that kind of life. Do you know what it's like to be so poor you have *nothing* to eat but brown bread and skim milk?"

Hilde smiled crookedly. "Do you know what it's like to have nothing to eat but ground up corn cobs?"

Sally looked shocked. "No! You didn't!"

"For awhile, yes." In mock humor, Hildegard boasted, "*Our* depression has been worse than *your* depression,"

Sally spoke seriously, "Then Hildegard, you've got even more reason than I have to do *anything* to get away from the kind of dependency that makes you a slave to other people. If you have to depend on others *or* take care of others, you're trapped. Have you ever thought of that? And what about the things that you, alone, have to give to the world? God gave you gifts and talents. Aren't you obligated to use them wisely, generously?"

"I haven't thought of that. Not really. Everything I've done for the last five years has been aimed first at survival, then at getting out of a country drenched in such poverty that people actually died in the streets. Do you know how rich you Americans are?" She shook her head. "Then the struggle of just getting here. And now, as I'm getting used to America, the Hasslems are kind enough to pay me for the help I give them. But, no. I haven't thought about what comes next. I'm still learning to talk, remember? " She smiled.

"Well, *do* think about it, Hildegard. This is a country where you can become anything you have brains to become. And you certainly have brains! It isn't like the old country where one's social and economic level predicts their station in life. Women here have a better chance than anywhere else in the world. Think of freedom, for a change. Think of being in charge of your own life. Think of challenges to your intellect and development of your talents. Think of what you can contribute that nobody else can, Hildegard. Your future can be a banquet for yourself and a boon to the world!"

As the next days passed, Hildegard found herself thinking very hard indeed. It hadn't really occurred to her until she listened to Sally that she not only *had* options in this country, but obligations to take advantage of them. Before, her day-to-day problems of living had taken all her attention. But now she gave thought to her future.

Every woman was supposed to marry, wasn't she? Eventually? But what kind of marriages had Hildegard observed? Her mother and father? What pain they had inflicted on each other! Even Opa, when he was drunk, swore at Oma, and sometimes hit her. Johann and Katarina had never been happy. Aunt Luisa had come to learn of her husband's compulsive gambling. Even dear Uncle Peter had never dared to take the plunge. Well, she knew why *that* was, but could he ever have found happiness with Mama? What married couples did she know who were joyful in their love? Well, she had to admit there were some in the Church who seemed happy. Art and Mary seemed to love each other. But you could never tell from the outside. Maybe Sally was right about choosing another path. Or at least about putting off marriage for awhile.

Hildegard continued to think while she passed diapers through the wringer on the washer. She pondered as she hung them on drying racks in front of every sunny window in the house. She considered while she ironed little dresses and shirts for the children, or stirred pots on the stove.

Housework definitely wasn't a challenge, she thought, pushing damp hair off her forehead as she boiled starch for the shirts. Well, getting it all done was a challenge every day. But how did it enrich the mind or the spirit? What would she do if she had all the options in the world? And the money, of course. Education cost money. What if she could do what she really loved? What *did* she really love? She turned off the burner and with potholders carried the pot to the back porch to cool.

Music. She loved music, and thought longingly of the piano lessons abandoned at age ten. And art. She had shown a natural proficiency that surprised her teachers when a girlfriend at Notre Dame had given her a set of watercolors for her birthday. She loved botany and growing things; that had come from her mother, she supposed.

But what could one do with such talents? Being a professional musician or artist was totally unrealistic, no matter how joyful. Could she teach them? Not at her level of expertise. And she wasn't interested in gardening or farming as a science. No, she would have to be more practical in her dreaming.

That evening after she bathed, she sat in warm pajamas on her window seat, looking out at the moon and considering practical options.

She could sew exceptionally well. Her grandmother had

made a good living creating expensive fashions and running a school of couturier. She imagined the lovely dresses her natural artistry could design, and anticipated the pleasure of praise from the women who would buy them. Grandmother's school had made her wealthy. Hildegard rearranged herself where she sat on the window seat, uncomfortably aware that she was basically shy, and would hate ordering and correcting women older than herself. Maybe she could just do dress design.

She had considered teaching at one time. Perhaps in America she could teach German. That was a stimulating thought, something she might excel at. But she would really rather work with younger children. The very thought of standing in front of a classroom of teenagers or college students brought an attack of stage fright. *My mother could do that*, she thought. *But not I! Mama was never afraid of anything. Why don't I have my mother's fearless drive?*

The following day she was folding laundry as she mused. *Nursing. Now there is an interesting possibility. I don't want to be doctor. I'm not like my mother. I don't want to be in charge of everything. Microscopes and blood counts don't interest me. But I do enjoy taking care of people.* She was holding a little undershirt for the baby, and inhaled the clean scent of freshly washed clothing. She smiled and thought of putting these tiny shirts over the wobbly head, and tucking the flailing arms into the little sleeves. *I like taking care of the baby. Its needs are so real, so important. I feel happy when I'm with the children. That's something I love, too.* She thought of her own childhood, and straightened with a little rush of pride. *And that's something I am better at than my mother ever was, for all her brains and drive!*

For a few minutes Hildegard let her imagination travel undisciplined down that path. *How would it be to have children of my own?* She smiled and imagined sewing little dresses for a daughter. Helping the children plant flower bulbs and watching together as they burst forth in the spring. She envisioned listening with them to Chopin and Liszt instead of the raucous music American radios played. She thought of giving them their own little sets of paint, and encouraging them to try anything they liked on the abundant supply of paper available in America. She thought of the endless questions Mary's children asked. *She* wouldn't put them off, but answer them truly, even if she had to go look up the answers in a book. Or she would send them to their father. Harris seemed to know how to answer every question in the world. No! She mustn't think about Harris! It was her own self she must discover here! She wrenched her thoughts back to considerations of how she might make a worthwhile mark in the world as an independent woman.

What can I do, Father? she prayed that night. *What contribution can I make which will be of worth?*

Suddenly the image of Elder Widtsoe came into her thoughts, just as he had looked when he spoke to her in Vienna. It was with a jolt she heard words in her mind, *"Why are you fighting this battle?"*

The inner voice disrupted her prayers, and troubled her mind. Why *was* she fighting it? Wasn't it a betrayal of her talents and intelligence *not* to seek a career, even for just a little while? But what was wrong with wanting to be a mother? Why was she fighting her feelings for Harris? Above all, why couldn't she seem to maintain the same desires and feelings for two days in a row? The confusion of her thoughts seeped into her very dreams.

❖ ❖ ❖

Harris went to the school's New Year's Eve dance. It wouldn't be as big as many other dances because so many students went home for the holidays. But those who were in Madison would want to spend the last night of the year having fun with each other. Harris tried to deny that his reason for going was the hope of seeing Hildegard there. He hungered to see her, even though he had sworn to leave her alone until she made some kind of decision for herself about where he would fit into her life.

There were more people at the dance than he had expected. Rather a lot of faculty, he noticed, and looked everywhere to see if the Hasslems had come. Harris danced a few numbers with girls he knew, but spent most of his time on the side, watching the dancers and hoping . . . hoping. Feeling a light touch on his arm, he turned. A man would have had to be blind, deaf, and half dead not to appreciate the sight that met his eyes.

"Wow! Hello, Dixie. Boy, you really look . . . very nice tonight." She wore a dress of fire-engine red, which went surprisingly well with her rich auburn hair. It clung to her figure like a second skin, flaring out below the hips into a swirling skirt. The shoulders were fashionably wide above sheer, puffed sleeves. A small corsage of holly drew the eye directly down the deep sweetheart neckline to a full and swelling cleavage.

"Why, Harris, you sweet thing, you."

That's as far as she got before she was inundated by other men, panting to fill her program. He watched as she dimpled, batted her thick lashes, and allowed her admirers to sign her dance card.

"No, no, *no*," she shook her finger at one. That's mah *waltz*, and Ah have saved it for Harris, because he was the first man to say something nice to me when Ah arrived." Then she turned meekly to Harris with a tremulous smile. "That is, if he *wants* to waltz with me."

"You don't want old Newell," joked her would-be partner. "He dances like a slug. I'm the man for you!" Dixie continued to look up at Harris under her eyelashes.

"Oh! Uh! Wow, Dixie. I can't imagine you'd want to dance with me. But, you bet! I'm flattered!" He signed his name on her little card, and watched while another man led her to the floor for a fox trot. She winked at him over her partner's shoulder as they danced away.

Dixie was immediately forgotten when Harris spotted the Hasslems entering by the opposite door. His heartbeat increased, and he felt both agony and ecstasy as a small figure dressed in soft blue entered with them. He watched her eagerly glance around, as if seeking someone, and quickly look at the floor when her eyes met his. He should have let her alone. He knew he should have. But he was drawn to her like a magnet. Art and Mary glanced nervously at him and at each other, but said nothing.

"Good evening, Art, Mary." Harris shook their hands and turned to Hildegard. More softly he said, "Hello, Hildegard. You look so lovely in that dress," and added in his mind, *and you look so adorable blushing up like that I want to grab you right here and kiss you.* He took a deep breath and steadied himself. "Would you think it unfair of me to ask you for a dance? I won't if you don't want me to."

Art interrupted with a lopsided grin. "Give her a chance, Newell. We just got here. Try again in a while."

Harris looked down at Hildegard, who was twisting her little card with uncertainty. She told him, "I would like to dance with you . . . later on?"

"Then I'll come back after the intermission and sign up, if I may."

She smiled and nodded before her hostess drew her away. He looked after her, drinking in every movement as she progressed across the room, smiling and being greeted by people.

Some time later another fellow punched his arm and reminded him that he was the most fortunate man on campus for ·the next dance. Harris suddenly remembered the waltz and Dixie. It wasn't hard to find her in her bright dress, and to be nearby when her current dance ended.

The music was dreamy when he took Dixie into his arms. He wondered bitterly who would hold his own little girl for this dance, and glanced around. He couldn't see the blue dress he sought. Very soon his attention was brought back by the soft, whispered drawl of his own partner.

"Why Harris! I do declare! You are *too* a wonderful dancer! How could that silly Bob have called you a slug?" She moved closer in his arms, pressing her soft, scented curves against him and letting her fingers make curlicue motions on the back of his neck. He gulped hard. As the dance progressed, Dixie seemed determined to melt into his body. He tried to lead her into other steps which would separate them, but each time she returned it was to bind herself to him more closely. It was not easy to ignore such a luscious morsel of womankind in his arms. Oh, if only if it had been the girl of his dreams, instead! Momentarily he closed his eyes and let his cheek rest against that of the woman he held, thinking of the woman he wished he held. Opening his eyes, he saw before him, not half a dozen feet away, the very girl in blue of whom he dreamed. Her eyes were wide with shock and hurt.

Harris started and jerked himself upright, realizing what Hildegard had seen and what she must have believed. He tried to release Dixie from the intimate hold, but she wouldn't let go. He watched helplessly as Hildegard turned and rushed for the door.

❖ ❖ ❖

Hildegard ran down the hall outside the ballroom, looking for a deserted corner in which to hide. Her eyes blurred with tears and a wrenching ache gripped the region of her heart. How could she deny the rapture on Harris's face as he embraced that . . . that over-painted hussy in the skin-tight dress! She had really believed him when he said he loved her! He had been so convincing, looked so devastated when she had broken their one-day engagement. He seemed to gaze so longingly at her each Sunday in church.

I'm such a fool! she cried in her heart. *And that girl is so . . . Oh! She's so beautiful! How could he ever look at a scrawny shrimp like me? Ooooh.*

Under a staircase in a dimly lighted, empty hallway, Hildegard found a hiding place. Groping in her tiny evening purse for a handkerchief, she gave way to tears of hurt. And anger! *I'd like to tear her hair out! Who does she think she is? Harris is mine! Mine!* Her tears flowed afresh. *At least he* was *mine, until I sent him away. Ooooh! I wish I were dead!*

For the next ten minutes her heart broke as she dwelt on all the lovely times she and Harris had shared. *How could I believe he would still love me when I've totally ignored him? And why should he spend a moment thinking of me when there are girls like that all around? Harris is brilliant, and . . . and handsome! Of course other girls will be after him!*

She sniffed as her pride rallied. *Well, if* she's *the kind of girl he's interested in, I'm lucky to find out now! What kind of love could be as true as he said* his *was, if it couldn't endure for a month? Oh, what shall I do? Oh, Harris, how could you? You said you loved* me! *Oh, Harris . . . Oh, Harris, I don't want anybody else!*

Through her misery and tears, Hildegard became aware of a great deal of muffled noise going on at a distance. Horns were honking, firecrackers popping, and people cheering. "Oh, my," she gasped, "how long have I been here? It must be midnight!" Her aching heart didn't care. "Some new year. Some new life for me."

She took a deep breath, knowing she would have to go back to the ballroom; Mary would be worried about her. Her handkerchief was sodden, and she knew her face must be swollen with weeping. Stopping at a drinking fountain, she rinsed and wrung out her handkerchief, and pressed the cool fabric against her face. Her lipstick was probably smeared, and she hoped it wouldn't be terribly noticeable.

In a few minutes she felt composed enough to seek her hosts, and found them worried, as she had expected. Pleading a headache, which was entirely true, she asked if she might go home.

❖ ❖ ❖

The instant the waltz ended, Harris rushed into the hallway where Hildegard had disappeared. Frantically he went from one end to another, searching every corner, sick with grief and guilt.

What must she have thought! Oh, the weakness of the flesh, that he had given in to it for a moment! But *she* was the one he had been thinking of! How would he ever make her believe that?

He had to find her. They had to work something out; he could not go on like this. His work was suffering. His grades were suffering. He couldn't concentrate on anything, and he didn't even want to eat. "Oh please, Lord" he prayed in a whisper. "Please let us work this out. I love her so much. Please make her believe that."

After ten minutes of futile searching, Harris returned to the ballroom. He walked around its circumference, stomach churning, eyes darting everywhere, looking for the blue dress. He saw the Hasslems, but they were alone, and he avoided them. It was no use. He may as well go home. But tomorrow! Tomorrow he was determined to find her and talk to her, even if she didn't want to talk. He would *make* her see the truth!

Harris rose after a nearly sleepless night. Surely the Hasslem's would be up by nine or ten o'clock. After all, they had little children. He would go there. Insist that Hildegard talk to him.

Mary answered the door and looked troubled when she saw who the caller was. "Hello, Harris. I suppose you want to see Hildegard. I don't know what happened last night, but she was awfully upset."

"Mary, please, will you let me talk to her alone for a few minutes?"

"I suppose I'd better. Art's still asleep. Why don't you go into his study. I'll ask her to join you there."

Harris sat down, stood up, and paced the floor. He sat down again, picked up a magazine and threw it back down, then stood to read the book titles on Art's shelves. About five minutes later he heard the door close gently behind him. He turned quickly to see Hildegard standing quietly, looking at her twisting, clasped hands.

"Hildegard!" he stepped toward her, but she backed away a little. His heart yearned for her. He spoke more softly. "Hildegard, please sit down and let me talk to you." They sat at opposite ends of the long sofa. "Please, won't you look at me?"

Her eyes flickered up for a moment, and a slow blush rose on her cheeks.

"Oh, Hildegard. What must you think of me? Will you ever believe me now? I want you to believe me. I'm telling you the truth. I love you. I've loved you every minute since we met, and I have not changed my mind for a second."

Her eyes met his, accusingly, but she did not speak.

"I know what you saw last night, but it wasn't what it looked like. The girl I was dancing with was Dixie Houston, Dr. Janowski's secretary. I've known her for the last two years, but she has never paid the slightest attention to me before. This must sound arrogant, but actually, *she* informed *me* that I was to have the waltz with her. I don't know why. She's pursued by dozens of other men. And I would much rather have had that waltz with you."

Hildegard was looking at her hands again, and Harris breathed a deep sigh of despair. "Hildegard, it was *you* I was thinking about at the moment you saw us. It was *you* I was wishing for. This is the truth, before God, and I do not say such things lightly. I ask you to believe me. I plead for you to believe me."

She looked up at him with a softened expression, as if, for a moment, she wanted to believe.

"Oh, Hildegard, I wish I could do something to make you understand what you mean to me! I've tried to be patient, give you time to figure out what you really feel, but it's tearing me apart! I can't eat. I can't sleep. I can't work." He moved closer to her and extended a hand until it almost touched her. "I love you. I love you more than anything in the world." He gently took her hand in his. She let it lie limply in his for a moment before softly withdrawing it. "Please tell me what you are thinking. What you feel. I have to know, or I'll go crazy."

Her voice was a whisper. "I don't know what to say. I don't know what I feel. When I saw . . . " her voice choked, and tears filled her eyes. He longed to take her in his arms, and reached toward her. Quickly she rose to her feet. "Harris, I believe you are a truthful man. But I need to think of this more." Before he could take another breath, she had slipped out the door.

As she left Arthur's study and hurried up the stairway to her own room, Hildegard's heart was pounding. But it was lighter than it had been. He loved her still! He said so with such fervor! But did he really? She had meant what she said to him about believing him to be truthful, but could she be sure? She thought of how much she loved her own father, a man whom in every other way had been entirely honorable. But he had not been a faithful husband. In a small way, during the past agonizing night, she had begun to understand the torment her mother must have felt for all the years of her marriage. Hildegard quailed. Could a woman ever trust a man? And if she did not, was life really that much worth living? She fell to her knees beside the bed and whispered out a prayer. But she hardly knew what to pray for. "Thy will be done," she repeated and repeated. "Oh, let me know what I should do."

For the next two weeks she was miserably empty. Painfully lonely. She didn't care if the young men who called her were handsome. They weren't the right *kind* of handsome. Her smiles were forced when she responded to their wittiness and compliments; she ached for a clear, enthusiastic explanation of verb tenses or kidney functions. She went on two dates, and they were fine; but right afterward she went home to bed. What was there to stay up for?

She didn't notice, on several evenings as she drooped beside the fireplace, that Mary and Arthur regarded her with worried expressions and shaking heads.

This is stupid. Hopeless, she thought. *All I'm doing is mooning around and feeling miserable. And for what? So I won't disappoint Mary and Art? So I can say I truly gave myself a full chance? All right. I've seen what it's like to live without Harris, and I don't like it. Why am I going on like this?*

With a little feeling of determination beginning to grow so far down in her heart she was barely aware of it, she rose to her feet. She went to the closet in the front hall. She put on her warm coat, wrapped a soft, woolly scarf around her head, and tossed the ends over her shoulders.

"Hildegard? " Mary asked. "Are you going out? It's almost ten o'clock, and it's freezing outside."

"I must take a little walk, Mary. I want to think. Go on to bed; I will be all right. I won't be long."

Instead of arguing, Mary nodded, a look of concern on her face.

Hildegard put her hands into her pockets and strolled in the general direction of the campus. Her feet seemed automatically directed toward that section where the object of her thoughts would probably be working right now. She remembered that he usually stayed there studying until midnight. It wasn't as if she actually intended to visit him. But it seemed natural to walk in that direction.

❖ ❖ ❖

Harris had fed the dogs an hour ago, and sat at his desk in the lab, trying to read the words in his textbook. He never got very far with his studies. Brown eyes floated in the air above his book, and made his own blur. A partly eaten sandwich languished and dried out on its waxed paper nest beneath the lamp. He had failed a test. He had actually failed a test for the first time in his life, because he couldn't study. He couldn't find it within himself to care.

Venus whined at him, as if speaking. He rose and ambled to her cage. She stood over her empty water bowl, looking at him with pleading eyes. He glanced quickly at the other cages.

"Oh my gosh! I forgot to water you! Sorry, guys. I'll get it now. He walked into the adjoining stock room where the supplies were kept, and lowered a tin bucket into the deep lab sink at the back end. Adjusting the faucet to cold, he waited while the bucket filled. The stock room was long and narrow, with just enough space for one person to walk between banks of cabinets and shelves on each wall. Lifting the full bucket, he returned to the main room, only to realize he had forgotten to turn off the tap in the stock room.

"Honestly!" he said with a half laugh, putting the bucket on the floor. "I've got to snap out of this before they commit me." He walked back into the stock room, and shut off the tap. Turning around, he was startled to see someone blocking the doorway of the small room.

"Dixie! For goodness sakes, what are you doing here?" He stepped forward, expecting her to go back into the large room, but instead she came slowly toward him. She had removed her coat, and was wearing a thin, silky dress which seemed incongruous for the cold Wisconsin winter, but which was obviously very attractive on her. As always, it clung to her body in an alluring way.

"Good evenin', Harris. Ah had some reports that needed to be dropped off at Dr. Martin's office for him to read first thing in the mornin'. Ah saw your light, and thought Ah'd stop in for a little chat. It's a cold, lonely evenin' and Ah thought we both might enjoy some company." She had continued to undulate toward him, and ended her sentence by touching the top button of his shirt with a long, manicured finger.

Harris stepped backward nervously, and Dixie advanced another step. "Aren't you a bit lonely up here all night, with nothin' but these little old dawgs to keep you company?" Her dimpled smile was warm, and she stepped yet closer. He backed up again.

"Uh . . . ah . . . , actually, I get quite a bit of studying done with no distractions at this time of night. B-but if you want to talk a little, I have a couple of chairs by my desk." He gestured beyond her. "There's more room . . ." Harris felt distinctly nervous as he backed into the wall. Dixie was near enough that he could smell her perfume.

"As a matter of fact," she drawled, tracing her fingertips over the chest of his lab coat, "Ah feel that sometimes a cozier space makes for better communication."

Harris thought he heard a footstep in the outer lab, and hoped Dixie might back off. But apparently her mind was elsewhere.

"Dixie, um . . . I think we should go out and sit down, or something." He nodded in the direction of the door behind her.

"You know, Harris, I never realized until you held me in your arms the other evenin' how very attractive you are. You *are* very attractive, you know." She gazed up at him through thick eyelashes, and dimpled a little smile.

"Ah . . . Oh, no. I-I'm really not. Really, Dixie. I'm nobody. You're very kind, but there's already a girl I'm . . ." he got no farther. She placed one fingertip over his lips, and laid the other hand on his chest.

"Now, Harris, y'all know it isn't polite to talk of other ladies when you're with one who obviously finds you very interestin'."

"Dixie, really!"

"Hush now," she sighed. "Just relax. You know, y'all keep it awful hot in here. Why don't you just take off that ol' lab coat, and we can both be more comfortable." She pulled the coat's lapels apart, and he clutched them together again tightly, frantically. Was that a scraping sound out in the lab?

"Dixie, no, please. Dixie, I think someone might be coming in."

"You silly thing. Nobody *ever* comes here at night. Oh, yes, it is *definitely* hot in here. My *goodness!*" Moving almost against him, she fluttered her eyelashes and breathed seductively. "So hot. And Ah believe it might get hotter yet." Her hands lowered to the front of her bodice and unfastened the top button. "Oh, yes. So hot . . ."

Suddenly a mass of water deluged both Dixie and Harris.

Harris gasped in shock and Dixie screamed. A chilly, accented voice came from the doorway.

"That should cool you both off quite well!"

Wiping water from his eyes, Harris saw the girl he loved standing a few feet away with an empty bucket, a look of fury on her face.

"Hildegard!" Harris cried.

"How dare you!" Dixie screamed at the same moment.

"Hildegard, wait! Don't go!" Harris tried to scramble past the sodden Dixie, who had taken the brunt of the soaking. The lab dogs were barking wildly. He saw the girl he loved turn away and rush from the lab.

"My hair! My dress!" Dixie cried. "Look what she did! Harris, stop pushing me! Ohhhhh!" Her scream rose as Harris squeezed past her and ran through the lab, determined that this time Hildegard would not get away.

Down the stairs he raced after her, and out into the icy January night. She was hurrying ahead, but his long legs caught up quickly. He grasped her arm and swung her around. "No! You will not run away this time! You will stay here and listen to me. I don't know what devil of fate always brings you to me when Dixie is around, but I did *not* invite her to come, and I did *not* make one single advance to her. Hildegard are you listening?" Harris, with damp clothes and no coat, was beginning to shake with the cold. "Please, please, darling girl! Please believe me! Oh! What can I do to make you believe me? I know how it must look! Oh, Hildegard, I love you! Why is this always happening to us? Hildegard . . . ? Hildegard, are you crying? Oh, darling, I'm so sorry." He took her unresisting form into his shivering arms.

"Don't cry. Please don't cry," he begged through chattering teeth. "Look at me, please." He lifted her chin, and was amazed to see not tears, but a face struggling to suppress laughter. His brow puckered in confused astonishment.

Her laughter burst forth. "Oh, Harris! I *know*! I heard what you both said. But I am so bad. I could not stop myself." She shrugged within his arms "The water was right there." Then she frowned at his chattering teeth. "Harris, you're freezing! We must get back into the building."

As they turned toward the doors, Dixie came raging out, her coat on, wet hair straggling onto her forehead. "You two! Ah hate you both! Ah never wanna see either o' you again!" She stalked off into the night.

Hildegard led Harris back inside. There she took off her warm coat and pulled the inadequate thing around his wide, wet shoulders. "There now. Come upstairs. Are there any towels in your dog room?"

Harris was still shivering and looking confused. "You believe me?"

"Of course I believe you." She smiled fondly and then lowered her chin shyly. "Harris, will we please be engaged again?"

Shaking as much with joy as with cold, Harris put his arms around her, and spoke fervently into her hair, "Oh, yes! Yes! If you'll have me."

Hildegard pulled his face down to hers and kissed him with a thoroughness that left no room for doubt.

❖ ❖ ❖

Mary Hasslem smiled at the girl busily writing at the dining room table. "Hildegard, you're a changed woman. You've been glowing like a light bulb for weeks, and you bounce around like a chirpy little bird. I suppose we were wrong to doubt you , but I'm not sorry you tested your feelings. Do you want me to help you address announcements this afternoon?"

"No, thank you, Mary. There are not so many left. And those that must go to Europe, I must do myself. They wouldn't recognize your round American writing." She returned the smile.

Mary glanced out the window at a sound on the porch. "Oh, here's Harris, anyway. I'm sure you don't want me around now. Come on in, Harris. Don't bother knocking anymore, you practically live here. I'll go change a baby or something." She went upstairs.

Harris had a look of eagerness about him. He could never hide his moods or thoughts for a moment.

"What's up?" Hilde asked, using his own phrase.

"Oh, nothing. Just an idea. Say, tell me the name of your mother's friend again. The one who won all that money."

"Aunt Steffie? She's Steffanie Greben."

"Are you sending her an announcement? Do you have her address?"

"Yes, right here in my little book. Why?"

"Just a thought. Nothing important at the moment. But here's something that *is* important at the moment." He lifted her from her chair and kissed her long and lingeringly. It was good that he held her so close; she would have found it difficult to remain standing when her knees felt like water.

A child's voice rang out from the stairway. "Hey, Mommy, they're kissing again!"

Harris laughed and let her go. "My mother said she sent you a letter. Did you get it?"

"Oh, Harris, yes! She is such a kind woman! She welcomes me so completely. Look. Read it. She has beautiful plans for the wedding and afterwards. And your sister, Eleanor, has said she would help me make my wedding dress when we get to Provo. I'm so excited! Oh, Harris, I've never had a *real* family before. Not since I was a tiny girl. And never a big one like this! Look. Your little sister Joyce drew me a picture of a bride in a wedding dress. It's awfully good! She really is an artist. I can't imagine this. All of your big family so loving! They're like you. I will love them, I know."

"They already love you. My father took one look at your photo and said I was obviously marrying above myself."

The weeks in Madison rushed by. Harris was planning some surprise, but wouldn't give Hildegard a hint.

❖ ❖ ❖

Utah, 1939

*W*hen the spring term ended in April, Harris and Hildegard drove the 700 miles to Utah with a friend. From Ogden they took an electrified train into Salt Lake City, leaving at midnight. They were almost the only passengers on the last leg of the trip heading south to Provo.

Harris's whole family turned out of bed at 2:00 A.M. to greet the new bride-to-be. The young ones cheered and capered around the room, the teenagers asked a hundred questions, Harris's mother enveloped Hildegard in a warm hug, and his father shouted vainly for a little less noise.

Overwhelmed, Hildegard shrank back against Harris's chest.

"They adore you," Harris murmured into her ear. "Don't worry, you'll get to like all this chaos."

June 21st was a gorgeous day. The sky was intensely blue behind the granite spires of the LDS temple in Salt Lake City. Hildegard and Harris looked up at the magnificent long windows and tall, carved doors.

"There, behind that window," he pointed. "Only a few more hours, and then eternity." He smiled and pulled her close.

Hildegard was very frightened. Oh, she loved this man beside her! Loved him more every day! But eternity? That was a very long time! She thought of her mother and father, and their bitter, angry years. She thought of Aunt Steffie, abandoned by a rich, famous husband in favor of her own sister; of Johann, tricked and trapped into a loveless marriage. She knew of Opa's drinking and abuse in earlier days. How did anybody ever *dare* to get married!

I can back out at any time, she told herself. *Harris said that I didn't need to go through with it if I ever didn't want to. Oh, I think I'd like to run away right now!* She paused and envisioned herself darting out of the beautiful garden, through the gasping guests and the high gates—*but only if Harris would run away with me.*

The image made her laugh aloud, and Harris looked down at her, questioning. She stood on her toes and gave him a sound kiss.

Later, across a pale green, velvet altar, Hildegard and Harris knelt with joined hands. Ornate mirrors covered opposing walls, sending their reflections into an infinite distance, symbolizing eternity. Rococo carvings in gilt and beautiful colors decked the walls and ceiling of the marriage room. Both were dressed in white, the color of purity, the color of truth. Morning sunlight flooded in, bathing the room with light. Surrounding them here in this holy place sat smiling people who loved them. The officiator asked them for vows of faithfulness to each other and to God, and promised them the blessings of heaven, for time and for all eternity. Gently Harris leaned toward Hildegard across the altar. She turned her glowing face up to his and received the kiss of a husband for his wife.

❖ ❖ ❖

London and Madison, July 1939

Rosa sighed and put the letter back into its envelope. Hilde and Harris were married and happy. So happy. She smiled sadly, as glad for her daughter as she was discontent with her own tedious and uninspiring life. After the cruel disappointment of the shop, nothing seemed worth doing anymore. But one had to live. She supposed she might go back to Austria if the economy were actually better now. Peter had written that everyone's finances were improving with the massive buildup of the military. But he had made another good point as well: it was safer to stay with the devil you knew for awhile than to leap toward the devil you didn't know. At least in England she had good food and comfortable shelter, a modicum of entertainment, and a few friends. She ought to be content. Instead, she was suffocated by boredom.

❖ ❖ ❖

In August, back in Madison, Hildegard walked from one end of their little attic apartment to the other, her eyes carefully envisioning what she could make of it. The whole thing was actually one big room divided by a partition. There was a little kitchenette built into one wall, and a half bath. They had to go downstairs to take a shower, but that was acceptable, considering the price.

Harris was at school. He said there was something important he had to check on right away. So Hildegard was free of the typical masculine impatience with decorating to decide for herself what she wanted to do to make this bare little place a pleasant nest for them. It couldn't be much. She could dye sheets for a bedspread and curtains, and embroider them richly as she had learned to do at Notre Dame. Maybe even a wide band of crocheted lace on the hems. If she pulled the furniture this way or that it might make the areas look bigger.

She was thus happily engaged when Harris burst through the door, glowing and grinning with excitement, holding a manila envelope toward her as if offering a plate of pure gold.

"We did it! We did it! They accepted it! I never dared to hope! Oh, Hildegard, wait until you see!"

He pulled her to the couch and explained. Confused at first, her eyes widened as she began to understand.

"Harris! *That's* why you wanted Aunt Steffie's address! And you've been writing to her all these months? Oh, that dear woman! Could anyone have a better friend? And all the *work* you've done!"

He showed her documents, letters, and forms, with the excitement of a child at Christmas.

Hildegard's eyes were moist when he finished. "Oh, Harris. Oh, Harris. You did all this! Was there ever such a man!"

He arranged the papers in order. "Now the only thing that has to be done is for you to write to your mother and explain everything. It needs to come from you. She might not believe it from anyone else."

"Yes, of course I will. But I can still hardly believe it myself! You did all this for a woman you've never met?"

He took her face in his hands and gazed at her worshipfully. "I did it for *you*, Hildegard. I did it to make *you* happy. Because I love you more than anything in the world."

Hildegard spent the next hour expressing her gratitude, endeavoring to convince him that she loved *him* more than anything in the world, too.

❖ ❖ ❖

Rosa's hands shook as she read the letter from Hildegard a second time; a third time. She rose unsteadily to her feet and paced across her room and back again, unable to comprehend or speak. She was panting, and swallowed to moisten her dry throat. She stopped and looked into the distance, imagining. *What if. . . .* Then shook her head and paced again.

"Can this be? How *could* this be?" She looked at the letter in her hands, but could not read the words for the tumbling confusion of her thoughts. "They never even said a word to me! They never asked! Why should they think . . ." She flopped into a chair. "This is ridiculous! I'm too old!" But she leaped up immediately, and paced again. "This must be a joke! A cruel joke!" Then she looked down again to read the words,

"Mama, I know you might think for a moment that this is a joke.
Please believe me, we would never joke about a thing like this."

Rosa began to laugh wildly, a note of hysteria in her voice. There was a timid knock on the door. "Come in," Rosa called impatiently.

It was Tilly, one of the upstairs maids. "Mum, I've come about the bedding for the blue room, like you asked . . . " she saw the agitation on Rosa's face and dwindled into silence.

"Never mind that now, Tilly. Go dust the furniture or something. I'll talk to you about it later."

The maid withdrew quickly, closing the door behind. Rosa locked it.

She straightened herself. Calmed herself. Became analytical and cool. Her hands still trembled, and she laid the letter carefully on her desk.

"All right then," she challenged herself. "Why should I *not* do this?"

"Well first of all," she answered herself aloud," this is only a letter inviting me to *apply* to medical school in America. That is not at all the same thing as full *acceptance* to that school." She paced around the room thinking hard before she answered herself.

"Perhaps not," replied her first voice. "But it was an *invitation* to apply. It says the staff are *impressed* by the records Steffie sent from the Medical School in Vienna showing all my classes and grades. *Impressed* with the letters of recommendation from my professors. That means they have actually *considered* me. They haven't just sent a bunch of forms. They wouldn't have said what they did without giving it consideration."

"Well, then, what about this?" countered the doubting voice. "They don't know you from Adam. Why should they give *you* any preference? There are who-knows-how-many other people, *younger* people, applying for entrance as well. Why should they choose *you?*"

The reply from the first voice was quick. "Well, they aren't idiots, after all! Surely someone who has fifteen years of training is a good bet. A better bet than a newcomer still wet behind the ears! Besides, Hilde says right here that Harris knows most of the faculty, and works with them, and they respect him. *He,* at least, is no stranger. And just *wait* until they meet *me!*"

She took another turn around the room, her eyes beginning to gleam, her heart beating fast.

Slyly the discouraging voice persisted, "Very well, think about this! You are thirty-nine years old. Medical school and internships in America will take you another ten years of your life. Why, you would be nearly fifty when you finally got into practice!"

Rosa's lips thinned. Fifty years old. An old woman. Her shoulders slumped, and she stared out the window. But slowly a smug smile grew to spread across her face. She straightened and spoke boldly, silencing the discouraging voice.

"Fifty years old, eh? When I finish my schooling in ten years I'll be fifty years old! Well, how old do you think I'll be in ten years if I *don't* go to medical school?"

Tilly was still in the upper hall when Mrs. Edler burst from her door and ran down the staircase, holding a sheaf of papers and laughing in an alarming way. Leaning over the banister, the maid watched the previously dignified housekeeper open the front door and rush onto the driveway shouting, "Yes! Yes! I'll come!" at the top of her lungs.

❖ ❖ ❖

Saturday morning Harris let Hildegard sleep while he went over to the lab and fed the dogs. When he returned, his wife still lay curled on her side with her long eyelashes resting against her cheeks. Looking down at her, Harris's heart was filled with tenderness and awe. He crawled back into bed and woke her slowly, lovingly. They lay close, her head cradled on his shoulder, his arms around her.

"Oh, Harris, what will it be like for us?"

"Happy," he replied, and kissed her. "Busy! Lots of kids!"

"*Lots?*" she asked timidly. "Harris, I'm just beginning to learn the first things about children,"

"Your heart is so kind, you won't have any problem. You'll love them all."

She chuckled, "Easy for you, growing up with eight others, and four dozen cousins around." She sighed. "I never had anybody. Sometimes I'm excited and sometimes so afraid."

"I'll help you. I know how to feed babies and change diapers, and cook meals, and do laundry. I'm great with a dishpan!"

Hildegard laughed out loud. "I can't believe you! I can't believe your family! I can't believe America! A proper Austrian male would die before he'd lower himself to do any of those things."

"Well, I *can* let you do them all yourself, if you insist."

"Don't even think such a thing!" she declared, burrowing a finger between his ribs until he yelped and jumped away. "If you're going to give me *lots* of babies, you can just stay around and help with them."

They cuddled back together, gazing into space, imagining the future together. Smiling dreamily, the two lovers eventually drifted into sleep.

The angels who had watched over them both for so many years could hardly wait to be born.

❖ ❖ ❖ ❖ ❖ ❖ ❖ ❖ ❖ ❖ ❖

Recipie Appendix

Wienerschnitzel
(Say: Vee'-ner sh-nit-sel)

This scrumptious Austrian national dish has *nothing* to do with hot dogs. It simply means "schnitzel which is made in the style of the people of Vienna," or "Wien," as they spell it. It is a thin, boneless cutlet of meat which is seasoned, breaded, and fried crisp with a bubbled crust. Wealthy people and many restaurants use veal. But the common people use pork or chicken, which costs less and has a much better flavor.

Usually, a half-inch thick cutlet is beaten with a meat mallet until it is about 1/4" thick. However, modern butcher equipment allows meat to be cut to that thickness to begin with, and saves the beating. The recipe below has been adapted for American cooking habits.

Ingredients:

Slices of pork loin, about 4 slices per person, cut or beaten to a quarter or third inch thick, fat removed from outer edges.

Flour, 1 cup, well mixed with the following, and placed in a pie plate:
Salt, 1 1/2 Tbs.
Pepper, ground black, 2 tsp.
Sage, ground, 1 tsp.
Onion Powder, 1 tsp. (not onion salt)

Then blend together and pour into a pie plate:
Eggs, 4, beaten with:
Milk, 3 Tbs.

Breadcrumbs, 2 cups of "Italian seasoned" in pie plate

Cooking oil, 1" deep in large frying pan (electric frying pan best)

1. Dredge each fillet thoroughly first in the flour, then egg, then breadcrumbs. Lay the breaded pieces on paper towels.

2. Heat oil to 300°. Temperature may vary with different frying pan controls. (I put my electric fry pan on the patio to keep heat and odors outside.)

3. At 10 minutes to eating time, lay schnitzel close together in hot oil. Cook on both sides until light golden brown with a bubbled crust. Watch the first piece to see how long this takes. It should take about a minute on each side. Raise or lower temperature of oil as needed. When browned, drain on paper towels. Serve immediately. Leftovers are tasty cold.

❖ ❖ ❖

Springerli Cookies
(Say: spring'-er-li)

These traditional Christmas cookies are prized for their sculpted prettiness, and taste delicious. They require a special, deeply carved rolling pin or cookie mold which can usually be found at cooking specialty stores. Or they can be made plain, like sugar cookies. Also, have on hand a clean, dry toothbrush and a clean, dry, soft brush such as is used for blusher (save one from your used-up cosmetics; wash it clean and dry completely). The mixing and rolling takes less than an hour, but the cookies must dry for 7 or 8 hours before baking, to set the pattern.

Ingredients: Thoroughly mix:
> **Powdered Sugar**, 2 3/4 cups (plus extra for rolling out)
> **Flour**, 4 cups, sifted or tossed
> **Lemon rind**, grated fine, from one lemon
> **Salt** 1/2 tsp.
> **Baking powder** 1 tsp.

Then beat in thoroughly:
> **Eggs**, 4 large

1. When ingredients are well blended but crumbly, turn out onto a clean, dry countertop and knead 1 minute to form a firm, slightly moist ball. Clean and dry countertop again.

2. Sprinkle countertop liberally with powdered sugar from a sifter. Place dough ball on top and pat and mold it into a large square, as thick as a finger. Dust the top of the dough with powdered sugar and rub it around to form a thin, even coating.

3. Prepare Springerle rolling pin or mold to prevent the dough from sticking: Press powdered sugar into all indentations and surfaces of mold. With a clean, dry toothbrush, scrub the powdered sugar out of the indentations. This will leave a fine film of sugar over all parts of the mold.

4. Placing the Springerle pin at the near edge, and pressing both hands firmly on top of the cylinder, roll the pin the full length of the dough. The finished cookies should be about 1/2 inch thick.

5. Using a pizza cutter or long, flat-bladed knife, cut completely through the dough between the cookies. Trim off excess dough, and with it repeat the process.

6. Before placing cookies on a baking sheet, use the cosmetic brush to brush away all visible powdered sugar, leaving the pretty design clean and bold. With a metal pancake turner, lift the cookies from the counter and place them 1/2 inch apart on a well greased cookie sheet. Allow cookies to dry 7-8 hours so the pattern sets before baking.

7. Bake in 275° oven for 15 minutes until edges are barely beige. Cool. Remove cookies and store in tight container.

❖ ❖ ❖

Apple Strudel
(Say: Sh-tru'-dl)

Real strudel has a 3-5 inch core of fresh baked apples with raisins, nuts, and cinnamon-sugar, wrapped in a few crispy layers of paper-thin crust. It's simple to make when you see it, but harder to describe in words. Making it is loads of fun for a bunch of people to do together, and even more fun to eat hot with vanilla ice cream.

Crust: (This process is messy, but entertaining.)

On a large clean countertop make a pile of **2 1/2 cups flour** with a large well in the center. Into the well drop:

Salt, 1 tsp.

Egg, 1

Oil, 2 Tbs.

Water, 1/2 cup

With clean bare hands, squish the whole mess together, squeezing, smashing, and kneading until it, amazingly, forms a breadlike dough. (Or use a food processor.)

Continue kneading 5-10 minutes until the dough is satin smooth. Flatten the dough into a hockey puck shape, coat with oil, cover with a bowl, and let it rest in a barely warm oven (90°) for 20-30 minutes.

Lay a cloth sheet over a table, and pin it tightly below. Heavily flour the cloth.

Filling: (Make while dough is resting. Keep ingredients separate for layering.)

Tart apples, about 12, peeled, cored, sliced thin

Cinnamon-sugar = 3/4 cup sugar, 3 Tbs. cinnamon

Raisins, 2 cups

Walnuts or pecans, 1-2 cups

Bread crumbs or cake crumbs, 3 cups, ground coarse, sauted 2-3 minutes in 1/2 cup butter until they begin to brown. (Spice cake crumbs are wonderful!)

Procedure:

1. Place the warm, rested dough on the floured cloth, and roll it to an 18-inch square. Then all participants at once (no jewelry!) may surround the table and lay their hands flat beneath the dough and gently draw and stretch it from the center outward, avoiding holes or tears. Quickly work all the way to the edges. It will expand to about 3 ft. square. When it is nearly transparent, lay it on the cloth and cut off the thicker edges. It may drape over the edge of the table a few inches.

2. In an 8-inch wide strip clear across the center, spread on the buttered crumbs. Over that spread the apples, then the cinnamon sugar, then the raisins, and then the nuts.

3. Unpinning the cloth, use it as a support to lift and fold the bare dough on one end over the strip of apples. Continue to lift the cloth so the strip of apples rolls over and over, wrapping itself in the remainder of the bare dough, forming a long cylinder. Twist and pinch the ends of the roll tight to prevent juices from escaping.

4. On a large greased cookie sheet or pizza pan, and with all hands lifting at once, lay the strudel roll in a U or a C shape. Compress the center curve rather than stretching the outside curve, or the strudel will split open. Brush with melted butter. Bake at 375° for 20 to 40 minutes until golden brown on top. Remove. Cool 10 minutes before slicing and serving.

❖ ❖ ❖

Austrian Sandwiches

This tasty canape' or sandwich filling can be put on any kind of firm bread. The secret is that any one of the garnishes tends to give the whole sandwich a different flavor than any other garnish will. These look very pretty and taste wonderful!

Filling: (Dice all ingredients very small to 1/4 size of a kernel of corn.)
>   **Red potatoes**, 2 cups diced, cooked tender
>   **Carrots**, 1 cup diced, cooked tender
>   **Baby peas**, 1 cup, cooked tender
>   **Celery**, 1/3 cup fresh, diced
>   **Onion**, 1/3 cup fresh, diced
>   **Bell pepper**, 1/3 cup fresh, diced
>   **Onion Salt**, 1/2 tsp.
>   **Dill weed**, 1/2 tsp.
>   **Black pepper**, 1/4 tsp., ground

Mix all the above with:
>   **Mayonnaise**, 1 cup

Bread: Buy a long, narrow baguette (French Bread) about 3 inches in diameter. Slice into quarter-inch-thick slices. Other firm specialty breads such as rye or sourdough may be used. Crackers make an interesting, crunchy base.

Press a heaping Tablespoon of filling onto each slice of bread. Makes about 5 dozen.

Garnish each sandwich with any of the following:

Black olive slices	Green olive slices
Sardines	Cheese, any kind
Bologna or ham	Red or Green Bell pepper
Jalapeno rings	Hard-cooked egg slices
Radish slices	Parsley or Cilantro sprigs
Sweet pickle slice	Dill pickle slice

✦ ✦ ✦ ✦ ✦

Notes About This Book

This story of Hildegard Edler is the middle section of a larger family saga which is based on real characters and situations. It is preceded by the amazing adventures of Rosa's childhood, medical schooling and romance in the book *Iron Rose*. After Hilde's marriage comes *A Rose in War*, stories of Rosa's years in a British prison camp, her return to wartime Austria, and events leading to her final fulfillment and happiness. If you liked *The Thorn Birds* and *Gone With The Wind*, you will enjoy *Iron Rose* and *A Rose in War*. Further in the future, we follow stories of Hildegard's decidedly off-beat daughter, and world-galloping granddaughter.

❖ ❖ ❖

Disclaimer

This is a novel, a work of fiction. Although many of the events depicted herein happened to a number of real people, they have been composited, altered, and fleshed out by the author's imagination to create a storyline which is not strictly accurate. All the names of characters on whom these events were based have been changed.

❖ ❖ ❖

Lorie welcomes your comments on this book! Please send E-Mail to: grandma-lorie@juno.com

About the Author

Lorie H. Nicholes has divided her lifetime between Utah and Michigan. She grew up near the top of a stack of ten noisy, opinionated children, and spent a lot of time telling them stories to prevent mayhem. After several changes of major at Brigham Young University, Lorie received a BS in Health Education, English, Dance, and Library Science. She worked as a high school teacher and librarian, and also poked around as a freelance artist, storyteller, and carpenter. When she first returned to BYU for a Master's Degree, she found a husband instead. They raised three gorgeous children in Michigan before her husband of twenty-two years died.

Back in school again, she earned an MS in Instructional Technology at Utah State, and spent four blissful years working for BYU, scripting educational videos, laser discs, and CD-Roms. In 1997 she took a leap at the dream of a lifetime, quit her job, and wrote a 700 page novel, 35% of which appears in this book. But there's more to this book . . . *there's more!*

Aside from writing and storytelling, Lorie is a fair artist and sculptor, a reasonable carpenter and cabinet maker, a creative silversmith, and an avid inventor of weird gadgets. She also enjoys clothing and costume design and construction. Her radio program, Grandma Lorie's Bible Stories, is slated to be broadcast on several Utah radio stations in the near future. Recently Lorie joined the Audiovisual Department of the LDS Church in Salt Lake City as a freelance multimedia director assisting with Church projects. She currently lives in Provo, Utah.

❖ ❖ ❖